Also by Mandy Haggith

Fiction

The Amber Seeker

The Lyre Dancers

Bear Witness

The Last Bear

Poetry
Castings

letting light in

Non-fiction
*Paper Trails: From Trees to Trash,
the True Cost of Paper*

THE WALRUS⊙ MUTTERER

BOOK ONE OF
THE STONE STORIES

MANDY HAGGITH

Saraband

Published by Saraband,
Digital World Centre, 1 Lowry Plaza
The Quays, Salford, M50 3UB
www.saraband.net

10 9 8 7 6 5 4 3 2

ISBN: 9781912235087
ISBNe: 9781912235223

*Printed and bound in the EU
on sustainably sourced FSC-compliant paper.*

Mandy Haggith is the author of several works of poetry, fiction and non-fiction, having gained a Masters in creative writing with distinction from the University of Glasgow. Her first novel, *The Last Bear*, was set 1000 years ago and won the Robin Jenkins Literary Award. An eco-activist and former scientist and academic, Mandy is Co-ordinator of the Environmental Paper Network and has lobbied at the United Nations. She lives in the northwest Scottish Highlands and teaches at the University of the Highlands and Islands.

The Walrus Mutterer is the first title in the *Stone Stories* trilogy, followed by *The Amber Seeker* and *The Lyre Dancers*.

ENSLAVEMENT

ASSYNT

Rian emerged from the broch, blinking. The light was almost too bright, but she found it impossible not to stretch into the morning sunshine. It was cold, but beautiful. Hardly a breath of wind. Snow had fallen four days before and still hadn't thawed much. For a couple of hours in the middle of the day it had softened, then re-crystallised. Moisture had oozed out among rocks and frozen into icicles and sheets of sun-glint.

She crossed the frozen yard to the midden and emptied out the contents of the pail: a slop of rinds and discards, soil washed off vegetables, scrapings and bones boiled white, the detritus of a winter night. A stink of rotting splashed up from the pile. A drake plumped down off the roof of the byre onto the heap, eyed Rian with its jet bead of suspicion, then guddled in her offering. She envied its bright colours, its effortless splendour.

Back to the broch. Back to the sweat-stench of people, bleary-eyed hangovers and the mental stains of yesterday evening's arguments.

Before she went in, she paused to savour the morning. At sea, a ship, sails limp, oars out, was creeping in from the south and making for their harbour.

She pulled back the door, pinning it to let some light and air in, and shouted. 'A boat! A boat coming into the loch. Red sail.'

Drost snapped out of his hangover into life and strode out. Danuta, his mother, followed, leaning on a stick. Other people started appearing from nearby huts, streaming out to get a vantage over the loch. All of Seonaig's children tumbled out, shouting and excited, and even their elderly neighbour Eilidh made her stately way out towards the headland to get a view.

It was a sizeable vessel, under oars, the red sail being furled. Drost raised his arm and a figure on the boat raised a staff in response, its tip catching the sun.

Drost's son Bael was running down towards the shore, slipping on icy stones, picking himself up and slithering on. Drost strolled towards the sheltered inlet where the rocks had been cleared so boats could pull up. Shouts and gestures were exchanged with the crew about the safe channel. The boat glided in.

Rian joined Danuta at the viewpoint just a few paces out from the doorway.

First off was the wielder of the staff. It was Ussa the trader.

'The women had better look to their menfolk,' Danuta said, as the merchant stepped over the bow of the boat onto the rocks in her high sealskin boots and long white coat.

It was a couple of years since Ussa had visited and Rian thought she looked rounder in the face than the last time. Under the polar bear pelt, she would no doubt be wearing enough gold and bronze jewellery to sink a coracle.

Behind her was a stranger, a slender man wearing tight-fitting fine leather clothes and a cloak made of thick grey fur. He had a short-cropped beard and hair tied back into a neat plait. After stepping ashore he was passed a wooden chest, which he carried under his arm, and a pole slightly longer than he was tall.

Ussa strode up the shore ahead of him, tucking her hand under Drost's elbow, and with a sweep of the other arm conjuring a blushing grin onto Bael's face. From the vantage point beside the broch, Danuta looked on, her eyes like stones.

A murmur of recognition from the villagers greeted the next to clamber off the boat: a thickset, dark-haired man, who helped a slight girl to follow him onto the shore.

'The smith's come,' said Danuta. 'Thank the stars, at long last.

3

Do you remember him?'

'Is it Gruach and Fraoch?' Rian said.

'That's them. You remember them then?'

'Oh yes. He's the dragon man and she's the dwarf.'

Danuta's laugh was like a tumble of water. She turned to the house, pushing Rian ahead of her. 'Come on lass, we really have got baking to do now.'

Ussa continued to stride towards the broch, Drost and Bael scampering to keep up. 'Danuta!' she called.

The old woman stopped at the doorway and turned to face the new arrival. 'So, Ussa. Welcome to Assynt. What brings you?'

'Trade, Sister, what else?'

'Who's the eunuch?' Danuta gestured towards the slim man picking his way up the icy rocks from the shore, his box clutched to his body, not putting his weight on his staff.

Ussa turned to him and shouted. 'Pytheas!'

He looked up, smiling at his name, and waved the pole. His face was full of rapture.

'He's my passenger,' said Ussa. 'He's Greek. Part child and part god and part, I don't know what. He's rich and charming and curious as a bear cub. You'll love him. Everyone loves Pytheas.'

'How long are you here?' Danuta watched Pytheas approaching, not giving Ussa the respect of eye contact. 'We've hardly enough food for ourselves. I don't know what you imagine we'll feed your crew.'

The crew of four men and a boy were hauling the boat up towards the line of nousts, hollows in the grass beyond the high tide mark.

'Just until there's a decent wind.' Ussa pulled her coat up around her chin. 'We'll hunt, no doubt.'

Drost stepped forward and wrapped an arm around Ussa's back which she leaned into. He ushered her past Danuta into the broch, with Bael close behind him. 'Come away in and get warm,' he said.

Danuta raised her eyebrows, then nodded towards Pytheas who had stopped several yards away, put down his box and knelt, lowering his head in an elaborate bow. He said something incomprehensible but his smile was wide and brilliant. He opened his box, took something out, then closed it. Danuta nodded at him again and failed to suppress an answering twitch of her lips.

Rian was right beside her, wondering at the elegant figure. His boots were of red leather, elaborately patterned, like nothing she had ever seen. Straightening up with his box, Pytheas gestured to her to come towards him. She looked up at Danuta, who tilted her chin up in assent. Rian took a pace forwards and saw that he had something blue in his hand, the colour of the sky on a carefree day. She loved that colour: darker than forget-me-nots, almost as deep as a milkwort flower.

'Pytheas,' he announced, touching the blue fabric towards his chest. Then he said something else in his own tongue and with his hand like a question he offered her the blue ribbon – for she could see this was what it was now that he let it unravel – hanging from his fingers, shining.

'Rian,' she said, and turned to check with Danuta that she could take the gift. The old woman gave permission with a simple wave of her hand and Rian realised she should ensure the strange man knew he was in the presence of someone important.

'Danuta,' she said, touching her arm. 'Our head woman.'

Pytheas pointed at them and repeated their names.

Rian giggled. His voice made their names sound funny, and he laughed too, gesturing to his own chest.

'Pytheas.' She liked letting her lips and tongue shape the strange sounds.

His delight at her use of his name was so excessive she thought he might be crazy. He put his box down again. What a nuisance that box was to him. He was still holding out the ribbon but now stepping towards her, saying something and reaching for her head. Before she knew how to defend herself he had reached behind her and pulled her hair into a bunch. His hands were strong but not unpleasant on her head as he smoothed her hair and tied the ribbon. Looking down she saw his red leather boots were inscribed with a fancy pattern of leaves. Then he had stepped back and was looking at her.

'Bóidheach,' he said. Then he said another word, which she didn't recognise.

'Rian Bhóidheach,' Beautiful Rian, he repeated, as if it was her name. She blushed and laughed at how ridiculous it was of this man to have picked her out for such attention. But now he was handing Danuta a piece of something small and gesturing her to put it in her mouth, as he put a similar piece in his, and she was eating the thing he offered and beaming back at him as if he were an old friend.

'It's sweet,' she said.

'Mhilis,' he repeated. 'Danuta Mhilis.'

They all laughed. Rian could see that what Ussa had said was true. They were all going to love Pytheas.

*

While the visitors were busy with unloading the boat, inside the broch it was a morning like any other.

Ducking back in through the narrow entrance to the broch, Rian tripped. The empty slop bucket span away from her across the room. Bael pulled his foot back and laughed.

Danuta reached from her stool by the hearth and stood the pail upright. 'What's all this? Leave her alone Bael.'

Bael took no notice, poking at Rian with a wooden spike as if she were a pig. She edged away around the central fireplace until she was out of reach.

The fire was sleeping. It was Rian's job to wake it. She stirred the peat ash, snapped some willow twigs and heaped them into a conical pile, then prodded a birch bark strip in amongst them and crouched down, out of range of Bael's stick. She breathed into the embers. They glowed and the kindling began to smoke. She blew again, and the birchbark flamed. With a crackle, the dry twigs caught and she reached for some bigger sticks to feed them, singing the morning waking song.

'Wake, wake breath of sun, sing the morning flame song.

Wake, wake limbs of sun, stretch the morning blessing.

Wake, wake soul of sun, warm our morning hearth.'

With each line, she reached her arms towards first the floor, then the walls and lastly the roof, encompassing all of the house in her greeting to the fire. Danuta nodded from her stool, then handed her a bowl of milk. She took it and laid it at Bael's feet. The boy sneered at her then picked it up and began to slurp. Rian retreated and Danuta passed her a smaller, but fuller, bowl and an oatcake to dip in it. She turned her back and hunkered down with it. Danuta patted her on her shoulder and Rian rested her head for a moment against her thick wool skirt.

'The fire is cheerful this morning,' Danuta said. 'We'll need to bake plenty today, so build up its strength.'

Rian nodded.

'Then you can come and help us with the cows.'

'Can I milk?'

'Of course. Beithe likes it when you do.' Danuta stroked her hair, then got to her feet, levering her stiff back upright with her staff. She stomped up the stairs between the two circular walls of the stone tower and rattled the door of her daughter Buia's sleeping room, one of several partitioned spaces on the first floor of the building. 'Buia. Wake up.'

A ragged woman with a sleepy, pockmarked face followed Danuta downstairs. She bowed to the fire, whispered, 'Morning,' to Rian, and limped to the water tank beside the hearth. She dipped the wooden cup and drank, then dipped again, groaning slightly, before downing another cupful. Bael edged away, keeping out of arm's reach.

'We need fresh water,' Buia said to him.

'Why can't she do it?' Bael poked his stick towards Rian.

'Rian is feeding the fire,' said Danuta, 'then milking with us. Go on.'

'The stream'll be frozen.'

'The Mother's blood never stops flowing.'

'But it'll have iced over.'

Buia turned and cuffed Bael. 'You impudent pup. You dare to contradict what she tells you about the Mother?'

'Sorry.' But Bael didn't look abashed.

Danuta stood with her staff raised, unmoving. Bael took the waterskin from behind the water tank and turned to go.

'Put something warm on you stupid brat, you'll freeze,' Buia said.

He turned back red-faced, glowering, and she tossed him a leather cloak with stoat pelt around the hood, an utter contrast to her own bedraggled skins. He took the coat and left, and Buia and Danuta chuckled to each other.

'That boy,' Buia said. 'Like father like son.'

Danuta nodded, following the younger woman out. Rian was left alone for a moment, building the fire to a crackling blaze.

A shadow fell across her as Drost barged in, blocking the light from the door. He headed straight for the water tank, without bothering to honour the fire. He reached in and splashed water onto his face, spluttering as he doused his head and beard. Dripping into the stone-lined pool in the floor, he ran his fingers through his hair, preening himself. Rian proffered an oatcake, which he took, barely registering her presence. He stood munching then gulped down a cup of water as she fed the fire and arranged the cooking stones around the hearth to heat up.

He ducked into his room and emerged wearing his newest jerkin and boots. 'You'd better find enough to feed the visitors. They're used to better fare than this rubbish.' Drost stuffed the rest of the oatcake in his mouth, turned his back and swaggered back out.

*

By the afternoon, the air was bitter. The new arrivals had eaten the meagre food that could be lain before them immediately – oatcakes and porridge – and were hungry and tired enough to be grateful for it. Ussa explained they had been sailing for four days, ice preventing them from making landfall and most of the time too little wind to enable them to make progress, powerless against the tidal streams, struggling to make headway northwards. And they had been cold, so cold they had feared that their fingers and toes and noses would freeze.

Gruach the smith and his daughter Fraoch went off to call on people they knew, Big Donnal and his four boys, who always loved to have visitors, over in the crannog at Clashmore. The skipper of the boat Toma, a wiry old character, and his apprentice Callum, ten years old, small for his age but wise-eyed and silent, had gone with them. Ussa insisted her three slaves sat outside, but Danuta took pity on them. Ushering them into the broch, she asked them their names.

'Og, Li, Faradh,' the tallest one said, pointing to himself, and the other two, in order of size.

'We can clear one of the rooms to make space for you,' Danuta said.

Buia reluctantly dragged her bedding to the chamber at the foot of the stairs, in beside Danuta's bed, and cleared her scraps of possessions from her own room.

Danuta produced a beaded bag of cowhide. 'Use this for them,' she said, pointing at the collection of shells and dried herbs, and the sticks Buia had been carving as part of her training in the arts of the Mother. It was recognition that Buia had achieved the status of a 'woman with a medicine bag' and typical of Danuta to make such a move without ceremony.

Buia took the bag, and bowed with it to the fire, then began to stash her herbs and amulets away. Rian smiled at her in congratulation, but Buia pretended to ignore the girl. Rian reached out to stroke the bag, intending only admiration, but Buia clutched it to her chest and turned her back.

Danuta winked at Rian. 'Watch those bannocks.'

Rian returned to her duties at the hearth.

After they had carried various bags and chests up from the boat, the crew settled down for a snooze. Bael gave up his bed for Ussa, and he and Drost set out to check their traps and snares. Danuta gestured to Pytheas to take Drost's room opposite the main door. He rose and bowed, then offered Buia a shiny bead in his outstretched hand, saying something in Keltic. Buia took it and held it between her thumb and first finger. It was perfectly blue, just like the ribbon he had given Rian. She smiled widely and he dipped his head to one side. Now all of them had been given gifts by him, and no-one could feel sorry for the presence of their guests. At least for the time being.

Quiet settled in the broch as the three women peeled and chopped, pounded and stirred, kneaded and shaped, and the visitors slept, all except Pytheas. Instead, he sat on the bed with the curtain open, scratching with a feather on a piece of animal skin. Rian was desperate to look at what the strange man was doing but something about his concentration made her hold back, as if he cast a spell around him, a circle like the moon creates, an aura of colour, a spread of magic. He breathed deeply and cleared his throat, staring out into the space in front and above him as if he was gazing far away with no focus or awareness of anyone in the room. Then, as if his dreaming had created something that itched the skin in front of him, he fell again to scratching.

She felt his eyes on her and realised that he was watching what they were doing, with an intensity that was embarrassing, as if he could see into their minds. It was such a powerful scrutiny Rian could hardly bear it and wanted to draw the curtain and shut him into her foster father's room. Something about his gaze, such alertness while others slept, made the women go even more quietly about their cooking.

'He stares like a heron fishing,' Danuta murmured.

Rian nodded, trying to smile, managing only a grimace. 'I wish I could hide under some seaweed,' she whispered back. 'What is he doing?'

'Writing, I think. But it's nothing like the ogham script.'

Rian tried to wind the quern stone as gently as she could, wincing as it squeaked.

'Go and check for eggs,' Danuta said. 'I'll do that.'

Rian slid the quern across the floor to the old woman, hurried into her boots, grabbed a shawl and fled, never so glad to have to visit the ducks and geese.

There were no eggs, so she tried to think of other things she could usefully do outside. She could fetch water, even though it was not her job. Then she hit on firewood.

She headed up into the woods above the broch to get some birch. They had asked the trees for permission to take their limbs and had cut many of them down in the early winter. Their stumps were still covered with snow. She felt sorry for the primroses that had showed themselves the week before only to be smothered, but then she spotted a couple in a sunny, sheltered spot where the snow had melted. Of course. They knew where to grow.

The branches were stacked to season. It didn't take long for birch. The cold had done its work and already the twigs were brittle and snapped easily. She took a bough off the heap and set to work, breaking off the small side shoots and dead wood. The main stem could be left aside, it was too useful to burn, but she bundled all of the smaller wood before starting on another branch.

She loved the way the twigs held their tension as she bent them, then sprang to obey her will once the force was enough. She loved the noise of the snapping wood, its sharp crack and tear. And she loved its smell. A robin came to watch from a rowan nearby, wondering what the racket was and whether it would bring food. Once it had established what was going on, it hopped down to check over the broken wood, scouring for insect prey. Rian greeted it. It cocked its head as if in acknowledgement and then returned to its inspection.

She kept her eyes on the slope above her, alert for movement. The stream was slow, its song muted, gurgling under a muffle of ice. She knew her noise would keep most animals at bay but an early-waking bear could be a danger. Hungry and bad-tempered, they took risks they would never otherwise take and – even close to the village – bear attacks were possible at this time of year. To be honest though, she was more frightened of being here when Drost and Bael returned from their hunt, especially if they had been unsuccessful.

She wasn't paying much attention to the path up from the village, so Pytheas was almost upon her when she noticed him. He was carrying his rod and he bowed politely as he passed her, continuing on up the slope towards the high point. She shifted her bundle so she could watch him, wondering if he knew about the bears, curious as to what he might be doing. He seemed so purposeful.

After a few minutes he returned down the slope, then beckoned her to follow him. On the flat ground at the top, he made her hold the pole as he paced around. Several times he seemed to be intent upon the shadow cast by the long stick. It had elaborate carvings on it, and she liked the feel of them under her fingers. It must be some magic that he was performing, but it was unlike anything she had ever seen anyone do.

After a couple of minutes, something in his manner suggested that he had done what he had set out to do and she returned to her wood pile. On his way past, he paused to watch her and then, pointing to one of the bundles of wood, made an offer to take it with him. He shouldered it as if it weighed nothing. He said something in his tongue and she shook her head in incomprehension. He waved his rod, pointing it up at the sky towards the sun. She had no idea what he was saying. He tossed his rod up, span it around, twirled it until it blurred, then tapped her on the head. It was a feather touch, but it still made her duck and squeal. He chortled, bowed again, and set off down to the broch.

She set about another bundle of sticks.

When she returned, Pytheas had lain down and seemed to be sleeping. The rest of the day was quiet. The somnolent guests cast such an atmosphere Buia nodded off in a corner and Danuta spent longer than usual in her afternoon meditation. The sounds of children playing down by the shore drifted in as if from some other world. Rian felt she was the only person alive. The blood pulsed in her head and every sigh of the wood in the fire was a warning from the spirit world.

The light faded. Above the fireplace the mask needed to be turned. Rian twisted it on its spike so, instead of the day face of work, the evening face of play looked down on the hearth. Although why the evening should be for play she had never understood, as that was when her hardest work took place. Someone had to serve the food and drink and clean up afterwards. Someone had to keep the fire happy and someone had to fetch and carry for everyone else's pleasure. That someone was her.

But, as the long dusk straggled towards dark, she was in for a surprise. The crew members woke, and although they spoke little they were remarkably helpful. The three slaves, Og, Li and Faradh, worked. Og, the biggest and friendliest, asked questions, practical things about food, drink and fuel, and then gave instructions to the others. By the time darkness was in, lamps filled and lit, most of Rian's chores were done, and more. The circle around the hearth was arranged for feasting; the slow preparations of food by the three women had accelerated into a production line of delicacies. Og transformed eggs into an exotic pudding using a grainy powder he brought out of a bag, one of several such treats which Danuta, Buia and Rian sniffed with curiosity, scepticism and wonder, passing the little bronze bottles capped with cork to one another.

The youngest slave, Faradh, had running sores on his hands from rowing in the cold, which Danuta dressed with her yarrow butter ointment. She was rewarded by great displays of gratitude.

Their loud good humour woke Ussa, who appeared from behind her curtain dazed and rumpled. She cast her eyes around the house in a groggy sweep as if performing a head count, then pulled back the door and stomped out into the dusk.

Shortly afterwards, voices outside heralded the return of Drost. Ussa made a grand re-entrance into the broch, ducking inside and standing, hand on hip, head high, dark hair spread luxuriantly across her shoulders, her eyes glinting. 'The hunters return victorious,' she called, stepping aside, and with a thrust of her hand conducting Drost through the doorway, bloodied and sweating but grinning, with a roe buck across his back, two delicate hoofed legs clutched in each of his hairy hands.

A space was made beside the fire. He slung the carcass down and stood back to revel in the chorus of appreciation.

Pytheas sat up bright eyed, strode forward, clapped Drost on the back and with a theatrical gesture towards the deer declared 'Bóidheach!' Beautiful! to a gale of laughter.

Behind Drost, Bael stood with two ducks and a string of four rock doves and soon he too was swept up in the praise and seated beside his father with a beaker of ale. For once the grin on his face even stretched to Rian as she handed him a warm bannock, dripping butter.

Og and Li helped Danuta and Buia to skin the deer and set up a spit over the fire. Rian plucked the birds in a corner, seeking invisibility now that her tormentor had returned. She was as alert as a fox for the signs of danger. But the atmosphere in the big round house was jolly. Not long after dark they were joined by the smith and his daughter, Toma the skipper and his boy Callum, as well as several neighbours. Gruach had brought some of his wares and bronze daggers, bowls and pins were passed around the villagers. Bael was sent for some skins and the trade began.

14

Danuta gained a bronze bowl and Buia a cloak pin for their hospitality, which would extend to supplying the boat with oatmeal for the onward journey. The barrels were getting low. It was a long time until the next harvest and they could scarce afford to be generous, but it mattered to feed their guests well. Pride was a lot of it but seafaring allies were a better investment than enemies. You never knew when you might be rewarded for a remembered act of generosity. Plus being on Ussa's bad side could be dangerous.

Drost fingered a bronze dirk with a knot-patterned hilt but put it down when Ussa opened her chest and produced a sword. It was sheathed in a scabbard with inlaid walrus ivory and the hilt was a twisted silver knotwork. The bronze blade was long and sharp enough to cut leather, as she demonstrated by nicking off the thong on Faradh's boots. Rian wanted to help him, but could only watch as he tried to hide his furious tears.

Drost held the sword across his lap, lust for the beautiful weapon turning his eyes wide and his mouth into an open drool. He waved at Rian. 'More ale all round!' Then he turned to Gruach and Ussa. 'How's this made so sharp? And the scabbard, there's a story in that I'll bet.'

He made to hand it over, but Ussa pressed it back into his hands. 'It was made in Belerion by the King's smith, Yberg, the greatest craftsman ever known on the western seaboard. You know he's lame? The King destroys the kneecaps of his most skilled makers so they cannot leave him. And people say that I'm heartless!' She gave a sideways glance at Gruach and laughed, a high percussive titter of pure malice. 'Look long and lovingly, Drost, for you can't afford it.'

'How much?'

'Half a queen's ransom.' She smiled. 'And cheap at the price.'

'Tonight we'll play craps and I'll win enough from you to buy it twice over.'

He handed the sword to Bael, who stroked it with reverence, then passed it reluctantly back to Ussa.

The food began to be passed around and the trade goods were stored for later. Jugs of ale emptied as fast as Rian could refill them from the vat in the byre. She was glad of the snow, for it stopped the night being too dark as she fumbled with the catch on the door. The cows smelled warm and their lowing was comforting between the mounting din of the revelry inside the broch. Each time she returned, she had to blink at the lamps and the gleaming reflections from new bronze and glittering silver.

Ussa had taken over Danuta's stool and was presiding over the feast, ordering her slaves to pass and carry, choosing the prize pieces of meat for herself or selected beneficiaries. She had shed her outer layer of clothes and sat glittering in a chemise of deep green, her skin shining, her arms decorated with silver and gold bracelets and an elaborate gold torc around her long neck.

After they had eaten their hunger into silence Danuta said, 'So tell us what brings you this way, Ussa.'

The big woman continued to chew. She swallowed, shrugging. 'Trade.'

'You'll not get rich from the likes of us.'

'You'd be surprised what some of the things you people think are worthless can fetch elsewhere.'

'Like what?'

'Sealskin. Antlers of a red stag. Even that hide there.' She pointed to the roehide, bundled ready for treating. 'Well-tanned, that's high value down in the farming lands further south.'

'So you're going south?'

'Not straight away.'

'You're always so evasive.' Danuta shook her head and moved to clearing some of the empty dishes. Rian jumped up to help.

'All right, I'll tell you my quest.'

Danuta paused, watching her. She handed the dish she held to Rian, who put it on the pile and sank onto her hunkers. Ussa was looking around, making sure she had everyone's attention. It would be a story.

'Go on then,' said Drost.

'I'm seeking Manigan, the Walrus Mutterer.'

'Who on earth's that?'

'He's a hunter. He travels far, far north to the lands where ice rules. He's the best walrus hunter there is.'

'What's a walrus?' Bael said.

Ussa laughed at him and he blushed, but Rian was glad that he'd asked.

Drost said, 'It's like a huge seal, and the males have big tusks of ivory. They're so fierce even the biggest ice bears cannot kill them.'

'That's right,' said Ussa. 'They are almost invincible, nothing except a few exceptional men can threaten them. There is never only one walrus. It's not as if you can pick one off like a seal. They live in huge packs. They huddle together like an army. Picture the biggest bull you have ever seen.' She looked around at her audience.

People nodded back, enthralled.

'Well, they're that big, that strong. Imagine a boat, not much longer than this house.' She gestured to help people to visualise. 'And half the width, and forty or fifty angry bulls trying to crush it. You wouldn't stand a chance.'

Drost was nodding. Even Danuta had put down her bowl and was rapt, listening.

'Well, Manigan, not only does he hunt walrus, he hunts the biggest males, the walrus Chiefs. And he does it alone. He talks to them. He does. That's why he's called the Walrus Mutterer. He's a kind of magician. He charms all but the big chief into the water. They say they're so calm about it they don't even make a ripple. They go swimming off and leave him alone with the leader, as if they believe he needs a word in private. You can hardly believe it.'

Rian shook her head and caught Danuta doing the same.

'He puts that big male walrus into a trance and gets him so dreamy and full of peace, he can walk right up to him and slit his throat.'

'Have you seen it?' asked Danuta.

Ussa shot her an acid smile. 'Once.'

Everyone knew she was lying, but it was a good story so she went unchallenged.

'And why are you seeking this mutterer?' Drost asked, a hint of jealousy in his voice.

Ussa turned her charm on him. 'I'd rather not have to ever see him again, if you want the truth, but he has something of mine he shouldn't have and I intend to take it back into safekeeping.'

'What?'

'It's a skull of stone, with three faces carved on it. They call it the Head of Telling. It speaks the future, so they say, but at the cost of a life for every question. To say you must be careful what you ask it is to rather understate the case.'

There was a hush.

'You'd be better off leaving it with him,' said Danuta.

'And why's that? Do you think I'm not capable of invoking its power?' She sneered at the old woman. 'Do you think you're the only one who can peer into the future?'

'Not at all.' Danuta's voice was mild. 'But I've heard of this stone. The druids revere it.'

'They do.'

'But they do not seek to use it. It's far too dangerous. Do you know its other name?'

'Don't you start,' said Ussa.

'What's its name?' Bael was frowning

Danuta looked at him, and paused for effect. 'It is the Death Stone. It is cursed. You should leave it where it is.'

Ussa rolled her eyes and turned aside to her chest of trinkets. Drost got to his feet and began offering the guests more to drink. Everyone seemed to be speaking to the people next to them about what they had heard.

In a pause in the hubbub, Pytheas demanded the attention of his hosts and, in an almost wordless mime, he thanked them for the meal. His manners delighted Danuta, who patted him and stroked his long pigtail.

He took her hand and then touched Drost's sleeve. 'You are his Mama?'

She nodded.

Then he pointed to Bael and Drost and said, 'Papa?'

They concurred.

Then his gesture was to Buia and Bael, 'Mama?'

At this Buia laughed and shook her head vigorously. 'He's no brat of mine, the mongrel.' And then she pointed to Danuta. 'Mama!' she said, imitating his accent and gesturing to herself. 'I'm Drost's sister,' she chuckled.

'Sister,' he repeated, then pointed to Drost.

'Brother,' they chorused to him. Then he pointed to Rian and Bael and said, 'Sister, brother?'

Outraged, Bael said, 'No way.'

Rian tried to shrink away into her dark corner, knowing that with her auburn hair, green eyes and pale skin she looked nothing like the dark-haired kin of Drost and Danuta. But Pytheas persisted, pointing to Buia. 'Mama?'

She crossed her hands in a dismissive gesture. 'She's not one of us.'

He swept his arm around the room, seeking someone to own up to being related to her.

Danuta said, 'She's a foster child.'

But even after one of the slaves said something to him in some other tongue, he seemed to be mystified.

Og said, 'So she is neither family nor slave?'

Danuta nodded. 'That's right. She came to us as a baby. It happens. I am the medicine woman. Drost's wife was keen to take her, but she died giving birth to Bael, and I took care of them both.'

Ussa's voice rang out. 'So who exactly was her mother? Who are her people? Where is she from?'

Drost nodded. 'Aye, you never have told us whose bastard I got fobbed off with.'

'It's not to be spoken of,' Danuta said.

There was another embarrassed silence. Rian wanted a hole to open up under her in the corner.

Pytheas frowned and then, suddenly, the cloud seemed to clear from his face. He gave an elaborate twist of his hands towards her and then his gaze circled the room, seeking the agreement of everyone, and he lifted his cup in a toast. 'Bóidheach!' Beautiful.

The slaves roared 'Bóidheach!' back in unison, with the laughter of a standing joke in their voices. They swigged from their mugs, emptying them, and the jug began to circulate again.

Rian sat red-faced in her corner, far too many eyes on her, desperate for something to distract attention away. She saw Li empty the jug into Bael's outstretched cup and seized her chance to flee. But reaching for the jug simply drew more attention to her. Li clutched it to himself in jest, then stood, indicating he would follow her out with it, to cat-calls from the others. Rian swithered, the laughter beating at her from all sides, until Pytheas tugged Li back to the bench and, murmuring something to him, extracted his fingers from the handle and passed the vessel to Rian. Any gratitude she might have felt blinked out as he winked at her.

She turned tail to the byre, back to the bovine warmth and darkness.

She left the jug on the barrel and shuffled over to lean her head on the shoulder of Beithe. The hairy cow made no gesture of interest, standing indifferent, chewing its cud. Rian stroked the top of its head, wishing people were more like cows.

The faint light from the byre doorway was blotted out by a shape. Rian tried to melt into the cow, holding her breath, feeling her heart like a scuttling mouse. The person loomed into the byre, went directly to the beer barrel and seemed to locate the jug on top.

'Rian?' It was Danuta's voice.

Relief flooded her. 'I'm here, Danu, talking to Beithe.'

'Come away in. They're thirsty.'

'I hate it. I hate them.'

'They're only having fun.'

Rian said nothing.

Danuta filled the jug. 'It is nice and quiet here,' she conceded. 'I'll take this in. Don't stay out here all night.'

Alone again, Rian tried to return to the comfort of stroking the cow but the fear of a shadow in the doorway remained. Her imagination conjured figures, all less benign than her foster mother, and eventually the horror of being found out there on her own by any of the others drove her back to the broch. She stood just outside the door, listening. A quietness seemed to be settling. Someone had produced a drum and one of the men began a song in a sweet mellow voice, a jaunty rhyming sea shanty with a chorus that everyone joined in with: 'A hoy-a, a hoy-o, the sea's a merry boy-o.'

Rian chose her moment and slipped into the room, threaded her way through the crowd of knee-patting, head-nodding people all singing along. She faded into her corner. Danuta's hand reached in and gave her toes a welcoming squeeze. She was invisible again.

The ceilidh continued. It was Og singing, and Gruach the smith was on the drum. After the shanty, Og sang again, another old favourite. Then Danuta asked for something slow and he began an elegy. The sweetness of his voice was made for such melodies and, as he led the tune along its mournful contour, people breathed, sat back, and allowed themselves to be carried to a place where emotion softens. The lover was lost, the lover was drowned, and the throng around the fireplace lamented. When Og reached the end of the song at last, they whistled and cheered, a few eyes were wiped, some surreptitiously, some openly.

Danuta was one of those who didn't try to hide her tears. 'Og, you'll break our hearts.' She shook her head. 'Who'll cheer us up after that?'

Og pulled a whistle out of his top pocket and began to pipe a tune for hauling rigging. Gruach joined in on the drum. With a whoop, Pytheas jumped to his feet, grabbed the youngest member of the crew, the captain's boy, Callum, by the hand and though there wasn't really enough room to dance they hopped and mimed the pulling of ropes, shinning up the mast and dragging up an anchor. The tune got faster and faster until they were scampering on the spot and waving their arms as if their feet were on fire. Everyone clapped along until with a shriek and a trill, it was done.

Then the drum started up a slow, regular beat with a skip like a sharp intake of breath, or a twitch of a hip. Og's whistle changed tone and out of his little pipe a reedy sensuous tune took shape. A slow, chromatic descent, a pause, and then all eyes were on Ussa, standing with one hand on her hip, the other raised like a snake about to strike, her bangles glinting. With eyes half-closed, eyebrows raised and a smile of abandon, she began to dance. The tune followed her arms and torso, or she followed it, and the drum seemed to be inside her hips. She became the music. All the light in the house seemed to glow from her skin as she writhed and shimmered and clicked her fingers with all the passion of moonshine. And then with a stamp she lifted her chin and sang.

Her voice was like the baying of a wild animal. She sang of love, of love no matter what, a defiant love dark as the forest's heart, deep as the ocean's depth, a love that nothing could release her from, a love that thundered, a love that broke her body open. Then, with a toss of her head, the slow dance tune returned and she became human once more, voluptuous, all hands and skin and breasts and pulsing hips. She felled the dance with a final stamp, the whistle trilled, and a snap of her fingers extinguished the music to rapturous applause.

She refused to dance another but instead, with every man in the building at her command, she called for drinks all round and a board and casket of ivory chips. The gambling began.

Rian was soon bored by it. She had curled up on a mat in the corner and was close to sleep when the shouting of her name pulled her alert.

'Bring her here,' Drost was shouting. 'She's nothing but a burden to us anyway, one more mouth, always in the way, bothering the boy.' Bael was sitting beside his father, wide-eyed.

Ussa reached for Rian's hand and pulled her to her feet as if demanding the next dance, spinning her into the lighted circle beside the hearth. All eyes, mostly blurry now, were on her. Drost was ablaze with drink, his eyes heavy in their sockets, cheeks red, voice loud. Something bullish raged in his body, aroused by Ussa. Rian had never seen him look so dangerous.

Bael, beside him, noticed her fear. A smirk spread across his face. She looked around desperately for Danuta, but she must have gone off to her bed.

'You'd better watch carefully girl, this next round could change your life forever,' Ussa said.

Rian tried to meet the eyes of Drost, who snarled.

'If your foster father wins, he has the sword. If he loses, you belong to me.' Ussa stroked Rian's hair. 'You're a pretty little thing.'

'What's happening?' Rian's voice came out as a squeak. Was she hearing right? Was she dreaming?

'It's quite simple,' said Ussa. 'You're the stake. Drost is betting you for the sword. I'm dragons and he is eagles. You'd better wish hard he wins. If you do, he'll be very happy. He'll have this lovely sword and he'll still have you to fetch his grog and tend his fire. And if he loses, I'll be very happy, because I'll have you and I'll still have my sword. So whoever you end up with will be delighted to have you.' Ussa smiled like a cat and nodded to Faradh, who had a kind of spinning top on the board with an elaborate pattern of ivory and bronze chips.

'Throw.' Ussa clicked her fingers.

The slave span the top and it wheeled among the pieces on the board, slowed, then settled, leaning on an ivory chip. He lifted the top and turned the piece. 'Dragon,' he said, pointing to the carving on the piece.

'You're mine, girl.' Ussa clasped Rian on the shoulder, her fingernails biting into flesh.

Rian pulled herself out of the grasp and ran out to the byre. They let her go. For the rest of her life she would regret not running further, not taking herself away while she still had the chance.

BRANDED

If Rian had been able to believe it was really happening she would have hidden herself in the woods, but when Danuta found her in the byre, where she had cried herself to sleep among the hay, the old woman said, 'It will be sorted out somehow. Drost was drunk. He'll see sense this morning.'

But Drost did not see the sense Danuta saw and no amount of shouting from her made an impact on him. He had taken Ussa to his bed and in the morning he was drunk on more than beer, and still drinking. Rian had no idea how but he had acquired the coveted sword, which he wore with a swagger.

The branding took place at midday.

Ussa, Li and Faradh cornered Rian and dragged her outside, positioning her opposite the door of the broch. She could see the fire she had lit earlier glowing and flickering orange in the hearth, and those inside could see her without having to come out into the cold. Bael leered out at her. It had frozen hard again in the night and the snow surface had crystallised.

Faradh and Li held her, one on either side. She tried struggling but received a blow to her head from Li, the bigger slave, that made her think twice about further resistance. She was so slight compared to the burly southerner.

The iron was quite a small thing with a short handle tipped by a wooden knob. Ussa dangled it from her hand like a decoration. 'Strip,' she told Rian.

Rian unfastened her belt, which Ussa took, eyed, admired and buckled around her own waist.

'Get on with it, strip.'

Rian shed her outer layers of hide and inner layers of wool. She stood naked, skin goose-pimpling.

Ussa poked at her like someone inspecting an animal at market, raising her arms to inspect the hair in the pits, then making her open her legs, probing.

Rian squeezed her eyes shut and tried to think of anything but what was happening to her. She listened for the robin, but it did not sing. There was no bird song at all.

'Open your eyes.' Ussa made her voice sound as if she was offering some kind of treat but it was more of the examination. 'Look up.'

Rian closed her eyes but the slap to her face made her do what she was told. After she had shifted her eyes in all directions, she had to open her mouth. Ussa poked about inside, looking at her teeth, holding her jaw tightly so she couldn't bite down. Rian shut her eyes again but not before tears had escaped. The smack on her cheek was on some distant part of her. She had retreated deep inside.

'Tears won't help you now, girl.'

Rian lifted her lids and stared. The big woman strode into the house and thrust the branding iron into the hottest part of the fire. She shut her eyes again.

When the iron touched the skin on her right thigh, Rian came back to herself. The pain was a kick of pure hatred. The enemy held the tool. She breathed in the stench of her own burnt skin and cooked flesh. A boulder weight shifted within her and she became light. Only the hands of the two men held her down.

The incline of her life, flat until that point, shot steeply upwards. She was a crag. Her childhood fell away. After that boulder, more rocks fell, a scree of memories tumbling from her, splitting and sharpening themselves as they slid.

When the iron branded her a second time, on her left shoulder, she was far above it, on a distant ridge, out of harm's reach.

She looked at her oppressor. Ussa had veins of hardship in the yellowed whites of her eyes and wrinkles below them where greed lived. There was bruising on her mouth from whatever she had done with Drost in the night. Beneath the glamour, an ugly person inhabited this body.

Ussa brought her eyes close to Rian's, too close to focus. 'I know you,' she said. 'And now you're mine.'

Rian tried not to breathe, but Ussa kept her face directly in front of hers. Her hot breath was fumy with drink from last night and with another smell, something green like cabbage. Rian didn't want it but her lungs were bursting. Ussa puffed out over the skin of her nose and her cheeks. Rian kept her mouth closed but eventually her body refused and, with a gasp, she inhaled. It was as bad as the burning on her shoulders and thigh to see the look of triumph on Ussa's face. The conqueror.

Yet Rian knew, also, that she was not conquered at all, that there was a high place she could go to inside herself where she was still free.

Ussa stepped aside and into the broch. The branding iron hissed as she dipped it into the water butt. She called out, 'Og. Dress her brands. I don't want them to fester.'

Rian heard Danuta's response. 'I will do it.' She hurried out to where Rian teetered, shivering. Danuta was white-faced, her bottom lip trembling as she unwrapped a leather packet. She glanced in towards Ussa. 'Vixen.' Turning to Rian, her face softened. 'Come in here, little bird.'

Rian didn't move, just stood, quivering. A judder went through her and Danuta put an arm around her waist. She allowed herself to be led into the broch, her eyes vacant, watching people as if they were some other species, her mouth slightly open, as it had been to take that fatal breath and as it remained after she exhaled the lungful of her enemy. Now each mouthful of air belonged to someone else. She felt its corrosion as it came in, its dirtiness as it flowed out. She obeyed instructions to move this way or that as

Danuta dressed her wounds with a salve of yarrow and seal fat, then found a loose-fitting shift to wear on top.

Ussa lounged by the fire, ordering the slaves to give her the best remaining morsels of the food from the night before. Putting down her bowl and wiping her mouth she announced, 'Today, I shall hunt.' She stood like a man, hands on her knees to rise, legs apart, elbows wide. 'And I shall take my new slave.'

Drost was by her side, willing as a dog.

Danuta frowned from her stool. 'To think that my own son could be so cruel...'

'Shut it,' Drost said.

Rian appeared not to hear them, then with a heavy slowness she turned, reached for the boots beside her bed. With her back to the eyes in the room she slid one foot into a boot, tugged a lace around her ankle and up her calf and tied a knot. The world was a sequence of actions without will. Another boot, another lace, a second knot. As the body of the girl made itself ready to go outside into the cold, Rian watched from her high place and let it happen.

BRONZE

She trudged behind them, her legs leaden and eyes unfocused, sometimes tripping because she could not be bothered to watch her feet. Her right leg was soaking wet after a slip into a boggy patch. The brands stung. Her feet slid on snow smoothed by footprints of the people ahead of her. The bag hung heavy on her back, something sharp inside it bumping into her sternum as she stepped, though she had stopped the worst of its bouncing with a rope borrowed from Og. She had been making good use of Ussa's spear as a walking stick until she had been told not to, and now it stretched first one arm then the other as she swapped it from hand to hand. She wanted to snap the damn thing, or ram it into Ussa's back.

Ussa strolled, unimpeded, beside Drost at the front of the party. Pytheas strode just behind her, chatting, looking about as they walked. Where the path crossed a burn, Drost carried Ussa, shrieking with laughter, then helped Pytheas across. After a glance behind, Pytheas stopped and waited.

He grinned and joked with the three slaves, Og, Li and Faradh, as they each splashed through the fast flowing water. As Rian approached, she tried not to look at him. She stepped onto the first stepping stone. It was slippy and she wobbled, bringing her second foot beside the first and bending down to grab hold of a boulder jutting out into the stream. The water gushed around her feet. The bag on her back slid awkwardly as she bent, pulling her sideways. The Greek man was speaking to her. She allowed herself to focus on him. He was gesturing to her to pass him the spear. Without thinking she let him take one end then used his balance to stand upright and rush across the other stepping stones. When she reached the far bank, Pytheas' face lit up. He slung the spear across his shoulder, patted her on the back of the head, thrusting her in front of him on the path, then proceeded to talk to her in his incomprehensible tongue behind her as she walked on. His tone was light but he was an enemy too and now he was armed. The anticipation of the touch of the blade between her shoulders kept her moving but it didn't come. Only his chanting voice and the sense of his eyes on her.

The hunt was fruitless: they were too many, too noisy, too stupid. Every prey animal for miles around had fled. Ussa was twitchy with frustration and everyone tried to give her a wide berth. Rian lagged behind, limping, the muscle of her branded thigh trembling, her back bruised by the weapon bag, her shoulder brand burning.

There was bustle when they arrived back at the village. Gruach was setting up his forge and a crowd had gathered to watch the performance. The fire was not yet lit but the paraphernalia of the forge was all laid out: a huge set of bellows and a long-handled pair of tongs, plus an armoury of stone, wood and metal tools. To one side crucibles and moulds were arranged as if they held offerings to gods. It was a cross between an altar and a stage and at the centre was the stack of wood that would feed the fire. Both Gruach and Fraoch were dressed in tough leather boots, trousers and sleeveless jerkins, their hair covered by tight hide caps, hands in sturdy but flexible cow skin gauntlets. Their upper arms, shoulders and backs were bare, and already beaded with sweat. Tattoos decorated Gruach's exposed skin: a dragon coiled up his back, breathing fire over one shoulder, licking down his right arm. His left arm was abstract: concentric circles, bands and diamond marks rippled up his triceps. On the tip of his shoulder, an eye watched, long-lashed and suspicious.

Rian stood apart from the throng, her bag at her feet. She wanted to sit down but the ground was slushy and she had no desire to enter the broch.

Fraoch spotted her, ran over to her and spoke with a strange foreign-sounding accent. She was pretty, despite her strange leather attire, with rounded features and smiling brown eyes. Like Rian, she was slight-framed, and her hair hung in a plait down her back. 'I'm sorry to trouble you. I am bleeding.' She pointed to her groin. 'I need something...' She gave a conspiratorial grin. 'You are Rian? I heard that Ussa... I'm sorry.'

The earnest frown of concern on her face was too much for Rian, who felt tears welling up. She turned, rubbing her eyes. 'Come. I can give you some moss.' She led Fraoch to the byre and found a box to stand on to reach up to where a roll of dried sphagnum moss was strung from the rafters. She tugged some from the bundle and rolled and smoothed it into a pad.

'There. I'll make you some more for later.'

Fraoch took it and began loosening her clothes. 'Thank you. If I can help you, ask me. Ussa is tough. You must be strong. Inside here.' She touched her chest, then her head. 'And here. She will try to break you in here. I don't know why she does it. Don't let her in. And be careful what you say. It is always better to be silent than to make her angry with words. She uses words against people. She makes weapons with them, sharper than my father's blades.' As she spoke she stuffed the moss down between her legs and fastened her leather trousers. 'Thanks. It's comfortable. You're a medicine woman too, like Danuta?'

Rian handed her half a dozen more of the swabs. 'I know some herbs.'

'Make sure Ussa finds out. But keep some secrets from her too. She'll hurt you less. Can you bring some healing stuff along with you when we go?'

'What do you mean, when we go?'

'We'll leave as soon as the forging work is done, before the embers cool, it's Ussa's way. You'll be coming too. You're one of us now.'

Rian had not thought about this consequence of what had happened. She said nothing.

'The day after tomorrow is my guess. It depends on the weather.'

Rian could not find any words to speak her feelings. Tears rose and she clenched them inside her. She turned away to the cow and stroked her.

'She is a lovely cow.'

Rian looked round at Fraoch. What did she know about cows?

'How old are you?'

Rian wanted to resist the question. Distrust was rushing through her veins. She did not want to be one of them. She was not like this girl. But 'fifteen' came out of her lips before she could stop it.

'Me too,' said Fraoch. 'I'll be sixteen at Beltane. And you?'

'Winter solstice,' Rian whispered. The few months that separated them in age seemed like an aeon that nothing would ever bridge. She looked back at Beithe, stroking the cow between its ears, wishing the girl would go away.

'I've got to go,' Fraoch said.

Rian nodded.

'Thanks for the moss. You know, in a way, I'm pleased you're coming. We can be friends.'

Rian hated her. Why didn't she leave?

'There's never been another girl on the boat.'

Rian wasn't listening. She just wanted her out of the byre. Now.

'Just leave me alone.' She turned to Fraoch, arms chopping. 'Get out. Get out.'

The cow, startled by her shouting, jostled in her stall. One hoof came down on her toe. Her voice rose to a wail. 'Oh just go!'

Fraoch's face crumpled into a pained frown. 'I'm sorry.' She retreated out of the doorway of the byre.

Rian buried herself in the hay behind the cows and wept. Once she began she wanted to cry for hours but the tears dried up and no more would come. She knew if she stayed there long enough Danuta would seek her out, but how long would that have to be? In the end, hunger drove her back out into the dusk.

A crowd had gathered around the forge and flames were dancing. Gruach was a huge silhouette, skin gleaming in the firelight. He had the crowd chanting an invocation. Normally Rian would have been mesmerised but nothing about today was normal. She stayed in the shadows, took the long way round the back of the broch and was about to enter. There were raised voices inside.

She crouched in one of the rooms off the entrance in the cavity between the two walls. Drost was sitting on a stool facing the fire. Across it, Danuta stood, her arm jabbing, finger pointed, shouting. Rian had never seen her shout like this. Her old face was red, veins stood out on her neck. She looked as if she might burst. A stream of insults flowed from her like some kind of song, not so very different from the invocation outside, but calling not on the fire spirits but on the spirits of mud, of bog, of mire and midden, the force of the sea bed, of sinking sand, the deepest powers of the ground. Danuta was calling on the earth to open up a pit and swallow him up and to fill the pit with venomous snakes, with cockroaches and fleas, with worms.

'You vowed to treat her as a daughter, you selfish boar. You'll rot in the belly of the Mother.'

With a jolt Rian realised this was about her.

'She's no flesh of mine and she's grown now, my obligation's done.' Drost was sitting firm on his stool but his voice betrayed him. He was close to whining. 'She's a burden. You'll see the difference when she's gone, how much more food there will be, how much less moaning.'

Danuta returned to the onslaught and Rian swallowed hard as the old woman reeled off the chores she did, a litany of work, season by season, hour by hour. She had never heard herself so appreciated and she sat back on her heels glowing with pride, her troubles forgotten, the brands suddenly soothed by the balm of Danuta's voice ranting a paeon of praise.

The cuff to her head sent her flying, face into the muddy floor, and before she could lift herself from the sprawl she was tugged up by her hair and a slap landed on her right cheek, twisting her head round, her lip burning. Her howl was cut short by another slap. 'So here's my workshy slave, sneaking and spying, not where it's wanted and not wanted where it loiters. This way.' The voices inside had stopped. Rian was spun and lurched forwards away out towards the forge, poked along by the bronze tip at the end of Ussa's staff.

'Wood,' Ussa pointed to the stack of logs behind Gruach. 'You know where it is. Get more.'

Rian turned but Ussa's talons in her shoulder stopped her. 'You take them with you.' Ussa was prising two of the slaves out of the crowd with her staff. 'And don't loiter.' The hand on her collarbone loosened. Ussa barked an instruction in the southern dialect. The two men nodded at Rian in acknowledgement of their joint mission. One was a burly, flat-faced fellow. The other was shorter and more slender, with a pointed nose like a marten cat and slightly crossed eyes.

'Li.' The bigger man pointed to his chest, then at his companion. 'Faradh.'

Rian felt she was expected to say her name, but these men had held her while she was branded. She would not speak to them.

They set off to the woodstack behind the byre. Away from the forge it was dark and the ice made the ground slippery underfoot.

'You were born here?' Li touched Rian on the elbow.

'No.'

'Drost not family?' he pursued.

'No.'

'Where are you from?'

'I don't know.'

'I'm sorry. My home is Lusitania, south.'

She didn't know where this was and said nothing.

'Faradh's home is Pou Kernou.'

She didn't know where Pou Kernou was either, although she had heard the name. The world was too big and too full of strangers.

'Where are you from?'

'I don't know.'

'How? How don't you know?' He grabbed her arm, but she shook it free.

What did it matter? Why did he want to know?

'I was found as a baby. Danuta found me, brought me here. That's all I know.'

'Of course. You're a fairy child, maybe!' he said. 'Faradh, Rian's a fairy child.' He said something in his own tongue or perhaps in Faradh's and they both laughed.

'Wood,' Rian said, picking up three big branches. Li took them from her, passed them to Faradh, then picked up two smaller pieces and laid them in her arms.

'Don't work so hard. Of course, work, yes, or Ussa...' He growled in imitation of some fierce animal. 'But work little, work gentle, or life is short.' Again he spoke in another language and shared a laugh with Faradh.

He picked up a third, small branch and balanced it with the others on Rian's arms. 'Fairy girl wood.'

He was being kind but she didn't want the sympathy of slaves. She threw the branches down, reached into the stack, pulled out two huge logs, and stomped away back to the fireplace. Li and Faradh's laughter scorched her back.

Her arms were burning with the strain by the time she reached the fireside and, pushing her way through the crowd to the woodpile, she felt people's eyes on her. Their scorn was worse than the pain in her muscles. She turned to leave but found her way blocked by Pytheas, who reached for her hand and lifted her arm, feeling the tension in her forearm. He spoke to Og, who said to Rian, 'He says you must carry smaller wood. Your arms will break if you take such big logs.'

She shook her arm free and ran headlong out of the crush of people and back to the woodstack, bumping Faradh as she passed him and swerving past Li, who tried to stop her. She would show them what she could do. She picked two more logs, even bigger this time, and trudged with them back to the fire. They needed all her body strength and she had to stop and shift their weight a couple of times, but she got them there. It was Danuta who stopped her this time.

'Rian, I need you.'

Rian glanced at Ussa, who was standing beside Pytheas, leaning in towards him as he gestured towards the forge, beating his finger in time with Gruach's hammer. Ussa lifted her nose, saw Rian and thrust a scornful finger in Danuta's direction. 'Go and cook with her.'

Rian let herself be led away by Danuta into the broch, arms trembling.

Inside it was dim, lit only by the central fire's glow. Danuta busied herself with sticks to keep it alive. Rian stood just inside the door. She had no momentum of her own. From high, high up she noticed her legs begin to sway.

Danuta blew a rush taper into flame and lit a lamp. 'Sit, sit. Look at you, oh just look at you, little bird.'

Rian let herself be pulled into motion again and wobbled past the hearth. Danuta steered her into her own sleeping area and sat her on the bed, then tugged the rigged up curtain between hers and Buia's spaces. She pulled the drape separating her cubicle from the rest of the house, leaving only a gap big enough to allow her to watch the door. They were alone, in a cocoon of cloth. The seal oil lamp's flame licked, its dance slowing, then stood. The shadows stilled. Danuta stroked Rian's head, then sat beside her. Rian let her arms rest on the bed, her fingers worked into the sheepskin, rummaging up to her knuckles in its softness.

The old woman tilted her head towards Rian's until they touched. Rian leaned into her shoulder and listened to her quiet sobs, feeling them shudder her frail body.

Danuta took a deep breath, pulled herself away and, taking Rian's face in both hands, she held her gaze. 'You're as dear to me as any child could be,' she began. 'You know I always wanted you to think of yourself as one of my family, and I can't tell you how angry I am at that brute son of mine. I don't know what I've done to make him that way. But you know yourself you're not his daughter and he's never really gone along with treating you like one. Anyway, one day you will know who you are and when you and all the rest find out where you came from I'll not be surprised if you charge them dear who've hurt you today. Drost included, even though he's my son. I make no secret he deserves it.'

'So who am I?'

'I can't tell you, little bird.'

'But you know?'

'Oh yes, I've always known, but I vowed I'd not tell a soul.'

'Not even me?'

'Especially not you.'

'Why can't you tell me?'

'I can't tell you yet, and the reason is part of the secret, which is why I've always made out I don't know anything and found you on the moor. But you might as well know that bit isn't true. I know fine who you are and you're no foundling.'

'So tell me.'

'No. You'll find out when the day is right for you to know.'

'But what if anything should happen to you? They're taking me away. What if I never see you again?' Rian's voice rose to a wail.

'Shush little bird. Nothing's going to happen to me. And there's another one who knows, so if it did, no harm's done.'

'Who?'

'A stranger to you, but a good man. Uill Tabar is his name. He is younger than me, and I've not seen him for a long time. He knows many secrets.'

'Uill Tabar? Who is he?'

'He lives far, far away from here.'

'But who is he?'

'He lives close to the southernmost tip of the land.'

'Will he tell me who I am?'

'He called the place Pou Kernou. I've never been there.'

That name again. She didn't mention the slave. Something, she wasn't sure what, made her hold back.

'More importantly, little bird, I need to check on those wounds she gave you, and make sure you've herbs so you can take care of yourself.' Danuta wrapped in seal bladder a patty of the yarrow butter ointment she had used to treat the slave's rowing sores.

Then she lifted the lamp off her medicine chest, opened it, and they began a ritual they had done a thousand times, Danuta laying out a package of herb, Rian undoing its fastening and sniffing then telling Danuta what it contained and how it was used. But this time Danuta had taken an old cloth, ripped it into small pieces, and from each package she took a sample and wrapped it up. The pile of little knotted rags mounted until Danuta said, 'There. Wrap them tight in something waterproof. No, here.' She rummaged in a box, produced a sealskin pouch and tipped its contents onto her bed. On any other day they could have spent a happy time now, sorting through the collection of amulets, bracelets and beads, but not today.

'For luck. Now, bundle all the herbs in there and tuck it away safely. We'd better look busy at the cooking.' Danuta swept all the other contents of the pouch into the deerskin bag she used every day, which hung on a peg above her bed, then pulled open the drapes and returned to the hearth.

Rian stuffed the pouch with all the herbs. When she emerged, Danuta had busied herself with making a broth of leftover meat from the previous night's roasted deer. She set Rian to chopping up wild carrot and silverweed roots and began on a dumpling mix. There was always plenty of seal blubber and the barley barrel still had enough to be generous. Danuta prided herself on never needing to rely on the success of a hunt to feed people.

Once the food preparation was well under way, Danuta sent Rian out to find out what was happening around the forge and when they might be likely to eat. She slipped out into the dark, creeping in the shadows, not wanting to be noticed. It was futile. Bael spotted her almost immediately and pointed at her. 'She's there.' He was standing beside Ussa, who had her hand conspiratorially in the crook of Pytheas' elbow.

'Come here.' She pulled the hand free and crooked her finger towards Rian with a smug smile on her face. 'I have news for you.' In her other hand she was rolling a ball of gleaming, flame-coloured jewel.

Rian approached, hoping to be able to stay out of arm's reach, but Ussa's hand swept her close. 'Here.' She pulled her in by sheer force of will. Once in reach, Ussa's fingers took purchase on her head, and swivelled her to look at Pytheas.

He bent down and said something to her in Greek. His eyebrows were lifted, eyes wide, and his grin pouched up his cheeks. Rian would have laughed at his expression were it not for the talons in her hair. He was ridiculous.

'Pytheas is your owner now, girl. He has paid me handsomely for you.' She rolled the ball in her hand. 'Look at this. Do you know what it is? Amber. He says it's the colour of your hair. Isn't that sweet?'

She spoke to Pytheas in some tongue and Rian looked from one face to the other. He nodded and lifted Ussa's hand off Rian's head, then replaced it with his own flat palm. He patted her like a dog and beamed. It was clear he expected her to smile back. She moved her face into some grimace that involved her mouth elongating sideways and bending up at the sides, feeling her cheeks stretch. She belonged to the clown. What did that mean?

'Pytheas.' He put his hand on his chest. As if she didn't know.

She complied and responded. 'Rian.'

He patted her on the head again. She was at a loss, so she gestured eating with her mouth and fingers. He nodded vigorously and, pulling Ussa's arm, indicated she should lead them into the broch. But Ussa shook him off, said something to him, and turned back to the forge to continue watching the sword being born.

Rian led her new master towards the hearth.

RÒN

They sailed soon after sunrise.

There was so much to do Rian did not have time to say goodbye properly to Beithe the cow, or to gather more than the most basic of her possessions. Danuta held a bag while she stuffed in a few clothes and made sure she had her new medicine pouch around her waist. Then she had to go, with only a quick hug from the wet-eyed old woman. Buia ran after her down to the boat offering a sheepskin but Ussa took it, laid it out on her bench and sat on it, saying, 'She's a slave. What does she want with things like that?'

As the ropes were slipped and Li and Faradh pulled on the oars, Rian waved to Buia, trying to smile.

'Be good,' Buia called, then turned away, one hand smearing her tears.

Ussa gave Rian a wooden scoop and pointed to the bottom of the boat. 'Bail.'

The water was stinking and its level did not seem to drop no matter how hard Rian worked. She had to stoop, fill the bailer, then stretch up and out to reach over and dump the water overboard. Once under way, sail up, the boat heeled and she had to be careful to ensure that what came out of the bailer didn't splash back onto Ussa. A mistake earned her a kick in her back that she knew she'd feel for days. As she bailed, her hands softened, wrinkling, and the wet wood became harder to grip. Her lower back felt as if she would break in two, but she dared not rest. The stench made her feel sick.

Pytheas and Og were laughing behind her. Og called her name. She stood and looked back. The boat was impressive, its four-pointed sail rounded and full of wind. At the stern, Toma the sailor stood with legs apart, hand on the tiller, talking to his boy, Callum, who was wearing a storm coat and hat identical to the skipper's except only half the size. Adoration filled the youth's face as he lapped up Toma's training, pointing to named landmarks to show he had learned them and jumping to tighten a rope so the sail was the perfect shape.

Just to the windward side of Toma, Pytheas lounged on a bench with his goose feather and the leather sheet that he scratched on. He patted the bench next to him. He was sitting on Rian's fleece, which by gestures she deduced he had retrieved for her from Ussa. He beckoned to Rian to come to him, then pointed back towards the land they had come from. The mountains were ranged out in a line like stumps in a crone's mouth, and Pytheas pointed to each one in turn with a question on his face.

Og said, 'He wants to know if the hills have names. I told him you might have some idea.' Then he lowered his voice. 'And you looked like you needed a break from the bailing. It's hard work for a short arse like you.'

Rian managed a smile. She pointed to the southerly ridge. It was a game she had played countless times with Danuta when they reached a high point on one of their many herb-gathering walks.

'Coigach,' she said.

Pytheas made an attempt to repeat it back and, once he was satisfied he had the sound, he dipped the sharpened goose feather in a little pot of dark liquid which he clutched in one hand and scratched on the leather, making a little squiggle of curves. Rian realised it must be some record of the name. She peered at the writing, intrigued. He grinned at her and pointed at the next mountain peak.

'Stac Pollaidh.' The squiggle was different this time.

And so it went on. 'Cùl Beag. Cùl Mòr. Suilven, Canisp, Quinag.' All went down in the Greek man's script with only one blot, despite the motion of the boat. She wondered what strange magic this was that he was doing and whether the mountains would be affected by it in some way. She hoped that what she had done was not wrong and asked the Great Mother silently to forgive her, if her naming the mountains so this man could write them down had been some crime she did not know about.

Pytheas asked Og something. He rummaged in a bag and gave them both an oatcake. Pytheas rolled up the feather and his leather sheet and stowed it in the box under his bench. Then he gave her a squeeze on the shoulder and leaned back beaming at the landscape.

Rian sat as still as she could, although the boat heeled towards Pytheas, and she had to grip the bench under her to try to avoid leaning too much against the man's body and to stop herself tumbling as the boat lurched on big waves. As they turned out of the bay, the sea's motion grew and from time to time spray showered the boat. Beyond them was open water, a great expanse of grey to the north.

As they approached Stoer Head, the boat rocked and tossed in the jabbly water. Rian was still nauseous from the bilges. Og pointed to the oatcake which she had left uneaten in her lap but she shook her head.

He picked it up and jabbed it towards her, patting his stomach. 'Best thing for it.'

She didn't believe him. But he kept thrusting the biscuit at her, Pytheas nodding, so she took it and nibbled and found to her surprise that she did feel better.

She looked about her. The boat was more commodious than it had looked when she first came aboard. From the vantage of Pytheas' bench at the stern she could see the whole vessel. The mast was closer to the front than the back and there were four rowing benches two on each side, to the fore and abaft the mast, and between them chests, presumably full of trade goods.

From what Rian could tell, Ussa was no longer in charge. Although she had barely noticed him on land, Toma was clearly in command of the boat. He and Callum were calmly making adjustments to the rigging.

Og saw Rian watching them and he shuffled her along the bench, squeezing her between him and Pytheas. 'Toma runs the show on the boat.'

Ussa was under a shelter of hide stretched across wooden beams at the bow. Rian could see her seal skin boots stretched out on a bench. From the waist upwards she was hidden from view but something about the way the feet were splayed told her that the trader was catching up on sleep.

Gruach the smith and his daughter were also in the shelter. Fraoch was curled up, a blanket wrapped around her, on a kind of shelf suspended above a bench on which Gruach splayed, head pillowed on his toolbag, mouth open, snoring.

Og pointed at them. 'The smith was working until dawn. It's always the same.'

'Are they slaves too?' Rian asked.

Og shook his head. 'No, far from it. Gruach is Ussa's cousin. He often travels with her.'

The two other slaves, Li and Faradh, sat on rowing benches, leaning against the side of the boat, hoods up, heads nodding. Callum was coiling a tangle of ropes.

Their route had taken them out into the Minch, towards the northernmost of the Evening Isles. Pytheas and Og pointed to them, speaking in Pytheas' tongue, then Og turned to Rian. 'Have you been to this island?'

'The Long Island. Yes, we go each year. To the Stones.'

Og transmitted this to Pytheas, who raised his eyebrows. 'What stones?'

Rian was amazed. Didn't everybody know? 'Over there, on the far side of the island, the sacred ring of Callanish.'

'Describe it,' Pytheas demanded. And Og repeated what Rian told him.

'They stand upright like stone people, a ring of them, and a double line where the road goes in. They were put there by the ancients. I love going there.' Rian stopped, suddenly self-conscious. Had she said too much?

'When do you go?' asked Pytheas, through Og.

'Beltane. People gather from all around.'

'And the stones? What part do they play?'

'They're the centre of it all.'

'And are there moon or sun readings?'

Rian wasn't sure what he meant and shook her head. Then something Danuta had told her came to mind. 'In midwinter, the Sisters do a sun ceremony. And there are moon dances. Is that what he means?'

Og translated and Pytheas nodded.

'Have you seen these ceremonies?' Og asked.

A memory, sudden and vivid, reached out of the past. She had not sought it. 'I once saw the moon dance, but I was very small. I didn't understand what they were doing.'

The Sisters had come for them in the afternoon. It was normal for Danuta to go and take part in whatever they did but usually Rian would stay with all the other children. It was a horrible day, driving rain on a cold north-westerly wind, one of those spring reminders of winter, like a growling bear woken too early from its sleep.

They went up to the stones. The big dome tent was in the centre, a plume of smoke issuing from the hole at the top. She had never been inside it. The Sister was about the same age as Danuta, though much shorter, dressed in a robe of pale cloth that made her movements seem fluid. She was light, fluttering along instead of walking, and her laughter was like the call of a little bird, a high piping trill. She and Danuta appeared to know each other well, though Rian had never set eyes on her. She was called, appropriately enough, The Wren.

At the tent, she said, 'No metal?'

Danuta unpinned her brooch, then pointed to Rian's belt, with the bronze buckle she had been given for her most recent birthday. It was her prize possession.

'Take it off,' Danuta said.

'Why?'

'We must not take metal into the Mother's womb.'

'But it's…'

Danuta was giving her one of those stares. She obeyed and stripped off the belt.

'I'll put them in a safe place, don't worry,' The Wren had said, examining it. 'Very fine. Is that Sorok's work?'

'Yes,' said Danuta. 'He stayed with us last winter.'

Sorok was Danuta's brother, a smith and a magician who travelled like most smiths, far and wide, searching for metals and trade and never settling for long. But he was getting old and spent his winters with them more often than not. He had not been well that last winter, coughing badly, and in the following autumn he had not come and word had eventually reached them that he had died on some far distant island to the north.

Now Ussa was wearing that buckle, ostentatiously, and Rian was reduced to a piece of rope around her middle. But the belt was hers, it had been designed for her, decorated with her favourite things, the twist of ivy and the tern. She loved the sweeping grace of a flock of terns, their massed flight like a wedding dance, the way one day they were here, the next gone. Although the day they left the shore was a void after months of their squealing calls, the joy they brought in springtime made up for it every time. Sorok said that they became snowflakes during winter. He also said that one day she too might fly. Looking at the main sail filling with wind, the ropes tugging, the boat coursing over the sea, she felt a little as if she was flying, but it wasn't what she had imagined when Sorok had given her her fate. She should be at the helm with her belt on and a good knife about her person, free to follow the terns. This was all wrong.

Rian shook her head and tried to return to the memory of Callanish. Her hand rested on her belly, remembering. These experiences had suddenly taken on a significance: the look of intrigue on the Greek man's face, a sense of this stretch of water being her place, the lands on either side her lands, the ceremonies that went on there being for the spirits of her people, the Sisters being her sisters. They had said she would be one of them one day. The Wren had said so that time in the warm tent when she had led them in, holding back the hide flap, then drawing it closed behind them.

It was dimly lit inside and Rian was bewildered by all the smoke and fumes. Something was bubbling on a fire in the centre and the tent was crowded with women. An argument seemed to be going on over on the far side of the hearth and everyone was watching. Rian was pressed to sit on a cushion next to another girl, several years older than her, who gave her a tense frown of irritation whenever she so much as moved. The older girl's attention was focussed on the shouting women. Danuta sat away over across the fire and was being whispered to by the woman next to her, a wrinkled hag. The old one pointed over at Rian and gestured to her to watch the fracas by the hearth.

One of the women was wearing a mask made of black wood with huge baleful eyes and a drooping mouth. Her body was flabby and wobbled as she dodged the shrieks and blows of the other, whose face was red and full of ferocity, snarling and ranting. She was wearing a wolf's tail and she reached behind her to catch it, then flicked it in the face of the other woman, who howled, grabbed it and pulled. The wolf-woman fell to the ground, her face to the floor, and the fat one stood over her, waving the tail.

Everyone seemed to be laughing. An ancient figure emerged from inside a cloth, silver-haired, pale-faced and all wrapped in white. Rian knew this must be the cailleach of winter. She sang a bitter tune in a thin, reedy voice, and then produced a little wooden whistle and played the same melody in an even thinner, reedier manner. The big woman swayed with the tail of the wolf in a sleepy kind of dance, then hunkered down, and the crone covered them both with her white cloth. Her piping had stopped but it left a painful feeling.

Rian gave an involuntary shudder and once more caught the eye of the woman next to Danuta. She winked. Rian shivered again. It was cold. It was too quiet. She didn't like it.

Then someone was poking her in the back, and she remembered what Danuta had told her when they had been walking to the tent. She had to take the whistle from the white cailleach and play the tune she had been taught. It was a very simple tune. Rian thought it was a bit stupid, just three rising notes, over and over, the first two close, the third higher. She knew lots of better tunes.

Now she had to take this old woman's pipe and play in front of all these women. The person behind her was pushing her to her feet and the winter cailleach was pointedly looking away, playing the odd creepy couple of notes on her whistle, then letting it dangle in her left hand, the hand closest to Rian.

She looked across at Danuta who was urging her on, smiling and tilting her head towards the white woman. She plucked up her courage and stood, stepped up to the crone, snatched the whistle from her hand and put it to her mouth.

It was bigger than the one she was used to. She had to look where the finger holes were. Then she took a breath and played the first three notes. The old woman slumped beside her. To her amazement, a chorus from the women, in full throat, sang her notes back to her.

'Spring will come,' they sang. Then there was silence.

She played the notes again. Again, they sang in response. Now the tune made sense. Each time she played it, they sang back in ever richer harmony.

With a clap and a rattle, the girl who had been sitting beside her got to her feet and began to dance. She had wooden beads around her wrists and ankles that made the rattling sound. Someone took the whistle from her hands and began one of the tunes she loved. Someone else led her back to her cushion. Danuta was beaming at her, clapping along. She found herself joining in. Everyone was singing. The girl danced with a big smile on her face, slowly lifting her arms. The song was about the flowers of spring, beginning with shy primroses in the woods. Each verse brought another flower into bloom: violets, celandines and wood sorrel, then bluebells blooming with their colour of summer sky. As the flowers were named, the girl's arms reached up over her head and she span, her skirt billowing out like the petals of a flower opening. Rian overflowed with love for her and her beautiful blossoming dress. She was magnificent.

'Math dha riribh! Math dha riribh!' The women shouted, cheering the Spring Dancer. She grinned shyly now she had finished and came to sit again beside Rian, sweating and out of breath. Rian adored her. They squeezed hands as the women whooped and called their praises. A drinking horn passed round, everyone taking a swig. Rian met Danuta's big smile across the fire and she glowed to be in the orbit of the Spring Dancer.

The cailleach was suddenly transforming, pulling her white hair off her head, then splashing her face from a bowl of water and wiping it with a ragged grey cloth: under all that white was a golden woman. She let loose a torrent of corn-coloured hair and stepped out of the crone's white coat to reveal a robe the colour of buttercups, embroidered and decorated with white and green leaves.

Rian was mesmerised by the transformation. She had seen the pupae of moths and watched dragonflies hatching by pools but now she had seen an equally magical metamorphosis of a woman. The yellow angel caught her gaze and smiled. She bent to the woman who had been playing the whistle for the spring song and said something to her. She nodded and handed it up to her. She gave a few toots and the women ceased their chatter and gave her their attention.

'You'll all agree our spring maidens have excelled themselves today. Rian, I hope you will be a Sister one day, and to help you on your way, here is the whistle you played so beautifully to herald the end of winter.' She knelt in front of Rian, drew her hand forward, and laid the little wooden instrument gently across her palm. Her fingers closed around its wonder.

The golden woman turned to the dancer but Rian could not take in what was being said. She blazed with pride and questions. Women were patting her on the back, touching her head as if she was a lucky talisman, stroking her like a kitten. Then Danuta was there and she could hide her flaming face inside the hug that she hadn't realised until then was what she really wanted.

The memory of it was enough to make Rian tremble still. Although she couldn't remember what had happened to the Spring Dancer that day, she knew what must have ensued. It had been her turn last year. She had danced the invitation and fulfilled the promise of her childhood.

But before she could follow the memory of that event she was interrupted by Pytheas. He wanted her, Og said, to describe to him if she knew of any other stones used for predicting the moon or the sun.

'Of course.' Then she bit her lip. How much of what she knew was she at liberty to tell this strange man? She wondered if Ussa knew she had begun training for the Sisterhood. Danuta had kept it from many people. There were few men who were allowed to know much at all of what the Sisters did – everyone knew that she had herbal knowledge and it was accepted that Danuta was passing it onto her as well as Buia. But the other lore – the ceremonies to invoke spirits, rituals for fertility and birth and all the moon-magic – that was never spoken of beyond the Sisterhood. Rian realised she wasn't sure exactly how much of what she knew was secret. It was better to err on the safe side and play dumb.

Og was waiting.

'There are lots of stones where the old people make offerings, but I don't know why.'

Og translated. Pytheas looked at her as if he could see her secrets.

'Does your foster mother make these offerings? She is a medicine woman, isn't she?'

Rian nodded. That much was common knowledge, but she would not be drawn any more on the matter of stones.

Pytheas spoke at length to Og, after which Og said only, 'He tells a story of some other Greek who bought a slave to stop some king from doing her harm.'

'Brisei.' Pytheas patted her on the shoulder. 'Achilles.' His other hand was on his chest.

'He wants you to know he means you no harm.' With that Og went into his galley area under the shelter at the bow.

Pytheas beckoned to her, speaking in his tongue, pointing to himself, giving his name, repeating a phrase over and over and clearly wanting her to say it back to him. She tried to pronounce the strange phrase, '*Onopa moi...*,' replacing Pytheas with Rian, and he clapped his hands, beaming, and corrected her. She tried again and again and eventually he was satisfied and moved on to teaching her how to greet him, and how to say goodbye. She learned happy and sad, cold and hot, and finally hungry. So began her lessons in Greek. 'Hungry', '*peinao*', was the trigger for her to seek Og in his galley, where she was set to work helping him to prepare food for everyone.

ERIBOL

By mid-afternoon they had rounded the Cape at the north and made their way east to a big loch where they began looking for somewhere sheltered for the night. Rian knew the people from here. A cousin of Danuta lived in a beautiful roundhouse known as Three Lochs, next to a trio of lochs with healing powers. But no-one on board asked for her help. Why would they? She was just a slave.

There was frantic activity for a while as the loch was sized up for a mooring spot. The sails dropped, oars were set out and all hands put to them, including Rian's. She loved to skull but this was harder than any rowing she had ever done in a coracle.

They pulled the boat up on the shore and set up a makeshift camp. They were on the far side of the loch from Three Lochs and no attempt was made to go over to greet the people. Rian wondered why, but said nothing. A spare sail was rigged from a rope between trees and two of the slaves set to cutting birches, with none of the customary ritual to seek permission from the wood spirits. Rian thought to intervene but, registering Ussa's bad-tempered pacing, decided it was better not to. She begged the Mother silently for forgiveness and spoke in a whisper as subtly as she could to the tree spirits, thanking them for their help.

She was put to work carrying sleeping rolls, food and drink from the boat to the camp. Then she was sent in the near dark to fetch water from the stream in two bladders.

Night fell swiftly and Ussa sat complaining to Toma while Og led the preparation of food.

Toma perched on his bedding roll with his hands clasped on his lap, his boy Callum beside him. 'Sailing in during darkness? Suicide. You've seen the rosts.'

Rian had no idea what a rost was.

Ussa rolled her eyes at him. 'Well, don't blame me if the people over there slit our throats in the night.'

Toma smiled. 'I can't help it if you've made enemies, Ussa.'

Rian wondered what Ussa had done to anger the Three Lochs people but, before she could listen more, Pytheas beckoned her to him. He began teaching her vocabulary for food – meat of various sorts, involving animal noises – until Ussa shouted at him to be quiet. He winked at Rian, who tried to shrink back into the shadows.

But Ussa saw her and snapped her fingers. 'Fetch my coat.'

Rian scampered to where she had seen Ussa drop it earlier, under the sail rigged as a sleeping tent. She carried it back, her fingers swallowed by the dense white fur. It weighed as much as a dog. She held it out to Ussa, who took it without looking.

Then Og asked her to help cook the bannocks, which at least gave her a chance to look after the fire and be tender to it and thereby perhaps appease the wood spirits. She looked up to see Pytheas' eyes on her. He grinned. She lowered her gaze back down to the patty of dough but could not help an answering smile breaking onto her face. Ussa said something in her tongue and everyone laughed. Rian wished Pytheas would let her focus on picking up that language, not the one only he used. It might be more use to her to understand the subtleties of Ussa's jibes and jokes. She could make out some of what was said, as the language they all used wasn't so different from her own, but they all had strong accents and strange intonation and she missed a lot.

Ussa tapped her on the knee. 'I said your master should be teaching you to speak Keltic properly so you can understand what we all want from you instead of us having to use your gutterspeak.' She opened her mouth wide to laugh, reverting to her

53

home dialect and clearly continuing to make jokes at her expense. She was sitting right next to Pytheas, rubbing up to him like a cat.

Rian was saved by Og serving up the meat he had stewed. The silence of eating descended.

She felt a bump as Fraoch sat down beside her. Og handed her a bowl of stew and Rian gave her half of the last bannock. They were good, and there were grunts of appreciation from around the fire. Li waved the remainder of his at Rian, his cheeks full, and said something, presumably his word for 'tasty'. She repeated it to herself in her head. While Pytheas taught her Greek, there was nothing to stop her picking up what she could of this other language too. It didn't seem so different from her native tongue and she had already noticed some familiar words.

Fraoch nudged her. 'They like your cooking,' she murmured. 'Don't mind Ussa's teasing. She's like that with everyone, but she has a heart of gold, really. She'll treat you well if you keep the crew's bellies happy.'

As soon as she had eaten, Fraoch went off to where she and Gruach were sleeping in their own shelter a little apart from the others, no doubt to get some peace and quiet. A flask of something foul-smelling was doing the rounds of the sailors. Ussa reverted to bickering at Toma. Rian was tired.

She woke to Pytheas leaning over her, pointing towards the tent made of sail. She dragged herself to her feet and gratefully made tracks to bed. It was starting to snow. Pytheas showed her where he had put his sleeping roll and indicated a hide mat and her fleece, next to him. He had lit a little oil lamp and, as she snuggled down, thanking Danuta for the extra layer of warm clothes she had given her, Pytheas got a square object out of his box, a tough leather casing beautifully embossed which opened out to reveal sheets of a smooth material covered with tiny markings. What other treasures were hidden in the luggage of this mysterious man?

'Periplus,' he said.

She frowned, mystified. He seemed proud of it, stroking it, and she liked him for his treasuring of this object. Perhaps if he was going to teach her to speak his tongue, he might teach her to read his script as well.

'Periplus,' she repeated, although sleep was making her tongue sluggish. He smiled down at her and put his hand on her hair with the same action he had used on the book.

'Good night,' he said. *'Hypíaine.'*

'Hypíaine,' she repeated.

And then it was morning. Or at least it was the part of the night when Toma decreed they must leave. The tide was back in, starting to lick the boat's stern timbers. In the half dark Rian rolled up her bedding and tied it.

Og was searching for dry sticks. 'We need porridge, quick.'

She gathered some slender birch twigs and dead heather stems. She breathed the fire back to life and fed it until the flames danced. Toma grumbled at Og but, when he saw the pot of porridge Rian was stirring, his shoulders dropped a notch and he almost smiled.

Li and Faradh emerged from their beds bleary and confused, and sat gazing into the flames until Ussa smacked them on the backs of their heads, cursing their excessive drinking in words even Rian could not fail to understand. She was beginning to distinguish the various tones that Ussa had in her repertoire: a coarse, guttural register for talking to slaves, a barking shrillness for those like Toma whom she considered should do her will, and a silken sing-song for anyone she was hoping to ingratiate herself with, which seemed to include Pytheas and for some reason Gruach. She is like a dog with three barks, Rian thought, one for sheep, one for the pack and one for the master.

Soon, porridge eaten, they were under way.

As dawn grew the tide lifted the boat free and the slaves began carrying all of the gear back down the shore. The snow had not been much but it was enough to make the stones slippery and there were curses as they slithered about, getting in each others' way in their haste to spend as little time as possible with their feet in the water. The sun rose behind the hill to the east as Rian clambered on board. The oars bit into the water. Toma called for the last of the ropes to be untied and a burst of sunshine blazed through the birches, crystals of ice glittering. Faradh and Li began to sing as they rowed. Callum tugged loose various ropes and Og joined in, hauling up the mainsail to the rhythm of the tune until Ussa snapped at them all to be quiet. As the sail caught the breeze, Toma allowed Li and Faradh to stop rowing.

Li minced about in a mockery of silence but the bronze tip of Ussa's well-aimed rod on his fingers took the smile off his face. After that Ussa sat alone in front of the mast and everyone else steered clear of her. Toma was the only one looking cheerful at first, but the beauty of the day could not fail to lift their spirits. It was one of those clear, blue mornings when then world is new again and seems ready for anything.

Toma called for Fraoch and asked her something, pointing at Rian. He showed her a tangle of ropes and she nodded, seeming to understand what was needed. Toma asked Pytheas and he gave a nod of assent. Rian watched with unease as Fraoch began tugging the ropes towards the bench where she had hoped she would be inconspicuous.

'Help me with these, Rian.'

Between the two of them the bundle slid easily across the deck. 'Do you know how to fix rope?'

Rian shook her head.

'No problem. It's easy. I'll show you.'

Fraoch sat down on the bench. Rian shuffled along to make room for her, then picked up an end of the rope to look at it more closely. It was much more smooth and flexible than the tough heather rope that she was used to handling.

'This is a blessing,' said Fraoch. 'Easy to look busy and a chance to talk to someone nice for a change.'

Rian didn't meet her eye.

'That was a compliment.' Fraoch nudged her with her elbow.

'Sorry.' Rian glanced at Fraoch. She seemed so confident, as if her muscles were somehow filled with a liquid hotter and more powerful than mere blood.

Fraoch nudged her again and nodded towards Ussa, imitating her sulking pout.

Rian let herself smile a little although she felt only dread. But she had nowhere else to go and so she sat very still and paid attention as Fraoch showed her how to mend the ropes. They were made of long, strong fibres: hemp, Fraoch said, which grew further south. It was a marvellous material, more pliable than heather twine and stronger than the nettle fibres she had spent countless hours plaiting to make halters for cattle and handles for bags. Fraoch's fingers were deft. She split the fibres of the broken ends of rope and twisted them back around each other until they held.

Rian was good at this sort of work and she was soon weaving almost as well as Fraoch. Though her hands weren't as strong, her fingers were nimble, and the older girl gave her the thinner, lighter ropes to work on. The bigger ones were plied and took the strength of two of them to twist right.

'It's satisfying, isn't it?' Fraoch said. 'When my mother died, Ussa told me to make rope whenever I'm unhappy.'

Rian's fingers slowed. So Fraoch was motherless, too. Her curiosity was piqued but she didn't want to be friendly. She had watched Ussa and Fraoch together and there was an ease between them that meant Fraoch must be suspect.

They were far out to sea, keeping well off the rocky coastline. Under the keel was a bottomless, black depth. The boat seemed flimsy. It rolled from side to side with every wave and the water slapping its hide skin was endlessly repetitive.

'When did she die?' Rian asked, eventually.

'When I was seven. Ussa taught me to weave my feelings into ropes, one twine of sadness, one twine of love, another twine of anger maybe, whatever I had inside me on the day. It all goes into the rope to make it strong. It works. I've always done it like that. Even when you don't know what to call the feeling, the rope understands.'

Rian tried twisting her hurt into the fibres in her hands, then the sickness in the pit of her belly, which she saw, once it was between her fingers, as fury: dark, bitter fury at Drost. Then there was the sorrow of not being with Danuta and Buia, not being with Beithe, not being in her secret place in the woods. She tried to stop the tears from welling up but they would not be prevented.

'It's good to wet the hemp a little sometimes. Let it come out, keep winding it all into the rope.'

Rian sniffed and kept her fingers working.

'Here.' Fraoch dug into a pocket on her jerkin and produced a cloth of soft material.

Rian took it and wiped her eyes and blew her nose. 'Sorry. It's lovely stuff.' She rubbed it between her fingers. 'Shame to snot on it.' She half laughed between her tears. Fraoch's concern stung her. There was such unbearable kindness in her face.

'You keep it,' Fraoch said. 'I've got another one. It's good linen, from Kantion, same as the hemp. It used to be an underslip of my granny's. She'd like me to be passing it on again. She's generous like that.'

Rian remembered the Sisters at Callanish and felt the same hot glow of adoration for Fraoch that she had felt sitting beside the Spring Dancer that first time. She blew her nose again then folded the linen square and tucked it inside her belt. The feeling for Fraoch was a float, buoying her along. She put her hands back to the rope, sniffed again, and heard the water hushing under the keel.

They sailed on, the breeze not quite directly behind them. For a while a cloud grizzled out the sun but then the sky cleared again, opening out into innocent blue.

Pytheas came with his box and squeezed onto the bench beside Rian as they worked the rope. The girls fell quiet. He seemed to be content to sit without talking, watching their hands, but Rian was conscious of his thigh pressing against hers. He opened his chest and took out his writing tools. He unplugged a bottle and dipped a quill into the liquid inside it. Rian watched with fascination as he scratched on the sheet of what must be parchment. She had only ever heard of it and wanted to touch its smooth paleness.

He spoke to Fraoch and she said, 'He wants to know if you can guess what he is writing.'

Rian gave a tiny shake of her head.

Fraoch and he conferred. 'He is telling where he has been. He writes down what you told him yesterday about stones. He is describing this coastline, where we stopped last night, the time of the moon and the high and low tide.'

'Why?'

Fraoch and he talked at length. Rian tried to follow but could only make out a few words. It was frustrating.

'I don't understand what he is trying to explain to me,' said Fraoch. 'He says the moon chooses the height of the tide but it is not because she is a goddess, it is something else.'

The moon was a powerful goddess. Rian had no doubt of that. She wondered what Danuta would have said to Pytheas. She also knew the tide was always biggest around the full and new moons. Should she say this to him? Before she could, he was pointing to a scratch mark on the parchment.

'He says this is moon.'

'*Selene.*'

She repeated it after him and, as she said it, he bounced his quill from tiny mark to tiny mark.

'Each mark has a different sound,' said Fraoch, and suddenly Rian understood. It was like Ogham, the script Danuta had taught her for carving into magic sticks.

He showed her another squiggle. '*Thalassa.*' He spoke so the vowel sounds were clear. 'ThA-lA-ssA.'

'A,' he repeated. He pointed to the corresponding marks and

Rian saw that they were the same. Then he scratched four symbols, emphasising the third, which was the A again. 'Ri-A-n,' he said. 'R-i-a-n.'

Her name was there on the parchment, a sequence of four marks. Would she ever get her soul back? It had fallen out of her mouth, which remained open. It was there staring back at her from the magic surface of the sheet spread out on Pytheas' knee.

Then he was handing her the quill, shifting the page towards her. It was almost more than she could bear. He wanted her to copy what he had written. She took the feather and, as if it was not such a marvel after all, she wrote her name.

SEAL ISLANDS

As they approached the Seal Islands the easy sailing came to an end. All the ropes and boxes were stowed away. The water became choppy.

'There are dangerous currents here.' Fraoch wound up the last of the ropes. 'Best not to antagonise Toma.' She put her finger to her lips and shrank into the corner of the bench. Beside her, Rian gazed out at the islands looming up out of the sea.

Toma began a convoluted song with a short chorus. Callum joined in but when Og added his voice to it Toma asked him to desist. Toma seemed to be using the words of the song to guide him along, as if it was a kind of magic to make the water safe, or perhaps just a way of teaching his boy the way to the anchorage.

Whether by magic or wisdom, before long they were into sheltered water, the sail lowered and oars out. They hauled the boat into a geo, a steep-sided inlet with safe shallow water for landing. A boat was huddled in a noust on land. After a brief, tetchy exchange with Toma, Ussa lowered herself from the prow. Og tossed her staff down to her and then followed. The two of them waded to the shore and headed away up the steep slope. Everyone else stayed onboard, readying themselves for disembarking but not actually going anywhere.

Pytheas indicated to Rian that she would carry both her bedding roll and his, while he carried his box and the long marked pole she had seen him use up the hill behind the broch. 'Gnomon.' He shook it. Then he handed it to her and taught her some Greek

61

instructions. 'Give me the Gnomon.' 'Bring me the Gnomon.' 'Put the Gnomon there.' 'Put it here.' The basics of command vocabulary. It was no doubt useful to know, but as they practised with Pytheas' box, his hat, his cloak, even his boots, Rian grew resentful. This was language for a slave, nothing more. When her attention slipped and she got one wrong, Toma, Gruach and Faradh, who were watching, jeered at her. Her cheeks burned.

Pytheas turned to them. 'Don't be cruel, gentlemen. She can't help being stupid.'

It was as if he thought she couldn't understand even simple Keltic.

'Sorry Rian,' Toma said. 'Your master has reminded us that we are not as courteous as he is.'

Rian looked up at Pytheas and repeated the phrase he used when she gave him what he asked for. 'Eukharisto. Thank you.'

The sun came out on his face and he threw an arm around her shoulder, pulling her towards him and ruffling her hair, saying things that could only be approval.

She shrank back. She didn't want to be petted like a cat.

Ussa was clearly not coming back in a hurry and the tide was still rising. After a while, Toma asked for the sweeps. They rowed a little closer in and Toma told his boy to let down the anchor. Pytheas conferred with Gruach and Toma and some agreement was made. Gruach was first over the side into the shallows and, as Fraoch began handing him their belongings, Pytheas gestured to Rian to join Gruach, ferrying things to shore. She rolled up her leggings and took off her boots. She knew the cost of wet footwear.

It took them ages to unload everything, Gruach cursing and swearing at having to wade ashore, but the sun was setting fast and they couldn't wait any longer for Ussa to come back with a better harbour option.

Rian's feet were numb as she slipped up and down the stony shore carrying tools, sacks and mysterious bundles of the bronze-esmith's trade goods, but she persisted and the thanks Gruach

gave her for her efforts made it almost worthwhile. 'You be careful here,' he said, as they sat on the rocks putting their boots on.
'It's a dangerous place for a young woman.' She wasn't quite sure
what he meant.

Behind their boat another vessel, longer but narrower than
theirs, was taking shelter in the geo with much shouting and
urgency. A man with sleek, dark hair to his shoulders, wearing a
coat with a furry collar and a substantial sword across his back,
swung off the bow and splashed up the shore.

Before she could look at him any further, though, he was on
her. Suddenly she found herself face down in the sward with his
arms around her. The grass was short and stiff and its sandy roots
were strong. Her hands attempted to get a grip and, her knees
sinking, she tried to butt him off her with her thighs. Then she
kicked out and made contact.

'You little weasel!'

She found herself squeezed tight, his breath on her neck. He
reeked of seal oil.

She kicked again but he had her calves pinioned. Elbows met a
grunt. She tried a trick she'd learned fighting with Bael. She went
limp and once she felt his grip loosen she squirmed into a ball
then burst out with all four limbs at full pelt. It worked and she
broke out of his grasp, her left foot inflicting a sharp blow that
had the required effect and let her roll free.

'Oh, by bladderwrack, who the hell are you?'

'Who the hell are you?' she retorted, panting and backing away
to what she hoped was a safe distance.

'I thought you were Fraoch. Ah, you bitch.' He clutched his
knee.

Gruach was looking on, shaking his head, a wry lift to his
eyebrows.

'What've you done with your daughter, you old metal-man-
gler?' he said. 'Have you traded her in for a prettier one?'

'Calling me old, you wee seal-shagger?'

Rian continued to back away as the intruder traded insults with Gruach, although both seemed to be thoroughly enjoying themselves in the exchange. Another man clambered down off the boat and made for the shore, miming drinking to the dark man, who swore at him as well.

With peals of laughter Fraoch ran ashore and dashed in to attempt a kick to follow Rian's, but her ankle was caught by the man and she took a tumble. She freed herself before he could gain the advantage and danced back and sideways towards Rian. 'Watch him! He's trouble, nothing but trouble!'

Then to the man she said, 'And you keep your stinking paws off my friend!'

He bowed. When he looked up at Rian, his eyes were forget-me-not blue. 'And who is she, this beautiful friend, to whom I owe an apology for my rude assault?' He spoke with an inflection that reminded Rian of some of the women from the south islands she had met at ceremonies with Danuta.

'Leave her alone, Manigan.' Fraoch clutched her sides, panting.

Rian started at the name. Was this the famous walrus hunter?

'But I threw her to the ground thinking she was you. She must think I'm a brute.'

'Aye, and that's where she'd be right.'

There was more splashing. Pytheas was heading towards them. Fraoch pointed at him. 'Her master. Now you can do apologies.'

He swung round to Rian. 'You're joking. You're enslaved? Oh beauty, beauty, beauty, always the slave of a rich man.' He looked at Fraoch. 'Ussa?'

'Who else?'

'Fraoch, come on.' Gruach was getting impatient but the man stopped her. 'Ussa's here? On old Toma's boat?'

Fraoch nodded, and waved her hand inland. 'In one of her strops, headed off as soon as she could get ashore.'

He looked back to his boat, then up the steep slope where Gruach was hauling his gear. 'Gruach,' he shouted. 'I was never here. I was

NEVER here.' He repeated it to Fraoch. And then he turned to Rian. 'Promise me you didn't see me, and I'll forgive you for my injury.' He clutched at his knee and winked, limping exaggeratedly.

She shook her head. So this was Manigan!

'Promise me.' He insisted.

'I never saw you, whoever you are,' Rian said.

He reached for her face with both hands, gave her a swift kiss on the nose and stared into her eyes, frowning. 'He doesn't deserve you, whoever he is.' Then he turned and paused, sizing up Pytheas in one glance. 'So is this the Greek I've been hearing about?'

Pytheas said something in his own tongue. Manigan drew his sword and swung it above his head in a circle, then sheathed it and pounded back out through the shallows to his boat, bellowing instructions to his crew to get ready to weigh anchor.

Pytheas bombarded Fraoch with questions that Rian couldn't follow and Fraoch gave monosyllabic grunts in response, then cut him off, gesturing towards Gruach whose shouted complaints could be avoided no longer.

Pytheas was as ruffled as Rian had seen him. He stuck his box under his armpit and, with his gnomon in the other hand, stomped up the slope after Gruach. He was soon using the measuring stick to lever himself up the steepest sections. Rian followed with the bedding rolls. Two was almost too much to bear. Pytheas' weighed more than anyone had a right to ask her to carry; there must be something other than blankets and fleeces inside it. But she lugged them anyway, slowly, thinking about Manigan. She looked down at his boat. There was a skirmish on deck, something was drawing raised voices. She could see the dark man tugging at the anchor, others tugging at him. She had deduced enough to see that he wanted out of there to avoid Ussa. And presumably not just because he owed her money. Many people, in many ports, owed Ussa. She made sure of that. Rian wondered, not for the last time, what Pytheas' business was with her. But soon the only thing she could think about was when she would reach the top of this cliff.

Li and Faradh were gaining rapidly on her and when they caught up Li told her to give him the heavy bundle. Gratefully she did so but, at the top of the slope, Pytheas stood shaking his head and told Li to take it back down the slope as far as he had carried it. He took Rian's bundle and sent her after Li, watching them closely.

'Of course, your master is a gentleman bastard,' Li said, handing her the bedding roll with whatever was stowed inside. Rian trudged back up, confused. He was like a March day this man who had bought her: sometimes sunny enough to bask in his warmth, then without warning capable of a hail squall.

Reaching the top of the slope, she looked back down to the boats. They looked like toys now, the people on them too small to recognise. The sea rolled away to the far distance, glittering. The earth beneath her was insubstantial. Her feet were becoming liquid, her ankles too. Slowly at first, and then more rapidly, she felt herself dissolve from the ground up and then, as the sensation made it past her thighs, she crumpled under her own weight. The other people's voices faded away and darkness engulfed her.

*

Rian was lying on her sheepskin in a strange place: next to a stone wall in an alcove off a big room. She was feeling better again. There had been nothing wrong that a bowl of soup and big hunk of bread and some honeyed ale couldn't fix. She was bleeding and sore but the ache in her belly was easing already. It never lasted long, the monthly pain, and a kindly round-faced woman had reassured her that she had nothing to fear from the faint. It was just the heavy load, that time of the month, nothing to worry about.

She was happy in the corner, trying to be inconspicuous. She had never been anywhere so busy and this house was richer than any she had seen. If she leaned to the edge of her alcove she could just make out a slice of the world outside the doorway: other no less substantial buildings, all thronging with people, bustling about with baskets and bundles and hanks of rope. There was a strong smell of fish.

Out in the big room, Ussa was storming with rage while Og tiptoed around her with plates of food, trying to placate both her and their hosts. Rian couldn't understand what Ussa was saying, although it was obvious enough that it was all about Manigan.

After Ussa stormed out, Fraoch tiptoed over.

'What's all the rage about?' Rian asked.

'Ussa's furious that we saw Manigan and let him get away,' Fraoch said. 'Us meeting him meant he found out she was here before she could jump on him.'

'Why does she want him?'

'Oh why does Ussa want anything? It's the stone. She's mad for it. Where's Pytheas?'

Rian pointed to the opposite corner, where he sat engrossed in discussion with two strange-looking men with long beards. They were all leaning over one of his parchments, poking at what was drawn on it.

'What are they all looking at?'

Rian shrugged, but her curiosity was enough to make her think she might be ready to get up.

Fraoch nodded over to Pytheas. 'Will he be staying here or going with Ussa?'

Rian shook her head. She had no idea.

'We're staying for a while. Gruach's got us a beautiful place. We've been here before. You should come and see it.' Fraoch laughed. 'Wake up, Rian. It's your life. No point just letting it happen to you. Look at the food here. Look at the clothes. There's so much to learn!'

Rian breathed deeply and said nothing. Perhaps staying in bed was the better option.

Og strode over. 'Try and get this lass on her feet, can you?' He had a horn cup and a hot buttery bannock, which he gave to Rian.

She tore it in two and gave half to Fraoch. 'We'll be going as soon as Toma's found, assuming he can stand. Are you fit for sailing?'

Rian nodded, her mouth full of bannock.

'Good. You keep eating. You're skinny as a weasel.'

'Ussa's as mad as a flea chasing Manigan,' Fraoch said.

Og looked around, wary of his mistress. 'It's all right for you, you're free to come and go as you please, you can say what you like about anyone. They all need your bronze.'

'Aye.' She chewed and swallowed. 'I'll miss you all though, it's been fun.' She grabbed Rian's hand. 'And I met you. I'm sure we'll be together again, even if you do go north now. You'll have to come back south sooner or later.'

She turned to Og. 'How long do you think? Have we got time to go to our place?'

Og looked over at Pytheas, at the door and back at his bundles of belongings and lifted his hands. 'I have no idea. If you can find Toma and buy him more drinks we'll have a few hours, otherwise we'll be off as soon as she shadows that doorway. It's not funny to keep her waiting at the best of times, and this isn't the best of times, not by a long shot. She's like a marten among ducks. No mercy.' He cuffed Rian. 'I'd get up and get ready if I were you. And go and be nice to Pytheas. He's talking stones and stars with those two old fellows but he's been asking after you.' He turned his back on them and returned to the cooks beside the hearth.

'Fraoch!' A woman was at the doorway gesturing. 'Gruach needs you.'

She flinched as if resisting a physical tug from outside. 'Better go. I'll try to come back, take you to see our place. If you can get away, or if Pytheas wants to come and see. Ask him. We're setting up the forge down on the flat ground by the river.'

She ran after the woman and Rian finished the bannock and ale. Og nodded approval and, while she rolled up her bedding, he replaced her empty drinking horn with a far more splendid one, frothing to the top, to give to her master.

'Rian,' Pytheas smiled. 'How are you?' He spoke in Greek.

She repeated her first lesson. 'I am fine.'

'I am sorry,' he said, holding his hand to his heart, shaking his head. 'Bed roll.' He pointed to his bundle, miming as he spoke. The meaning was clear. 'Too heavy.'

Rian shrugged. 'I am fine,' she said again, handing him the drinking horn. He patted the bench beside him and she shuffled in to watch what he and the bearded men were talking about. She might as well have been trying to understand the song of a thrush in a treetop but the patterns drawn out on the sheet of parchment before them were intriguing and strangely beautiful, the irregular lines and complex shapes reminding her of lichens on rocks at home.

After a while Ussa had still not appeared, so Rian got permission from Og to venture outdoors in search of some herbs to make a salve for the rowing sores on her hands. There was plenty of plantain growing nearby and while she was out she took the opportunity to gather some dry moss, yarrow and lady's mantle. They might go off in her pouch but it would be better to have them wilted than not have them at all. She was too shy to go looking for Fraoch and spent the afternoon and evening making poultices and drying herbs beside the fire.

In fact Ussa did not return until the next morning. No-one knew where she had been but her face was composed again and all trace of rage had left her. She was accompanied by a huge, burly fellow. Another man, a very hungover-looking sailor, was standing at the doorway. Ussa commanded everyone to get ready to sail. Og gestured Rian to come over.

'Toma is away to the boat, she says, and we have an extra man coming with us, one of Manigan's crew.'

'What, the giant?'

'No such luck. He's just here to collect some tin his master has bought from Ussa. That one.' He pointed to the weary-looking character at the entrance. 'We have to feed him, fast.' He lifted the lid on the pot. 'I told her you'd made your good porridge. Can you warm it up for him?'

Pytheas was scratching on his calfskin while Ussa leaned over him asking him questions, brushing his shoulder with her chest. Rian could make out enough to understand, 'Are you coming with us?'

Her heart sank as Pytheas nodded and smiled. With his top teeth over his bottom lip like a child offered a delicious thrill, he started packing his parchment away in his box. He turned to his bedding but Rian got there first and was already rolling it up. The hessian bag of whatever it was he kept wrapped up she left separate, but Pytheas shook his head and insisted that she unroll the blankets and wrap his load inside them. It became, once again, a burden rather than a bundle.

Pytheas was looking at the giant and, after conferring with Og and Ussa, his bedding roll was handed to the big man who carried it as if it was as light as Rian's.

The sailor squatted by the fire finishing his porridge in silence, looking up at Ussa who was growing impatient, then back down to his bowl, spoon working back and forth scooping the sweet mush into his mouth. As he chewed, Og scraped the last of the oats into his outstretched bowl, then he took a jug with him outside to wash out the pot.

The man smiled at Rian. 'Hey sweetheart, I hear you're an Assynteach. I'm almost your countryman. I'm from the Summer Isles.' He was thick-bristled and squat but his eyes twinkled. 'Braddanach of Tanera, but you can call me Badger, most people do. I got separated from the rest of my crew, had a bit too much… You make damn fine porridge.'

'Rian,' she said to the unspoken question.

Having made his greeting, he returned to eating.

Badger established to his satisfaction exactly where in Assynt she was from and remembered Danuta from one of the Long Island gatherings. He shook his head when she confessed to having been gambled away by her foster father. 'It brings shame to us, the selling of people. I don't care what anyone says, it's a sin to trade a person. It's not right.'

As soon as his bowl was emptied, Rian followed Og. Outside on the muddy street he poured water into the bowl. She stirred slowly with her fingers, loosening the sticky dregs.

'Who are they?' she whispered.

'Who? The sailor, or the big man?'

'Both.'

'The heavy is the chief's man, getting to complete a trade deal Ussa made last night. Tin. It's on board the boat. He's to carry it.'

'And the sailor?'

'He's one of the walrus hunters. He went off on the drink and got left behind by Manigan who was in such a hurry that he left without him. He's coming with us to the Cat Isles.'

'The Cat Isles.' She mouthed the name like a sweet treat in her mouth.

'You'll not have been there?'

'Isn't that the land of the whale people?'

'Aye. Come on.' They finished rinsing their pots. 'Time to sail.'

The sailor was leaving the house just ahead of Ussa. She told Og to hurry up.

Pytheas was with the giant who was carrying his bundle. 'Quick,' he said to Rian as he passed her.

They hurried to get their bedding and Og packed the pots in the food bag. Then they chased after the others back to the boat.

Pytheas looked relieved to see them. Faradh was lugging sacks up from the hold and Li was manoeuvring them over the gunnels down to the big man. Li made the sacks look as heavy as corpses, then the giant swung them ashore like toys. As Og and Rian reached the high water mark, one of the sacks split as the big man dumped it down. Knuckle-bone shaped lumps of grey tumbled out and he evidently swore. Og and Rian helped him gather the spilt tin ingots. As they splashed out to the boat, Og called to Li to

71

throw them a spare sack. The giant nodded his thanks.

Before Og could climb aboard, Toma told him to bring stones from the shore as replacement ballast. Li, Faradh and Badger, the new sailor, were sent to help, and with the muscle-power of the giant they were soon ready to go.

Ussa was in high spirits. What she had gained in exchange for the tin was anybody's guess. Perhaps she was paid in gold, perhaps in promises. Whatever it was it didn't take up much room. She sashayed about the boat. Rian stayed out of her way.

Pytheas beckoned Rian under the shelter at the bow and showed her that where Fraoch and Gruach had been sleeping was now their space. It was an airy spot but it was undercover and there were straps to stop the motion of the boat pitching a person out of their bunk.

Badger was chatting to Toma, looking closely at the rigging, getting familiar with the boat. There was an easy familiarity between them and Rian guessed they were not strangers. As soon as everyone was on board Toma ordered all hands on oars to get them out of the geo and into open water. The blisters on Rian's middle fingers and palms broke open as she rowed. She realised too late she should have bound them.

Once they were clear of the rocks, the sail was hoisted and the rowers could relax. Rian was pleased to find herself assigned with Badger to the never-ending task of fixing and binding rope.

'So you met Manigan.' He settled himself on a chest opposite her, the pile of ropes between them.

She picked up a frayed end of rope. 'Not really.'

'What did you think?'

'How do you mean?'

He was scratching behind his ear and looking around. Was he trying to signal to her, to make some sort of secret hint?

'Well, what did you make of him?'

'I didn't.'

He raised his eyes as if she was as dim as a sheep.

'Come on, you must have thought something. You don't meet Manigan and then come away and have nothing to say about what you think.'

He waited. She wound the fibres of the rope together and racked her brains for what she might be expected to say.

'Did he speak to you?'

'I can't remember.' Had he? She could only recall his touch and his eyes. She wound a string of sinew around the rope end. This one would never fray.

Badger leaned in towards her with a conspiratorial wink. Whatever she had failed to say seemed to have been eloquence enough. 'Say no more. That's how he operates.' Nodding, he picked up a rope end from the pile and untied a knot in it, pulling it little by little out from the heap, coiling as he went until he reached the worn section which he hung over a peg. He pulled the remainder of the rope out of the pile, leaving two neatly coiled ends, the worn section to work on in easy reach. He repeated the process as Rian plaited and plied, wove and tied, and the result was that the heap, tangled and chaotic, transformed into a few clear mending tasks, tidily stacked and ready.

As he wheedled the rope into order, he talked about Manigan. Just hearing someone speak her own dialect was a balm. The man she had met was brought back into their presence by the story. Was it the unlikeness of the tale or the solid certainty of its telling that made the hours pass like clouds, unnoticed? As her fingers worked, her mind rested. Within the boat upon the northern sea, Badger's story was another vessel floating on the ocean of his oddly familiar voice, and on that story boat she allowed herself to sail away.

MUTTERING

'I first met Manigan when I was just a boy. His mother had died and he had run away from his foster mother to join the walrus hunters and he was the boat hand on the handsomest boat I ever saw. It sailed into the bay on Tanera one spring morning just ahead of a storm, and we took in the crew and fed them and listened to their stories for what seemed to be days. We'd been hoping for the first spring flowers and didn't usually like to be kept indoors at that time of year, the days lengthening, everything to be done to get the year's growth under way. But we didn't mind so much with the walrus hunters as our guests, their tales were so good. And it was Manigan who told the best ones.'

Badger stretched his arms out along the gunnel behind him and braced his feet against ribs of the leaning boat, settling himself. 'I remember he related a story about his Great Aunty Onn and the man called Ultuk, who was the Walrus Mutterer, out on the ice in the far north, their boat seized up in the freezing sea for a whole winter. They were chasing narwhal when the ice folded in around them and they hadn't been able to make it back through the floes to the open sea.'

'What's 'narwhal'?' Rian asked.

'They're sea-unicorns with a great long pointed horn.' His hand demonstrated a long spike coming out of his own forehead.

Rian nodded, wanting him to continue. She had finished mending a rope and while he paused, she picked up another and started picking apart the fibres where it was worn.

'They had been trapped for a while, then a crack opened up and instead of trying to follow it and get mown down by a berg – these are mountains of ice with evil spirits inside that chase you down and try to crush you – instead of that, Ultuk told them to take the boat out of the water. The crew scrambled out onto the floe and got ropes to the boat and used them to lift it up and as they did so the ice helped them up. The crack squeezed closed and the frozen plates lifted the keel of the boat up, helping the sailors to pull her up onto the top. Then they turned the boat over and lived under it for the whole winter. They made walls of ice and used the boat as a roof, and it soon covered in snow and they were snug as bears in a den. At least they were until the bear came along who wanted to use it as a den. But that's not the story I'm trying to tell you.

'That story was the one that Ultuk told while they were there inside the boat shelter. It was after they had been there for a month or more, more most likely, and the food supplies had run out and all they had was the occasional seal they could manage to catch. The crew had all started dying, some of them faster, some of them slower. It depends on how much fat a man has, but most of all it depends on the mood of each person when the Death Spirit pays a visit. And you never can tell when that might be. You can be sick as a dog, but if someone has just said something funny and you've cheered up enough to chuckle, the Death Spirit sees you laughing in its face and skedaddles. Yet a cheery soul with nothing wrong with them can be caught short needing a pee in a storm and feeling sorry for themselves just for a moment, and that's them finished. Doomed.'

Rian wondered where he was going with this story. Badger took off his woolly hat and scratched his head, then put it back on. He was clearly in no hurry, and given where they were, out in the ocean, why should she be worried if he took hours to tell the tale? Her fingers wove the rope together as he wove his words.

'Anyway, eventually starvation got them all except old Ultuk and Manigan's great aunty Onn. What she was doing there in the first place I can't remember for the life of me. You'll have to ask him that but, well, you've seen Ussa. You've seen what a family they are.'

'Family?'

'Aye. They're cousins. Did you not know?' It wasn't really a question, as he carried on with the story. 'You know Manigan tells this story to everyone. He says Ultuk told it to his Aunty because he'd never told it to anyone all his life and he thought he might be the next to die. He said to her, "If I don't tell you it'll die with me," and she told Manigan on her deathbed the same thing. And Manigan says that for a while it was like knowing a wonderful secret that no-one else knows, but then he couldn't bear being the only one to know and so he told someone and then he told another. He says it's like a magic chest: you can keep on doling out the treasure and it never runs out.

'He has us all rapt, you know, waiting for his golden words, holding out our hands for the treasure, and he loves it, he revels in sharing it out. Except, he says, inside the chest is a wee jewel box, and he'll give out the treasure to everyone and anyone, the more the merrier, but he won't share the key to that wee casket. Inside it is a gem, he says, but he's saving it, and Mother bless us, let's hope he doesn't die with it. Anyway, that's getting ahead of myself, or behind, he usually says all that as a kind of introduction.'

Badger turned his head and looked down at Rian. 'I'm not really any good at this story telling malarkey, am I? You should be getting it from the horse's mouth. He'd have you spellbound.'

'I like it.' She lifted the piece of rope up as if to show she had nothing else to do but listen while she worked.

'Ach where was I? Oh yes, Ultuk and Great Aunty Onn in the upturned boat, adrift on the pack ice, everyone else dead, polar bears chewing at their corpses outside the boat. One night, with a storm raging, Ultuk starts on his story. And it goes like this. Are you following?'

She nodded.

'Good. Right. There was this whaler man and in a storm he was flung out of his boat and washed up on an island in the northern ocean. There was nothing to eat. He'd found a few berry bushes but it was spring and he'd starve before they fruited. He had nothing but a pocket knife on him. There were no trees on the island, nothing to make a spear with. And his few rags of clothes weren't enough to make a net to catch a fish. He found a spring of freshwater and hoped he might find a frog or something to eat. But the island was barren. There weren't even any birds nesting there. The only other life on it was a herd of walruses, and each day the man went to watch them, wishing he had a spear, trying to imagine some way of being able to kill one and eat it. But a walrus is a huge thing, bigger than a bull, and they look after each other. Not even a polar bear can pick off a walrus from its pack and there is no greater hunter than a polar bear.

'The stranded whaler man chewed on seaweed, but it made him so thirsty he stopped. He became weak and his mind wandered with hunger and he spent more and more time with the walruses.

'One day, crazy with starvation, he started talking to them. They had got used to him now and let him come close by. He started telling a story, but one by one they got bored of his voice, or maybe they just wanted a swim. Anyway they slithered off and away into the water until there was just one of them left on the island. All the others were bobbing about just off-shore, listening, and the one left closed his eyes and seemed to be at peace.

'So the man saw, as he reached the end of his tale, that the walrus had given himself up. Trembling with hunger, he crept up to the snoozing walrus and got his knife out and slit its throat, gentle as a mother putting her baby to sleep. And so he lived to tell the tale, as they say.'

Badger grinned. Rian tried to put the pieces of the story together in her head, but she couldn't see the connection between what he had told her about Ultuk and the man who killed the walrus and Manigan. She frowned.

Badger carried on. 'I guess now you're wishing I'd get on and tell you the tale that made all the walruses leave except for that one, and what it was about that story that made the one left there go to sleep. But the real story, the one you tell to get the walrus, that's the key to the little box inside the treasure chest that Manigan's saving until he's scared he'll die with it. That's the one that makes him the Walrus Mutterer. And I hope I'm not the one who hears it, for it'll be a sad day when Manigan has to give up the key and pass on the gem, although in another way of course I wish I knew it. Wouldn't we all? Treasure, is it ever enough for us? Don't we always seem to long for something more?'

'What happened to Aunty Onn?' said Rian. She had finished binding the ropes.

'I don't know.'

'But she must have got back from the ice to tell Manigan.'

'Someone must have found her, or the ice melted. I don't know. You'll have to ask him.'

Rian took a deep breath. It was like being stretched up on one leg, straining to reach a bunch of berries on a high branch and not being able to reach them.

'It's a good story, eh?' Badger wanted her to praise him, she could see that.

'Good enough,' she said. 'But it's only half a story so far.'

'Nah, you want the little gem box. You women are all the same, you just want the jewels. But what about the rest of it?'

'Well, a bunch of people get eaten by bears on the ice. It's not exactly happy.'

'I don't tell it right. If it was Manigan you'd be rapt.'

'What are you two slackers gossiping about?' Ussa was awake. 'And what would Manigan be doing?'

'I was telling her about the walrus muttering.' Badger did not seem remotely in awe of Ussa, although his left hand moved up his thigh and as it reached his hip it clenched around the handle of the long knife he wore slung on his belt.

'And where will he be now, do you think? Which way will he head?'

Badger blinked slowly. 'Cat Isles.'

Ussa tapped Rian on the side of her head, just above her right ear, with the tip of her staff. 'Help Og.'

Rian scuttled forward to help Og under the awning, making food. Then clearing up. Then making Pytheas' bed. There was always something to stop her returning to Badger for more of his stories.

THE CAT ISLES

By next morning the weather was poor, the sea choppy, visibility bad and the motion uncomfortable. The boat slewed across big waves, which sprayed over the bow. The sailors were busy keeping watch. Pytheas grumped in his bunk. Rian was put to bailing the bilges again. It stank and was dispiriting work. There was no way for her to get clean or dry. As the day wore on, the sea became even wilder but Toma's mood was ebullient. He seemed to love it when the sea rose and snapped and writhed. The boat alternately bucked on and sliced through waves as if it could not decide if it was riding or riving the sea.

Ussa sat under the shelter looking back, getting up from time to time to peer ahead northwards. There was nothing visible.

Rian asked Og what Ussa searched for.

'Manigan's boat, not that we could catch it. Or land. Ostensibly land.'

And eventually land came, looming out from under the cloud. They made their way along parallel to the shore.

Ussa dressed to take off but it wasn't necessary: a boat heading out of the harbour told them all they needed to know – no Manigan. So on they went away from what the sailor in the other boat told them was 'the Fairest Isle' – to the Cat Isles. It was no time to stop for mere beauty.

The wind dropped away, which was a relief to Rian, but not to Ussa or Toma or Badger. They spent another night on the water making little progress. Ussa wanted to arrive without notice. She began to talk about how they could conceal their vessel and allow her to get ashore in secret to surprise the people.

Next morning, they entered a patch of sea that roiled and broke, and Toma turned the boat away the way they had come. 'The Roust', he called it: dangerous water caused by the tide. Pytheas questioned him intently as he sailed away for an hour and then back again, by which time the sea had calmed and they could continue.

Closer into shore the sky filled with seabirds. Cliffs towered above the boat and thousands of gannets somehow found footholds and even nest sites on cracks in the sheer rock. A constant stream of the white birds launched themselves from their perches, their huge black-tipped wings outstretched, beating out and up then soaring. Rian had watched gannets many times from her home on the western coast but had never imagined so many could congregate in one place. What could they see with those egg-yolk eyes? They must have been able to spy fish in the water below because they would suddenly tip down and fall like knives. The water all around the boat punctured as they dived.

As they sailed away from the gannet cliffs, a group of dolphins leapt ahead and led the boat northwards until eventually peeling away. They passed two boats with a net swung between them. Close in, seals lolled on skerries and as they turned into a wide inlet a grey seal surfaced with a snort just beside the bow and watched them placidly, huffing, used to being greeted with a fish.

Instead of entering the main voe, Ussa asked Toma to seek out a cove to drop anchor. He must have known the shore well for he found a place to conceal the boat without any difficulty. Li risked his life jumping onto a wave-washed rock and then helped Ussa ashore. They pushed off and Toma anchored the boat at a safe distance.

Once Ussa was out of sight, Badger sidled up to Toma and a murmured negotiation took place, punctuated by long, grumpy pauses. Eventually Toma relented and Badger hauled the anchor while Toma and his boy rowed the boat back to the rocky shore, where Badger jumped ship.

The rest of the crew prepared to wait. It could take Ussa and Li several hours to walk to the nearest settlement and gain the intelligence she needed. She may well not return until the next day, or the next. It was anyone's guess what kind of reception she would get.

Og got straight on with cooking as soon as they had anchored, and demanded that Rian helped him. 'We have to use these times,' he said. 'Plenty days at sea when you'll eat nothing but dry tack, and the mood of the crew depends on nothing more than food.'

Pytheas had been keen to go with Ussa but she had refused him. He sat sulking on deck, back to the mast, until Rian brought him a cup of wine and some cheese on a hot pancake. Pytheas took his cup and gazed at Rian as he sipped. 'Beautiful,' he murmured. And then again, in Greek, 'Beautiful.'

As she handed him the pancake, he bent and sniffed her hands.

'Clean now.' She held them to her nose to check.

He sniffed again.

'Soapwort, and yarrow butter for my sores.'

He said something in Greek that ended with 'Mama,' and the puppy-dog look in his eye forced her to conclude that her herbal remedy was making him homesick.

He tore the pancake in half and insisted she ate half of it, then made her sup from his wine cup. She didn't know how to tell him this was a sacrilege: a man and a woman drinking from one cup without saying the blessings of the Mother. She said them in her head and then made an addition, 'but he doesn't know what he is doing, and it is not the nuptial cup.' She didn't like the long gazing stare of the man, the way his eyes lingered on her, the way he drew his tongue across his teeth behind his upper lip and then back along the lower as if in preparation for some kind of delicacy.

Smiling his most beguiling smile, he began another lesson: the parts of the body. 'I touch my head.' 'You touch my head.' 'I touch your arm.' His hand stroked from her shoulder to her wrist, to show her. Then on down, 'I touch your hand.' He held out his palm. 'You touch my hand.'

Rian tapped his thumb, tentatively.

He was all glee. Then he grinned with a gleam that she did not like at all. 'I touch your leg.' He showed her he meant the whole length. Then it was toe, foot, ankle, calf. She would never remember it all. Shin, knee, thigh.

She would do anything to end the lesson.

Hip. Belly. Perhaps she could run. He reached around her. Back. Could he not see her discomfort? And then, his gaze uncomfortably close, he lifted her hand and placed it on his chest. She could feel it, like a trapped animal.

'Heart'. He said it again, quietly. 'Heart'. And then a third time, quieter still. 'Heart'.

He was looking at her with an intensity she had not seen before. The necessity was to repeat what he was saying. That was what the lesson required.

'Heart,' she said. *Cardia.*

It thumped beneath her fingers. Beating. Trying to get out.

'You touch my heart,' he said.

'I touching heart.' She knew she had it wrong.

His hand imitated hers. His hand was on her chest. His big hand. Her shrinking breast. 'I touch your heart.'

She could not meet his eye. She wanted only that his hand lifted, that this weight on her was removed, that this moment ended. She looked about. Was anyone watching them? Was there any way of escape?

Toma sat at the prow, chewing, looking out to sea. Og and Faradh were sleeping in this moment of calm. The hand pressed on, demanding words.

She grabbed his hand and slapped it on her crown. 'You touch my head.'

She flinched at the flicker in his face as he registered what she had done and then she was falling back against the mast with the force of his slap. Her cheek blazed and sparked as if it was a log splattered by fat from a spitted animal.

She looked around again. No-one had witnessed this change in him. He sat, looking away up to the headland then out to sea, then back to her.

'I'm sorry,' he said.

She knew this phrase well. *Syngnōmēn ékhe.* He used it often.

He touched her cheek. 'I'm sorry. I touch your cheek, to say I'm sorry.'

Rian assumed this was what he meant. She was catching onto this language of his. It was not so difficult. Perhaps. Not as difficult to understand as touch. No, she understood that too, she just didn't like it, not from him. But the words, she loved them. She wanted to know them all.

HEALER

They spent an uncomfortable night at anchor. For several hours the tide ran strongly north and the boat tugged as if trying to break free, pitching forwards and rocking back, a motion that seemed to be exaggerated when Rian lay down to try to sleep. She worried about having drunk from the same cup as Pytheas.

The next morning Pytheas spent a long time trying to get Toma to explain to him why the current had been so strong, questioning him until the skipper was exasperated. Eventually his interrogation was cut short by a shout from the shore. They all manned the oars to bring the boat close into the rocks so that Ussa and Li could clamber on board.

Ussa was in a vile temper. She had got wet trying to get into the boat and Manigan had evidently departed. She told Toma to head north through the islands and he argued with her about a safe route through the tidal channels.

Rian's hands had suffered even from that short time on the oars. She undid the bandages she had improvised and dabbed on a little more salve. The yarrow butter that Danuta had given her, even in sparing amounts, eased the smarting.

Thus began Rian's role as the ship's healer. They all had rowing sores on their hands. The poultices she had prepared during their stop in the Seal Isles were good and she used linarich seaweed to keep the ointments in place and reduce chafing on the wounds when they were at the oars. The effects were dramatic. One after another, Og, Faradh and Li came to her for treatment.

Shortly after they left the Cat Isles, chasing Manigan north, Og cut the ball of his thumb trying to slice dried meat on the rolling boat. He bled profusely from the wound, which he feared would leave his hand useless, and he gibbered oaths with the pain in a language only he knew. Rian cleaned the cut, stitched it with three knots of gut thread, bandaged it and checked daily that it was healing.

From then on they came to her with all their aches and injuries. Her grasp was firm but her fingers were small and soft compared to the men's and she could tell that even the act of touching them was soothing. They showed her old wounds and groaned appreciation as she salved them.

When they first left the Cat Isles behind, the wind was steady and the sea motion slight, but gradually the wind eased and the periods when they were merely drifting became longer.

They were far from land. Nothing except ocean had been visible for days. Who could tell where they were? The sea had been calm for how many days? Rian was no longer sure. Five, perhaps six.

They seemed not to go anywhere much. The sail hung limp. Ussa ordered them to row in the morning, but by afternoon when the slaves' anger at their sore hands and their sheer exhaustion made the atmosphere on board intolerable, Toma let them rest. They drifted.

Each day they rowed for a shorter time. One morning they did not lift the oars at all. Who knew where the currents would take them? Og said Toma knew and he seemed unperturbed by their slow progress, sitting at the helm in contemplation or teaching his boy Callum ever more complicated knots.

There wasn't enough food on board the boat and they were soon starting to wish for something other than dry tack and mutton. Their fishing hooks caught nothing so they put out lines for seagulls. Almost immediately a herring gull took the salted fish bait and Ussa hauled it in. It was her prerogative as the leader of the expedition. But the gull had not lived on the ocean for decades without having the ability to fight and it was not going to give up its cruising days without a battle.

Once on board its full size became obvious. It flapped and struggled with wings strong enough to fly into a sea gale, beak and claws sufficiently sharp to tear the skin of a whale. It fought Ussa and won, battering her with its feathery limbs, tearing the arm she put up across her face to shield her eyes from its beak. She flailed and yelled for help.

Li grabbed the bird by the neck and with a swift yank and twist it lay limp in his arms. Ussa's swearing turned to a howl as she realised the damage to her arm. The skin was torn almost all the way from the elbow to the wrist.

Og pushed Rian ahead of him. All eyes were now on her, full of expectation that she could do something to mend the bloody gash.

'Bloody sea devil, bitch of a bird.' Ussa let herself be pressed down to sit on a bench. Rian took her arm in one hand and eased back the tattered sleeve to examine the wound. It wasn't as bad as it looked.

'What is it like?' Ussa's hand trembled. Her eyes were wide and straining, her voice a rasp.

'You'll be fine.' Rian held her arm. 'It's just on the surface. If it stays clean, it'll mend in no time.'

'Are you sure?' Those wide eyes, still staring.

'I can go and get something to clean it with.'

Ussa nodded. 'Make it stop hurting.'

Rian was about to say she couldn't do that. Ussa sounded like a child. Then something came to Rian that Danuta used to do when Drost was moaning about his sore back. 'I'll fix you a draft. It'll help to ease your pain.' She filled her voice with an imitation of sympathy. 'You're strong, your body's its own best healer.' She got up, resting Ussa's hand on her thigh. 'Sit with Ussa while I get my medicines,' she said to Li, amazing herself with her bravado. 'In case she faints with the pain.'

Ussa nodded her head with rapid jerks.

'It's a nasty wound,' Rian said. 'But she's going to be fine.'

'Of course.' Li gave her a half-smile and played along, crouching beside Ussa, concern written all over his face.

Rian fetched her herbs, took them to the galley, put a pinch of yarrow in a cup, added a dash of mead and soaked it up in a cloth to swab the cuts and staunch the bleeding. Brewing up a painkiller would be more difficult, but she crumbled a dried mint leaf in some mead then dunked a hemp rope in it to give it a more pungent flavour: it would taste odd, vaguely medicinal, and the alcohol would do the trick.

Back on deck, she concentrated her attention on the lacerations, clucking and cooing as she swabbed them, urging the once invincible mistress to sip her drink and relax, let it take effect. Miraculously, it did.

'This yarrow butter will staunch the bleeding.' Rian smeared it thinly down the cut, then wet some of the linarach fronds and bandaged the arm from wrist to elbow. 'And this will keep it clean.'

No thanks were forthcoming, but Ussa was at least passive for a while. For Rian there was comfort in realising she was not completely powerless.

*

The seabird killing seemed to break the spell of calm. A band of cloud thickened in the eastern sky and soon the first drift had clouded the sun. As it sank towards the horizon it became a primrose blur. A dense, misty rain began to fall and the sails tautened. Water trickled against the hide as the boat achieved motion. Toma took the tiller in his hand, murmured instructions and ropes were loosened, adjusted, tightened.

In the gloom of dusk, Rian sat on a chest under the shelter, her legs dangling. She was in the way of anyone who wanted to get into the galley and kept having to squeeze aside as Og went in and out, but she could see both Pytheas and Ussa from here.

Ussa was on her bunk looking pale and sweaty. She had insisted on eating some of the bird's giblets raw, saying something unintelligible as she had swallowed the heart of the animal. Rian felt queasy at the thought of it – a sea bird was not the same as a land mammal. She knew, she wasn't sure how, but she did, as if from an ancient memory, that the bird's innards should all have been offered to the sea. But Ussa had consumed them and now she looked as if the sea was taking its revenge. She was lying with her bandaged arm on top of the covers, being sorry for herself.

Pytheas was writing, catching the very last light, then lighting a lamp which spluttered viciously as the boat leaned, its sail heavy with wind, tilting the oil so it threatened to spill. Toma shook his head and muttered threats, but Pytheas made stalling gestures and scribbled faster and faster. Why, after all those days of boredom, he had waited to get the urge to write until a wind was rising Rian failed to understand. But increasingly she was able to follow what he was doing and she had grasped that his scratchings were a record of their voyage. When at last he put his writing instruments away and blew out the lamp, Toma relaxed.

Pytheas fastened his box and Rian took it from him, jumped down and stowed it under his bunk. He peered down at Ussa. 'She's sick?' he asked.

Rian nodded. "The heart of the bird is bird.'

'The heart of the bird is bad,' he corrected.

'The heart of the bird is bad.' The repetition of his corrections of her Greek had become automatic.

He asked her something she didn't understand. She shrugged. He didn't repeat it.

In her medicine bag she had dog lichen, a good purgative. It might be worth making Ussa sicker in the short term to prevent her dying of some slow poison. She mixed it with a little wine and told Ussa to drink it, then sat by to wait for the effects.

Within a few minutes Ussa had thrown up. Rian waited for her to finish then lugged the wooden pail out on deck and washed it out overboard. Ussa wailed and Rian hurried back. Another spate of vomiting followed, Ussa groaning as her stomach emptied its contents. A final retch, then she lay back on her bunk. Rian gave her a sip of water. Ussa's eyes were watery and her hair straggled over her clammy forehead. With the bucket washed out a second time, Rian sat on the bunk opposite Ussa. Her breathing calmed and her forehead relaxed. Rian thought she might be dropping asleep until her head turned. When she opened her eyes they were clear.

'What are you looking at, little witch?'

'Do you feel better?'

'Yes, as a matter of fact I do. No thanks to you and your poisons.'

'Your stomach needed to void. And your arm? Is it feeling better too?' She lifted it, and unwound the seaweed bandage. The cut was clean. 'If you can keep it clean and dry and open to the air, with loose sleeves, it'll scab up and mend in no time.'

Ussa said nothing at all, rolled onto her side, shut her eyes again and seemed to go to sleep. Rian caught a glimpse of a cockroach scuttling in a corner. She wished more than anything that she could get off the boat.

She sat and let the darkness deepen. The wind's song in the sails, so welcome earlier, had become thunder.

The sailors' voices were drowned out by creaking wood, water on hide and wind in ropes. Before long she felt Pytheas beside her. He smelled distinctive, although she could never put a name to the scent. But now what came to her was that his cloying odour was from the ink bottle, whatever its contents were.

His hand was on her head in the dark, stroking her like a cat. She felt the hairs on the base of her neck bristle, a tightening of her shoulders as if she would arch her back and scratch him. She resisted the urge, forcing herself to endure his touch. After a while his hand drifted to a halt, he gave a stretch and yawned. She stood, released her clenched back and curled onto her bunk.

The rocking boat was like a cradle but sleep did not come to her. The rolling seemed to become more intense as the night deepened. One lurch set the boat on edge and she tumbled right out of her bunk. She had resisted using the straps and felt stupid now. She heard shouts on deck and struggled to cling to an upright as the boat lunged back the other way. Spray battered the hide cover they were under, and every now and again there was a weightless feeling as a mountainous wave lifted them, then let them go. She was aware of Faradh and Li bailing and she wondered if she should go out and help, but the fear of falling overboard kept her in her bunk. A banshee wailed in the rigging and the timbers of the boat juddered and creaked. There was no question of sleep.

Dawn brought relative calm, although the sea had built up a motion that made even the simplest deeds awkward on the lurching boat. Og had a bruise on his forehead and was in a foul mood, as the shelter had split where he slept, soaking his bed and the stores of food. The flour sack was ruined with sea water.

Ussa was back to her normal self, a linen scarf wrapped loosely around her arm. She sat watching Rian serve Pytheas his breakfast, then came the daily language lesson. Today it was teeth, tongue, nose, hair, ears. Ussa sat on her bunk with her head turned away but her posture made it clear she was listening to every word.

When Rian stood up to take Pytheas' beaker back to the galley for a refill, Ussa turned her head. Rian got the drift of her remark. 'I'm sure you can teach her all about the body.'

Pytheas laughed. 'You have a one-track mind, Ussa.'

Rian brought his cup and he tried to catch her around her waist with his arm but she slipped aside, span around and returned to Og's cooking space, as if she had forgotten something. From there she watched Ussa perform.

Her eyebrows were raised and her eyes wide and fixed on the Greek like a dog waiting for a titbit to be thrown. Ussa licked her lips slowly, then lowered her eyes to linger on his body, before lifting her line of sight to his face. She murmured something so he had to lean towards her to hear, and as he did she placed her hand on his wrist. He shook it off but she placed it back there, her fingers long and straight. She stroked his shirt as if it were fur, then said something else, widening her eyes again and tilting her head with a raised shoulder.

It made Rian feel sick to see them but she didn't want to look away. Pytheas was saying something back to her and his laugh was deeper than normal.

Ussa kept stroking his shirt, then she stood and crossed the narrow gangway to his bunk. But as she tried to sit down beside him he turned towards the galley and called 'Rian,' waving his cup at her. She couldn't refuse his call and went to take the beaker.

'Come.' Turning to Ussa he put his hand to her forehead and pulled it away as if it was burning. He said something to her that Rian didn't understand, and then he laughed, his mouth wide. Ussa did not laugh back.

He buttoned up his coat, then headed out on deck. Rian took the cup back to Og, but Pytheas called her name again. There was no escape.

Ussa was holding her left fingers to where Pytheas had touched her forehead, lips narrowed. She grabbed at Rian as she passed, her eyes too close. 'Hussy.'

Rian juddered away.

Pytheas was chatting to Toma who was pointing into the distance, except there was no distance. Nothing was visible except water, with a swell out of proportion to the wind, and cloud. Dense cloud. Every direction was the same. They were enveloped. Out in the middle of nowhere.

CLOUD

Only cloud in all directions. All that remained of the universe was the boat and that was just an animal hide, tensioned and tautened over oak slats and rods. The breeze was light, ruffling the water's surface and filling the sail. It was enough to propel them forwards in a gentle burl. As the swell rolled, the boat lolled up and over the water's undulations, the sail tight and full of wind. Yet the cloud, the blurred horizon, and the rocking motion all brought a feeling of calm. The keel folded each wave over into a slosh of bubbles which rose, hushing, by the stern and left a wake of foam behind them.

The sailors were all at ease. Li was mending the part of the shelter that had taken a battering during the night. Faradh sat beside him watching, lending a hand to stretch the hide or to hold a tool as Li worked.

Callum, the skipper's boy, sat beside Toma, gazing out into the cloud ahead. Rian wondered if there was a way of befriending him but he and the skipper were wrapped up together, an inseparable unit, and he clearly felt no need to interact with anyone else.

The boat's hull hummed as the vessel cut through the sea. The tensioned wood seemed full of energy, its curves gripping its skin, poised over the great ocean depth, rich with potential. Expectation was in every lashing. The water was in total contrast to the boat: baggy and untensioned, its surface in constant motion, jabbling and tickling, loose. And the sky was even looser than the sea. Misty strands of cloud drifted like snagged fleece. The sun cast a glow to the east.

Pytheas came up behind Rian and put his hands on her shoulders, propelling her towards the mast. She had to duck under the sail. Every surface was wet with mist or still soaked from the storm. She did not want to sit down and get damp again so she crouched, her back up against the gunnel.

It was time for another lesson: action words. Pytheas is standing. Li is mending. Og is cooking. Pytheas is walking. Rian is sitting. Rian is standing. Pytheas and Rian are dancing. Pytheas is laughing.

'Pytheas and Rian are making me mad.' It wasn't necessary to see Ussa's face to know that she was not joining in the fun. She pushed past them, pinching Rian hard on the upper arm as she elbowed by.

'I should have let her die,' thought Rian. It was a bad thought, but she enjoyed having it.

The clouds continued to thicken. Even though it was early in the day, the sky darkened. The glow of the sun dimmed, faded to grey then bruised away.

Out in the distance there was a vessel, or was there? Was it Manigan's boat? Ussa got excited briefly, staring out ahead, but as visibility declined and there was no repeat of the glimpse, her frown became a scowl.

Snow began to fall. Li said something miserable. Ussa turned to him and Faradh and began ranting in the southern tongue they all shared that Rian did not understand. A tirade spilled from her down-turned mouth. Faradh kept his head down, fiddling with a rope. Li kept his face turned towards Ussa, his eyes not making contact with hers, his gaze intent on the point just to her right. She got to her feet and glowered over them, asking questions. By the sound of Li's monosyllabic answers they were mostly rhetorical, but finally one response earned him a slap on the face. Faradh inched away but Li seemed simply to take the abuse. He lowered his eyes and turned his attention back to the piece of hide he was mending. Ussa kicked it aside and tried to get him to focus on her, but he shook his head, pointed to Toma, and pulled it back onto his knee.

Ussa stormed past Rian and Pytheas again and began ranting to Toma. In measured tones he responded to her questions.

'Ussa is not happy,' Pytheas murmured in Greek.

That seemed to be the end of the lesson. The first few flakes of snow were turning to sleety rain. He indicated that he and Rian should retreat under the shelter where Og was making food smells.

There, Pytheas got out his box and took out his beautiful bound set of parchments. 'Look. Periplus.'

She remembered the word. He showed her a sheet with markings made in ink.

'Assynt.' He was pointing to some lines on the middle of the sheet, on the left hand side. 'Winged Isle.' His finger poked further down. 'Cape Wrath.' A sharp corner further up from Assynt. 'Sea. Land.'

She got it. This was a diagram of their route so far along the coast. There was the Long Island drawn off to the west. She watched with amazement and not a little fear as he traced his finger around the north coast to the Seal Isles, then the Cat Isles, and on to where they were now, somewhere further north.

There were more islands to the northwest of the Cat Isles. With trepidation, wondering if there was magic in this diagram that could be dangerous, Rian pointed to them. 'Faroes?'

Pytheas nodded. Saying something she didn't understand he circled his finger around in the sea to the north and over to the west and shrugged. Then, seeing her bewilderment, he tried to explain, but other than hearing the names of Ussa and Manigan, his long, slow speech failed to mean anything to her and his swirling finger patterns on the chart made her more confused rather than less. Was he saying they were going to find Manigan out in the ocean?

Og peered over at the chart. Rian pleaded at him with her eyes for help.

'Pytheas says we're lost,' Og said, going back to his bannocks.

Pytheas rolled his eyes at her stupidity and flicked his fingers in dismissal, rolled up the map and put it away. He began sharpening the end of a feather.

She sidled towards Og who emptied the sack into a bowl. 'That's it for meal. The other bag was ruined when the shelter leaked. I don't know who thought that would last with this many on board. I told her.' He winked at Rian. 'And we're lost. Good eh? The mistress...' He paused, stirring water into the meal. 'It was obvious we'd failed to catch Manigan ages ago. I don't know why we even bothered. And now we're lost. Faroes could be north or south, east or west, Toma says since the night of the gale he hasn't a clue. We should've passed them by now and we could have in the night and been none the wiser. So now we're just going on northwards into stupidity because the mist...' He stopped kneading, then restarted. 'Well, anyway. We're lost. And these are the last bannocks so let's hope we're east or south of the islands and we bump into them sooner than later.'

'And if not?'

He tensed his lips and shook his head. 'We will be lost and hungry.'

'Sorry, stupid question.'

'Stupid everything.' He punched the dough.

Sooner or later the smell of baked bannocks brought everyone to Og's iron fire pan under the shelter. When Toma ducked in to investigate, he stomped his feet with cold then tugged a fleece out from under a bench and thrust it at Rian and asked her to make wool pads to go inside his boots.

She was happy to comply. The greasy fleece smelled of home, of land, and it was warm on her fingers as she tugged and pulled, fluffing and straightening the fibres. It brought back memories of sitting between Danuta's knees by the fire, her fingers tugging through her hair after a wash.

When the bannocks were ready, Toma went back outside chewing hot bread and Ussa came for her share. She looked at the five remaining rounds of baked dough Og had made, took two for herself and, pointing to each bannock in turn, told Og who was to eat the others. Pytheas got one, Toma and Callum could have another. The last was to be shared among all the slaves. She tucked her second bannock into her bedding and sat there chewing with her mouth open.

Rian finished a roughly foot-shaped pad of wool and went out on deck to see if it was what Toma wanted. He nodded at the felts and gestured to her to make some more for his boy, Callum, who smiled at her with his pale eyes and, as always, said nothing.

Toma was scanning about as if the boat's behaviour had him baffled. The sea was calm now. Too calm. The swell had dampened and snow-clouds wrapped them up into an intimate world of quiet. There was no land nearby. No birds came to the bait line hanging off the stern, no fish or porpoises rose to the surface of the water. Their world seemed uninhabited by anything except themselves.

∗

They were barely trickling along, one small boat in the vastness of the ocean, one crumb on the puckered blanket of the deep. Only the line of bubbles behind them showed that they were moving at all.

Staring at the water, Rian drifted into a daze. All the crew seemed touched by the calm in the same way. Li and Faradh played a slow, thoughtful game of counters with none of their usual squabbling. Pytheas chewed the second quarter of his bannock with evident concentration. The water rolled with an ever gentler swell.

'Pfffff.' It was the sound of a huge vat full of fermentation letting out its fizz. A shower of spray touched Rian's face. She wiped her cheeks. Everyone was shouting until one bark from Toma silenced them all. An island rose out of the sea beside the boat.

Rian ceased to breathe.

The island was dark-surfaced, deep blue, with signs of scraping or scratching, hoeing or ploughing. As it rose, seawater poured off it. At first its tip was at the beam but either they were being dragged towards it or it was moving forwards. Soon it was alongside, stretching out both in front and behind, easily twice as long as the boat.

Then it began to sink and as it did so a huge thing reared vertically out of the water. What was it, a root? A flag? A weapon? A wing? It plunged under the surface. The sea boiled.

It was a sail, Rian realised. It had not been an island after all. It must be a huge, upturned boat!

She dragged her eyes from the sea and saw Pytheas staring, mesmerised. Ussa stood beside him with both hands on the gunnel, shaking her head and muttering. Og had come out from the shelter and was smiling into the distance. Even Li and Faradh had got up from their game and were pointing, rapt. Everyone's attention was riveted on the space in the sea where the apparition had been.

And now a sound began: a bird-like wailing. She turned and saw that it was Toma, at the helm, making a noise that was a mix of a gull's cry and a kind of chanting. Its tonal patterns somehow echoed the giant physical presence. Its rhythm was the slow pulse of awe.

The song filled a gap in her chest. She wanted to run to Toma and cling to him but she was motionless with wonder. He sang on, hand on the tiller, eyes scanning left and right, head turning to give him the widest possible view. Rian could see he expected the island-boat, or whatever it was, to reappear. As his music filled the chasm inside her she understood that what they had seen had been a great spirit, a vast living spirit from the depth of the ocean, and that this was Toma's way of worshipping it.

She listened, and as the notes repeated in his song, she let out trapped air from her lungs to join the melody. He looked at her and nodded. They sang the chorus together. She did not know if it was words he sang or only sounds, but they came from her throat in unison with his.

In the distance, water plumed as the island-boat rose and sank again. Its sail or wings or tail fluked out of the water and dived below like a wave of farewell.

Toma's song fell quiet. Suddenly everyone was talking, gesticulating and laughing.

Rian edged over to Og. 'Do you know what song Toma was singing?'

'To the whale?'

'It was a whale?' She had heard people talk of them, but had not imagined any creature could be anywhere near that size. 'It was so big.'

'It was one of the deep spirits. The sea's creatures are...' He tailed off.

Rian was confused. 'Is it a creature or a spirit?'

'Do you know the difference?'

She had no answer to that.

It didn't take long for the flurry of excitement at the whale to die away. The little that had been happening beforehand continued, hushed and diminished. Under bruised clouds, the sea shone.

Snow began to fall again. Flecks touched the sea surface and vanished. On the boat, snowflakes half-melted and the deck was soon a slither of sleet.

Where the sea spirit had been was now blurred. As the cloud horizon drew in, the visible world shrank. The afternoon light dimmed to a cold, wet gloaming.

After the huge presence, Rian felt only absence and longing. She hunkered down between a bench and the gunnel, making herself small. Each sound made by the crew seemed like a physical blow. She wanted only to hear the sad, beautiful song Toma had sung. It rang on inside her.

Under the skin of the boat, the sea held onto its secrets, but

Rian could sense hordes of living beings, a seethe of spirits, waiting in their mist-world beyond the edge. Somehow she knew the boat had slipped out of time, over the lip of reason, crossing the cusp of the world into a place of limitless danger.

CALM

A dense boredom settled over the boat, stealing their breath. Their wake fizzled into nothing as their forward motion ceased. The sail hung loose, slapping only with the swell, until Toma asked Callum and Li and Faradh to pull it down.

Og began a story about a time he was on board a boat in the western ocean that drifted in the doldrums for weeks until their fresh water supply ran out. His voice faded without completing the story.

Ussa paced along the deck, three steps forwards, spinning on her heels, placing her feet in the same three spots on her return. Her presence became unbearable.

Rian slipped off to her bunk and lay down wide awake, contemplating the vast danger looming around them. Like the cockroaches, it showed itself only when it wanted, and hid when noticed. You could go for hours without acknowledging its presence. She thought back to the first hour on deck the morning after the gale, when Toma must have known they were lost, yet seemed so calm. She had not sensed any hazard then. What had happened to create this sense of danger? Had the sea spirit brought it? Or had it been on board all along, unobserved, like a rat?

She could taste the danger, rusty on her lips. She breathed out slowly, feeling it leave her body and go roaming. Did it inhabit only her? Everyone else appeared to be at peace. Even Ussa, bored certainly, did not appear fearful.

As dusk grew, the slaves' bannock was ceremonially divided

by Og. Rian distributed the pieces. As they were eating, she saw that Pytheas took out his third quarter and gobbled it down with none of the care with which she had seen him relish the second. Og had made a soup from dried meat. It was thin but warm. It brought a song to his lips, but no-one else joined in.

Callum was looking queasy and did not want any soup. Rian took his bowl back to Og who shared it with her.

'Have you heard Toma sing that whale song before?'

Og shook his head.

'Would you ask him for me?'

'Ask him what?'

'Ask him what the song was.'

'Why don't you? You sang it.'

'I'm scared to.'

Og raised his eyes. 'I suppose I've got nothing better to do.' He stomped down the boat.

Ussa challenged him.

'I'm going to ask Toma something.'

Her retort was obscene, but it didn't stop Og.

He conferred with Toma at the helm then returned to Rian. 'It's called something like Free Spirit. It's an Inuit song.'

'What's that?'

'Inuit, the people of the ice.'

'Who are they?' She wondered if this had anything to do with the story Badger had told her about Manigan's Great Aunty Onn.

'They wear clothes of polar bear fur like Ussa's coat, and they live on seals. Most people don't believe in them but Toma claims to have lived with them. It's his only story.'

'Tell me.'

'Not now. Ask me when I'm really bored.' He turned his back and retreated to his corner. He pulled out his bedding roll. Rian waited. He saw her watching. 'Go to bed.'

She lay down on her bunk. The tiny portion of bannock and watery soup, plus one stale oatcake, was not enough. There was an ache in her belly. She put her hands over it and hoped she would sleep.

Li and Faradh squabbled over their game until Ussa told them to quit. Quiet settled.

In the night she woke to a touch on her head and smelled Pytheas. His face was close to hers. He was bending down, looking at her in the dim light. She could see the sky had cleared. There were stars.

The next day nothing at all happened, except Rian learned to count from one to ten in Greek. The day after she reached twenty and they caught a common gull, little enough food for them all, but welcome.

The morning after that, Callum was dead in his bunk.

DEATH

Rian was wakened by Toma giving her a shake on the shoulder. He woke Ussa the same way. Og was already getting out of his bunk. It was still dark but the first grey of dawn was hinting in the sky.

Toma stepped to the bunk of the boy and pointed to him. 'Is he dead?' He was looking at her. 'Or can you wake him?'

Rian took a deep breath.

Pytheas had stirred and was sitting up in his bed. 'What is it?' he asked in Greek.

Rian stooped and put her hand to the boy's neck. She didn't know anything about him except his name. It was as if he had been invisible. 'I don't know.' She said it in Greek, then in her own tongue, then in Greek again, and then because she seemed to be able to do so now, in Keltic as well.

Now Li and Faradh were awake too. Li said he had heard coughing in the night. Callum's body was cold, stiffening. He was not waking up.

Ussa pushed Rian aside and made her own assessment. 'He is dead.'

Rian crouched beside the body. She found herself smoothing his hair and pulled her hand away. It was impossible to understand what had happened to him. He was not old enough to die. He had not seemed ill. He had never complained.

Li, Faradh and Og sat on their benches discussing the death, Li and Faradh saying it was a bad spirit on board, Og blaming the sea.

'Shut up!' Ussa wrapped her coat around her.

It was snowing, big grey flakes that stuck to every surface of the boat.

Og shook his head but after Ussa had barked at him he nodded slowly. His slave nod, as Rian had come to think of it, the one he used to obey Ussa, the one that expressed all the shame of his position. Rian hated that nod.

Li and Faradh came and stood looking between Rian and the boy. Ussa turned her back on them and went to lie back down on her bunk. Toma touched Rian on her arm and indicated she should return to sleeping. Then he and Og took one end each of the boy's small body and hauled it out and back to the stern. There was a scuffling noise and then a splash.

Toma's voice wove another of his strange songs. He did not return under the shelter but stood alone at the tiller.

Og came back frowning, and tossed a bundle of snowy clothes at Li before retreating to his bunk where he lay, face hidden, legs bunched up to his chest.

Why had Callum died? Why had Death chosen him of all of them? Danuta would have known, would perhaps even have seen it coming and healed the boy. Had the sea spirit taken him? Was this the way of this place? Was a person's soul so vulnerable here that you could simply go to sleep and never wake up? Were they going to be picked off and fed to the fish one by one? If so, who would be next?

Perhaps because of the offering of Callum's body to the ocean, the cloud lifted for a while that afternoon. Pytheas and Rian went out on deck. It was a raw day and the sail hung thick with frozen hoar frost. They sat on the narrow bench under the mast, but sitting proved too cold, so Pytheas got Rian pacing and chanting numbers to keep warm. Then he took to tracing out symbols in the snow along the gunnels and making Rian learn them – a sign for each number. He switched between fingers and signs until Rian could remember them all and repeat them back without faults. She was trying, but a meagre oatcake was not enough to keep her from shivering.

Toma crouched by the tiller, chewing like a cow at its cud. He had his own supply of dried meat of some sort, which he did not share. It made his breath smell foul and by his mastication it was obvious that it was tough. Og told Rian that it was the skin of a whale and he chewed it to give himself the spark of the great sea spirit. When she looked at the skipper again, she saw that he was crying.

ICE

In the morning everything was frozen: the drinking water barrel, blankets, ropes, deck planks, benches, boots, coats, toes, fingers, tears. Even the sea.

Faradh's nose froze. He cried. He buried himself in his bedding roll. Li wrapped himself around him to try to keep him warm.

Ussa strode the length of the boat wrapped in her polar bear coat. She was a pacing fury. Sometimes Pytheas paced with her.

Toma stood at the tiller, chewing. Periodically he said something. Rian heard him say it over and over, not knowing what it meant. He was saying it to Ussa and to Pytheas. Eventually he said it differently and something changed. Rian did not know what it was.

Og said, 'Thank the Mother.'

Toma came and stood over her. She closed her eyes so as not to have to see him. But he tapped her on her shoulder. She looked through him, but his face was that of a seal and it drew her gaze. He was holding out a piece of the whale meat he chewed, offering it to her, and then he hummed, bringing his face close to her right shoulder so she could feel his breath on her neck. He hummed almost inaudibly into her ear the song he had sung to the whale. Staring at her, wild eyed. Tugging her out of herself.

She reached a hand out from under her blanket and took the meat. She curled her fingers around it and closed her eyes again. Her hand retreated with its gift under the blanket. Toma gave an insistent poke. She resisted, then lifted her lids. He pointed out on deck, and then touched her lips with a feather touch. His eyes spoke. 'Come.'

Something in her decided to accept the challenge. She allowed him to pull the puppet inside her and to do his bidding. She was, after all, only a slave now.

They were sailing towards the sun and the sea was milky. They were among an archipelago of ice islands. Everyone was looking to the right. A white bear was ushering two cubs away across the ice, looking over her shoulder at the boat and striding purposefully away, her two followers scampering to keep up. At the edge of the floe she poured herself into the water and the cubs splashed in after her. She let them climb onto her back and swam off. Before long she was swallowed into the seascape, a blur, a dot, gone.

Rian's attention returned to the ice. Near to the water line it was translucent blue. The pieces ranged in size from large plates to small islands. They were all, subtly, in motion, a teeming yet inanimate hoard in a bath of jade green sea.

A seal with a frozen moustache lying on one of the ice slabs regarded them with curiosity but no fear. Another, closer, slid into the sea. Two kittiwakes flew by, tilting sideways to get a better view of them.

The boat nudged its way though slush and Toma began to sing the free spirit song. Rian joined in and let her voice escape out over the freezing ocean.

Ahead of them a sea spirit with a single-horned head lifted from the water, puffed and rolled back under, showing them the way. Toma had taken over the tiller from Li, who moved between the ropes, tightening, slackening, keeping the sail taut with the breeze behind them. It seemed to be helping. Li did not sing, but he pointed to the water where the creature had been and breathed its name. 'Narwhal.'

Ussa did not sing either. She sat slumped in front of the sail, closed to the world.

Pytheas perched at the prow, casting excited, if anxious, glances overboard. She could see him watching the ice, following slabs with his gaze as they approached and were gently shouldered aside by the boat like partners in a slow, elegant dance.

Toma was focused not on the ice but on the water. She could tell from his singing that his attention was on the liquid flow, following it as if he had some extra sense none of the rest of them had guiding him between the ice, showing him the free passage, allowing him to detect liquid. She heard the fluid in his song and flowed with it, abandoning herself. She gave herself to her voice.

Her voice trusted Toma.

She could feel the ocean's current barrelling under the boat. The slush scraped the hide, but stronger still was the water carrying them through. They rode the current and the wind's hand thrust them along it.

The ice wanted to trap them but the current and the wind wanted them to be free and for now, the ice spirit was on their side too, coursing along ahead of the boat, showing them the way. She sang to it and felt the thrum of its greeting in the timber below her feet. The whole boat was humming.

The narwhal surfaced, its horn lifted in salute. Then it pierced the water ahead of them and sank below. Without warning they were out of the ice and back on water, and its motion was a jabble that tossed the boat from side to side uncomfortably, the sail slapping and flogging.

Toma's song stopped abruptly. Rian heard her own voice alone for a moment like a bird. It got out before she could stop it and it hung too long, echoing.

Toma, Li, Faradh and Og reset the sail to ride the open sea.

The new motion set the bilges slopping. They stank. Faradh was sea-sick and Og did not do a good job of clearing it up. Soon enough it would be her job again.

Rian gave Faradh her remaining supply of lady's mantle to stop his nausea. They had so little firewood left she couldn't brew it up and suggested he chew it. He chewed, wincing at the taste, then threw it up.

Perhaps she had lost the ability to heal. She stood by the mast, hanging onto a block she didn't know the purpose of, trying and failing to understand what she had done to deserve all of this.

THULE

The cloud must have been thinning for a while. It was the change in the texture of the water that Rian first noticed. The slow swell lost its glassy sheen. It crumpled like cloth, as if an invisible hand were puckering it.

Toma called to Li and Faradh and they roused themselves from their beds. He made them beat the sail with oars. They were showered with ice and cursed, then turned it into a game until a snarl from Toma finished it. Stumbling back to their benches under the shelter, they were stopped by a shout from Pytheas.

'Look!' He pointed before them to the prow and pushed past beyond the sail.

Out of the thinning cloud, shapes loomed. There was a weird glow in the sky. Was it the sun?

Pytheas called to Toma, 'What do I see?'

Rian put her back to the mast and looked out. There was land ahead.

The calm was easing. A trickle of water murmured under the keel. The sail twitched and tensioned.

It was like wakening from a dream.

Unfolding out of the cloud was a coastline unlike any that could be real. The land was made of impossibly black rock. It smoked. Catching an acrid smell on the air, Rian breathed it in and understood that this was not the world. It must be some sort of nightmare and they had not woken at all.

'Where is this?' Pytheas asked.

Nobody answered.

Li, Faradh and Pytheas were all agog, standing forward up on the gunnel straps to see more.

Toma caught Rian's attention. 'Ussa.' He indicated she should go and rouse her.

She ducked her head under the shelter. To the single word, 'land', both Ussa and Og reacted as if struck by some physical blow. Ussa jumped into motion, grabbing her white coat. Without bothering to tie her boots, she was up and out on deck. Og was a breath behind her.

All on deck they stared at the impossible, furious, seething place.

'Where is this?' Pytheas asked again, but once more no-one seemed to hear his question. It was as if they were all made into statues by the sight ahead of them: the fuming, black slick where the sea touched whatever kind of land it was.

The air smelled rotten and burnt. It reminded Rian of the smell of the forge, only darker, as if something foul were being created. She shuddered. Callum had died and now they were sailing beyond the edge. They had not even noticed themselves cross the threshold. There had been no membrane to pierce, just cloud. The sea had taken them too far. The sea had taken them beyond the edge of the world.

Rian clutched a rope tied to a peg at the mast, as if it could attach her to reality. Why did no-one apart from her seem to want to go back?

'Go back,' said Og. 'We should go back.' He was kneeling, with one arm around the mast. Rian wasn't sure if anyone else heard him.

The sail snapped to life with a shower of ice flakes as the wind picked up a little more. Toma kept the boat a constant distance from the shore, not approaching, not backing off, just skirting along, watching what emerged as they picked up speed and the land flowed by. The cloud continued to lift. The black smoking sludge gave way to rock, spattered with orange and green, just like the lichened crags of home. A swirl of gulls suggested there was life here of some sort.

As the cloud cleared, it revealed a mountain looming. At first it was a glow though drifts of mist, then more clearly a blaze, belching a torrent of filthy smoke into the sky.

'Where is this?' The question was more insistent.

Rian let go of the rope and drifted back to the stern. Behind her back, her hands clutched the gunnel on the side of the boat away from the land. She leaned against it, wanting to be as far from this sight as possible, needing the support of something strong. The boat seemed impossibly flimsy compared to this vast rock dragon, breathing fire.

Toma must finally have heard Pytheas. 'Thule.'

The Greek caught the word and span round to nod assent. 'Thule,' he repeated, awe in his voice. He went to his box and brought out a little bottle, poured a few drops of a liquid into the water. Rian heard him muttering in his own tongue, but most of it she didn't catch or understand, until he turned, made a theatrical gesture at the smoking mountain and said clearly, 'Of course. It is a volcano.'

A skua flew so low over the boat Rian could see its eagle beak and yellow eye.

Og ducked as it swooped over him. 'Thule,' he echoed, but in his voice it was a warning of something fearful, a naming of a disease, a death threat spoken and irredeemable. He crouched below the level of the rowlocks, hunched up with his head in his hands. 'Go back. Please, let us go back.'

But Toma showed no interest in retreating. They continued skirting the shore of this strange place. As the night drew in and stars began to pit the sky, the temperature plummeted. Rian felt her will leaving her as she grew colder. Og retreated to his corner. Their firewood supply was dwindling, but he lit a little fire to brew up a weak soup. Ussa and Toma consented for the slaves to be given an oatcake each. A line trailed behind the boat, baited, but the gulls showed no interest. No fish rose. The sea mocked them.

Having cleared the sky, the wind faded away again and with it their motion ceased.

Pytheas was enthralled by the hellish landmass and stood questioning Toma as dusk set the mountaintop to ever more terrifying proportions. He wanted to land but Toma said it was out of the question. So the Greek appealed to Ussa. What if the Walrus Mutterer was here? But she too was unwilling to set foot on the place, saying she could smell its evil.

As night grew, molten metal, or some similarly fiery material, smeared down the mountain's flank. The black land glowed in the dark.

When they drifted closer, the temperature rose and a hissing sizzle became audible, presumably where the smoking material reached the sea. Toma ordered the slaves to the oars and they rowed, wearily, out to sea. Rian was glad to be making the monstrosity shrink, but her limbs were weak and the effort of trying to row in time with Og, Li and Faradh set pain running in her arms so they also seemed to be on fire. Sweat poured down her face, down her sides, down her chest, until she felt she might explode with the agony, or collapse.

But it was Faradh who first lost control. His oar splashed. He lost the rhythm and then let go, slumping forward with a groan. Ussa grabbed him by the hair, tugged him to his knees and let fly with her whip. One stroke was enough to flatten him. In that one lash, Rian learned much about the woman. What drove her on, what fuelled her rage, what fed her talent for terrorising others was not strength or power. As the woman lifted her arm in its thick, polar bear pelt and raised the leather handle with its snaking sinew, her face traversed from the fire-spewing mountain to the flaccid sail and her eyes carried a light in them of a cornered prey. It was fear that Rian saw there. Ussa was afraid, not only of this island, if an island it was, but of anything in the world more powerful than her.

Faradh, shielding his head with one arm, got to his knees, then took his place back on the bench behind Rian. They resumed rowing again until Toma's call relieved them. They were empty anyway.

The mountain had shrunk to a distant glow. Pytheas had not taken his eyes off it.

When Rian stopped rowing and her breathing settled, her clothes were wringing with sweat. It took no time for shivering to begin, her teeth chattering. She tried to get to her feet but after all that work she was wobbly. She sat back on the bench, holding the oar, trembling. She had not known such intense weakness was possible.

Pytheas was her rescuer.

He gave her his coat, took her down to her bunk and wrapped her in a blanket.

But the cold deepened, her trembling continued until he took her to his wider bunk and shared his body heat with her.

She calmed eventually, warm enough to drift off into sleep.

She woke in the darkness to his hands on her skin.

And then he hurt her.

And Rian understood what it meant to be a slave.

SLAVERY

AFTER

Rian crept back into her own bunk, rolled over to face away from the world and sunk into herself.

Pytheas had done to her what was not his to do and now she was defiled.

Her hand moved towards her crotch. She wanted to hold herself, to make herself whole again, but it was impossible. Ice gripped her fingers. She tucked them into her armpits, crossing her arms over her chest. She brought her knees up to her belly, moving with slow, barely noticeable shunts until she had pulled herself into smallness. Within her body, she continued to shrink away. She faded, withering like a flower does. Autumn came to her and she allowed it to take what it would. It wanted flesh, so she gave herself to it. She was only meat, only a body. She let herself be devoured.

A voice used her name.

She ignored it.

She slept.

*

When she woke, she breathed slowly until she slept again. She did not want to wake. Finally, it was impossible to sleep any more. It was dark and she was wrung out with hunger. Thirst too. Everyone else seemed to be sleeping. Dread tormented her. Bad had become worse. Enslavement had become slavery. Her body was no longer her own. How long would it be before he did something to steal her spirit? They were beyond the edge of the world. She was lost.

She tiptoed to the water barrel, wobbling. It was low. Og snored nearby. She dipped the cup and drank and felt it course down into her gut. Goodness, but not what she needed. There was nothing of what she needed.

She drifted on her melting legs onto the deck. Toma was at the helm, staring at the sea. Did he never sleep?

The sky was blurred with cloud, dull and starless. Grey water slugged the hull. The sea's huge thoughtlessness seemed a refuge, a place to find respite from this small and incomprehensibly overcrowded boat. There was a tightness in her that needed the looseness of the dark water.

She gave way to it and offered herself to the ocean. It was simple to do. She took off her coat and her boots. It would be wrong to send them, skins of animals, to the depths. But, without them she could go.

She would go.

She went.

STORM

Toma was furious. Rian had not seen him like this. He said nothing, but there was iron where his face had been, and fire in his eyes. He breathed out hard, snorts of mist that hung in the air over where she lay, prostrate on the deck where he had thrown her. The back of her head was sore where it had smacked down. He stood over her, one foot on each side of her, legs in the stance of a sea-rider. The hand that had let go of her was still stretched out in front of him, palm down, fingers open.

She couldn't read his expression. It was not only anger. It was something worse. Scorn? No. His eyes were as changeable as the weather. Perhaps it was sorrow.

Would he sing again? Would he ask her to join him?

No. Not that either. Nothing like that.

He had pulled her back from going overboard. A crowd of voices were babbling in her head. Danuta was telling her to pull herself together. A child screamed. A slow insistent voice spoke only of filth and darkness. The screaming child wailed and Toma nodded.

The screaming was her own. It was coming out of her own mouth and now Ussa was standing over her, Pytheas too. He was tugging at her shoulder but Toma's outstretched hand prevented any movement from her somehow, as if he could press her to the deck just by gesture. He was talking. Ussa interjected with shrieks and barking. Toma finished what he had to say, and now the only sound was her wail.

A hand clamped over her open mouth and she tried to bite

it, but it was a strong hand. It smelled of ink. She gagged and whimpered. She was being lifted. Pytheas had her shoulders off the deck. Toma let go of his hand gesture and lifted her feet. They swung her like a sack between them, shuffling until they could sling her on her bunk. There were more words and then she felt rope: her ankles trussed, another across her chest. Toma tugged her fleece out from under her body and laid it over her. There were incomprehensible clouds in his eyes now and he was shaking his head. She could feel her face wet but couldn't lift a hand to wipe it. She could roll though, onto her side, her face to the darkness. She closed her eyes and stared in.

It was a tumult, a barrage, a storm. She let it rage.

It was inside at first, but then the world answered with its own tempest. She lay in the dark listening to the sail howl and a shrieking in the rigging. There was flapping, then a rip. Shouts. A jangle of ropes and shackles. More shouts. When the boat tipped, the ropes stopped her rolling from her bunk. Pots clattered. Swearing from Og. A thump. Faradh groaning. The smell of puke. Water smacking. Splashing. Wind roaring. Everything roaring. Water sloshing everywhere. The world coming to an end.

It never ends. There is no edge to the world to fall off, not until death. Thule is always just another beginning. It is cold, dark, wet and miserable but it brings no conclusion.

Beginnings, the universe overflows with them. They are thrust perpetually into life.

Begin again.

Begin again.

Always begin again.

Faradh died in the storm. They found him face down in the bilges and threw him overboard with his clothes on. Li cried but no-one else had any strength to mourn him. The water barrel had toppled. They were certain to die if land did not appear soon.

Pytheas did not look at Rian nor speak to her.

SLAVERY

It was Ussa who eventually untied her and told her the new situation.

'You belong to me again now. Pytheas doesn't want you. You've seen what he does: takes a piece of parchment, scratches away a few words, then tosses it away, starts afresh. Get up.'

Rian barely had the strength to roll over. She made eye contact and what she saw shocked her. Ussa had aged. She was haggard. The flesh on her face had withered, yet as the skin slumped it was as if it had drained all its power into her eyes. They were moons burning through cloud and their pull was extraordinary. Rian found herself sitting up. An obedient part of her wanted to follow those eyes, to be tugged in their tide.

Ussa had already gathered Og and Li in the galley. 'It is time for me to take over from Toma. Look where he has got us. We need food and most of all water or we will die. Is there any water left at all?'

Og shook his head.

'It will rain, and we must be ready to catch it. Can you rig a sail or something?'

Og and Li exchanged glances and nodded.

'Of course,' Li said.

Rian was unsteady on her feet. She sat on Og's bunk. No-one seemed to mind.

Ussa pointed a finger at her. 'You clear up this mess. It will make you feel better.'

The galley was a shambles. Everything that could move had been tossed about in the storm

'I am going to catch a bird. We must eat.' Ussa stomped off, the bear skin coat swinging, its bulk commensurate with her will.

'You are one of us again.' Og passed her a cloth.

They all stared after Ussa. She stopped and turned. 'Move it.'

As Ussa predicted, it did rain, and Toma helped Li to rig a spare sail to catch water. He did not appear to mind Ussa taking control. It was cold and drenching and the swell after the storm made the boat lurch about. But they had water to drink, a whole barrel full in no time, cause for much celebration. They drank it at first as if it was fine wine, and then beaker after beaker.

Og caught a razorbill on his line. They ate it raw. Rian was surprised that the tiny mouthfuls she was allowed could give her such pleasure. She was alive. After that, Ussa caught a puffin, then two more, and before long they had a dozen – a feast of raw bird flesh.

Rian felt sick afterwards but she knew it was only the effect of food after so long with an empty stomach. She drank more rainwater.

Pytheas had eaten and drunk less than everyone else and sat on his own, not meeting anyone's gaze, then went to his bunk, looking unwell.

Ussa picked flesh off a bird wing. 'Toma says he knows where we're going and we will make land soon, but I do not know if he is lying or not.' With every bit of her bird she returned more and more to her old, belligerent self. She wrapped an arm round Rian. 'I'm going to sell you to the first person I see.' She laughed, mouth wide open. 'You skinny little bitch. You're bad luck, so you are. Now get back to the bilges where you belong.'

It was the foulest job possible: the slurry sloshing about in the bottom of the boat was now a disgusting mix of leftover food, scraps of feathers and guts of the seabirds they'd been eating, puke and piss. Rian gagged with each scoop, but bucketful by bucketful she hauled it out and threw it into the sea. It was exhausting. Her arms strained with the weight of the bucket.

Og lay down full of bird meat, looking sick. Rian scooped and tried not to retch. She filled the bucket again and again. Ussa sat at the foot of the mast, scanning the horizon. Li was at work tidying ropes, following Toma's orders to trim the sail. A good wind had got up and Toma had an air of purposefulness as he steered towards the midday sun, adjusting their heading so the sail filled in a steady reach. The boat cut through the waves with a rolling gait.

Back in the galley, Og and Pytheas were talking quietly. They broke off as she passed them. Pytheas was looking at her. His hair was plastered on his head as if he was sweating.

'Are you sick?' she asked. He nodded and indicated that he was nauseous by gurning, his hand on his belly.

She thought about what she had left in her medicine pouch and what he had done to her. She had nothing to help him anyway, without any means of heating water to brew up a purging drink. She could give him some dried mint to chew or she could just let him suffer. She hauled another bucket from the bilges and considered what might happen if he started vomiting into it.

When she gave him the last dry mint leaves and indicated he should chew them slowly, his face was a contortion of emotion. He took her hand and kissed it as if she was a princess. She pulled it away.

Of course it had to be that moment that Ussa chose to relinquish her post. Her voice was a vixen howl. 'What is going on here?'

The staff cracked onto Rian's shoulder, knocking her to her knees. The bucket, which she had set down beside her bunk, rattled into the bilges. She scuttled after it, but Ussa grabbed her hair and yanked her up, shouting, her face too close.

'Answer me. What is going on? You little slut.'

'Nothing.'

Her head lunged to one side as the slap made contact.

Ussa towered over her. 'You ravenous little whore. Do you think you're some kind of princess? Eh? You keep your slutty hands down there in the bilges where they belong.'

She said something to Pytheas in her southern dialect of Keltic and Rian found it obvious what she meant because Ussa's gestures were so eloquent. Pytheas was being warned off Ussa's property.

In a way Rian was relieved. She didn't want his attentions. What he had done to her in that black night, spreading her legs and forcing himself into her, that was enough contact for a lifetime. She should have known better than to help him with her herbs, but the instinct to offer healing was too strong; all her life she had been taught to do so. It was the way of the Mother.

The relief was short-lived. Ussa had not finished with her.

'What sort of a punishment does a slut deserve?' She spoke loudly enough so everyone on the boat could hear her.

Og looked up. 'Bilges is the worst job on the boat, is that not enough?'

Ussa looked at him as if he was a boy. 'So now you're trying to protect her as well.' She shook her head, reached for Rian's hair, tugging her out onto deck. 'Strip.'

Rian began to unfasten her jerkin, hands trembling.

'Get a move on.'

She speeded up a bit.

Toma asked a question and Ussa told him to shut up and mind his own business.

Rian was down to her underclothes.

'Get them off.'

Rian turned her naked back. Her face was crushed against the mast and she was tied around the thighs, ankles and neck. The wind was cold on her skin and the rope dug in.

The strap whined before it bit, then whined again and bit again. Leather lacerated skin. Rian was only conscious of the pain and then she clawed her way mentally back to her high place. She would not submit to that woman, no matter what. She felt the pain, and it was only pain. Her hatred of Ussa was stronger. She balled it up like dung and saved it away inside her.

CLICKIMIN

She came round in her bunk to a touch on her head and Og's voice. 'Land, Rian. Land!'

She was lying on her front and as she tried to turn her head she felt the wounds on her back reopen after the night's quiet effort to crust them shut again. As she rolled onto her side, her shirt, stuck to the flesh, peeled off scabs, filling her eyes with self-pity. But land, the sight of land, was worth agony. Land meant the possibility of an end to this nightmare. It might even mean escape. Land, any land, was bound to be better than this.

She hobbled towards the deck, drawn by sheer instinct, ignoring the pain that raged from her neck to her knees.

And there it was: a green line, already shaping itself into a rocky coastline, with hills beyond. Land, grey, solid and bathed in sun.

Rian closed her eyes and opened them again. It was still there. The sea glittered and waves splashed white, landwards. They were on a broad reach, the sail full across the boat, blocking her view if she stood. So she crouched, looking below it. They were heading into a loch, or a channel between islands. Soon rocky shores were visible.

She breathed deeply. She could smell the land. After all those days at sea – how long had it been? – there was the scent of life in the air, the mother-fragrance, earth-breath.

She inhaled to the top of her lungs, feeling her back sting, and exhaled all the way, letting it go.

Toma was relaxed at the tiller, with the appearance of being back in familiar waters. He was murmuring away to himself, no doubt a navigation song or story, his lips moving even though there was no longer a boy to teach it to. He caught her eye, tilted his head and with a lift of his eyebrows, conveyed some kindly question to which she responded with a pucker of her chin. She had to bite back tears.

Li stopped himself just before slapping her on her back. His smile was full of bitterness and desperation. She had no smile to return.

Og patted the bench beside him but there was no question of sitting. She clutched a thwart and stayed where she was, crouching.

Pytheas and Ussa were together, mostly hidden by the sail, leaning forwards, hair blowing as if it was they, not the wind, that was propelling the boat towards safety.

They passed an island and entered a sheltered channel, gliding in on smooth water. Ahead, smoke. A settlement.

Og asked and Toma answered. He knew this place. 'Clickimin. The Black Chieftain lives here.'

All Rian cared about was whether there would be butter and yarrow and anyone she could trust enough to touch her wounds.

The settlement was on an island. It grew before their eyes, the broch dominant and surrounded by stone houses and barns, smoke signalling occupation. Soon there was the frantic activity of making landfall. The sail came down and they had to row into the harbour.

Rowing. There was no escape, no matter the agony of it. Rian nearly fainted as with every tug on the oar her wounds tore open. Eventually the pain rang so loudly she ceased to feel anything and she rowed like a beetle pushing its ball of dung, oblivious to the world.

Eventually, they came alongside a boat and halted and the thronging harbour swam in and out of focus. Rian eased herself off her bench and stood. Ussa was already clambering onto the next vessel, drawing all eyes to her as she made straight for dry land.

Now that they were safe, there was suddenly too much to do. Food was the first priority. Og was immediately at work, interrogating people at the shore. He returned to Ussa's boat, grinning, with a loaf of bread and some salted fish. He shared it out between the four of them who remained on Ròn; Toma and Li grabbed their pieces with glee and Og split the other half loaf with Rian. She realised Pytheas had gone, although she had not noticed him leave. She thought bad thoughts, wishing him away for good, or dead, then her conscience pricked. Danuta had taught her that the mother knows what we wish and sends our unkind thoughts back to do to their evil on us. Still, she couldn't bring herself to do anything but wish him gone.

She munched on the bread slowly. It was fresh and smelled of sunshine. Although the day was cool and grey, the air carried the scent of flowers. The tide was high. A line of lichens on the rocky shore showed where the sea would never reach except in storms. Og and Toma were talking supplies. The fisher-people around them chattered, fastening boats, working on repairs, arguing over catches. She didn't need to understand it to feel its comfort. The boats were mostly like theirs, hide curraghs, and there were some smaller, sturdy-looking wooden craft.

Rian was desperate to get off, to touch dry land, to lie still somewhere and rest and heal. Now the tension of the sea journey was easing, a tide inside her rose inexorably, higher and higher until she could hold it back no more and it began to spill from her eyes.

Og saw her though she tried to turn away, to face out to the water, her back to the men. She felt his hand on her shoulder and winced. He snatched his hand away, saying, 'Sorry, sorry, poor Rian, poor Rian,' over and over, grimacing, wanting her to stop crying so badly it was almost funny, but she wasn't able to stop.

'I want to get off.' She heard herself wailing like a child.

Og said, without hesitation, 'Go. Go girl.'

Toma nodded.

Og was halfway out of the boat, beckoning to her. 'Come on, the boss could be gone days. Shore leave!' He was grinning and gesturing with an excess of comedy and something close to desperation. She followed down the wooden pier where the boats were tied up onto dry land for the first time in weeks.

CAKE

When her feet touched the ground her legs no longer knew how to hold up her weight. It was as if she was listing and then she was down on her knees touching pebbles, stones, tufts of thrift and grass, iris spikes, mud. Mud! Its softness. Stones, with all of their density and their stillness. She touched and touched and the plants gave her their smells and people passing smiled curiously at her. They were perhaps seeing a girl in ecstasy at touching land after a long journey but to Rian it wasn't that at all. They could not possibly understand. The mother offered life to her soul and she supped on it like a baby at a breast, realising only now how close to dying she had been on the boat. No matter what happened, whatever she had to do, she would not go back aboard.

She needed to be able to survive on land again. She had the medicine bag that Danuta had given her around her waist; it was so empty she had taken to wearing it as a belt. There was her fleece but it didn't matter. She could survive without bedding. Wherever she was going, summer was coming.

'So where shall we go?' Og held out half a dozen little polished shells. 'There'll be people with food, there might be some trading, though it is late in the day.'

They strolled, Rian wobbling and giggling at her clumsiness. Whenever they paused, she felt she was swooning, as if her body no longer knew how to stand upright. The only answer was to keep walking. She gazed around her. She had never seen anything like this. So many boats and so many people. A hubbub of ropes and baskets, fish and bones. Houses built of stone with doors wide open and everywhere people calling, guffawing, examining goods or rifling through baskets. A woman stood looking out to sea. A boy ran past, a dog on his heels. A line of four slaves with heavy baskets strapped across their foreheads marched up from the harbour towards the broch, their ankle chains rattling.

A big buxom woman with a basket of cakes hanging from a leather strap around her shoulders showed them her wares, tempting them to something sweet. 'Will you buy a honey bun for your honey bun?'

Og giggled like a naughty boy. He nudged Rian and pouted for a kiss.

'Get lost!' But she laughed, and he handed over a shell and they got a cake each.

'Don't tell Ussa, whatever you do. This is…'

The soft honey-flavoured cake was so delicious Rian thought she might cry again. She stuffed it into her mouth, feeling its nectar flood her. Her mouth, nose, belly and blood all swam with its sweetness. Her cheeks bulged with it and she had to close her eyes to stop the outside world from interfering with the wave of panicky joy that filled her. She opened them again to see the cake-seller laughing, her face lit with delight, her basket jiggling in front of her.

'Best cake ever, eh?' Og's mouth was full too, and he had an arm around the shoulder of the woman, looking as if he might be about to do something extravagant like burst into song, perhaps, or dance.

'Yum.' It wasn't exactly expressive but blinking at the woman she saw it was enough. Her hunger, her pain: she didn't need to explain any of that. She wished she could stay with this woman and not ever have to see Pytheas again, or Li or Toma. Even Og, she thought, can go now too. The longing was to be in the company of a woman and not a tyrant. Ussa wasn't a real woman. A motherly woman like this one, how she wanted that! But Og was saying his thankyous and goodbyes and they were parting company with the cake seller, and all Rian could do was make her reluctance to go obvious, and the woman nodded and smiled as if she understood.

Further on a fisherman was selling a basket of crabs. He had attracted a crowd of children with his antics. As he waved a crab about, enthusing about its excellent eating qualities, the other crabs in the box would begin to clamber over each other trying to make their escape. Rian knew how they felt. She too was looking for a way to run away. The man would almost clinch a sale and then turn to rescue his miscreant wares. He made a great show of being nipped by their claws, howling as if they had bitten off his finger, and the crowd tittered as he clutched his crotch and mimed a huge pincer with one hand. He was off on a story about a crab 'so big', his arms wide. Children stood mouths agape in front of him, backing away and shrieking when he waved a crab too close to their noses, giggling as he mock-hopped from a crab that he let get close to his toes. Meanwhile a cheery woman with a line of baskets of fish did a brisk trade from their mothers.

Rian wished she could giggle along with the children but the press of the crowd kept catching the wounds on her back, stinging like wasps. While Og haggled with the woman, exchanging some more of his shells for fish, Rian looked for somewhere she could slip away to, but as if Og could read her mind, he grabbed her by the arm and tugged her after him. As they turned they saw Ussa, and before they could merge back into the crowd she saw them too. Even at a distance they could tell that what she was saying wasn't exactly an endearment.

SALE

'We're in for it now. Don't say anything. I'll try and talk us out of it.' Og strode towards their owner.

Rian dragged herself along in his wake, glancing to each side, trying not to miss anything, wondering if there was anywhere she could run to.

To her amazement, though, Ussa only sent Og back to the boat. She scoffed at the fish, took all of his remaining shells off him, or those he showed her, and then grabbed Rian by one ear. 'You come with me.'

Rian stumbled beside her along a muddy passage between houses, up some rough stone steps and into a kind of courtyard surrounded by open-fronted buildings. Inside them and spilling out across the yard a market was in full swing: fabrics and clothes, skins and hides, food, drinks and trinkets. One whole side of the square was taken up with animal skins of all colours and sizes, from small gleaming otter pelts to huge brown bearskins. One corner had the stench of tanneries and mountains of leather goods were stacked behind ferocious-looking men armed as if for battle, not just for bartering. At one side a bustle of traders haggled over bolts of rough woollen cloth and Ussa led her towards them.

Nearby a woman clucked and minced around a customer, making a great show of measuring and pinning. Behind her was a rainbow of cloth and, through the drizzle of her pain, Rian tried to appreciate the wall of fabric. There were so many colours in it she could not imagine how they were all made.

'Time to dress you up for sale.' Ussa led her up to the woman, whose round face lit up with avarice at the sight of her. When she had dealt with her customer, she ushered Ussa into her stall, stroking the white pelt of her coat. As Ussa gave short, guttural instructions, the tailor turned her attention to Rian, nodding. She reached out and touched Rian's hair, then her gaze ranged up and down her body, sizing her up.

After an agreement was reached, Rian was taken behind a curtain and ordered to scrub herself clean. The woman spoke to her in Keltic and Rian knew enough now to be able to tell she was trying to be kind. She tutted over the lashmarks on her back and made Rian stand still while she smoothed fat onto the lacerations. It stung. The sleeveless dress the old woman dressed her in was plain, but woven through it were threads of yarn the colour of primrose leaves, and it was belted with a pale leather thong. There were sandals of a similar leather – Rian had never worn anything so delicate on her feet – and a pale green shawl. 'Green like your eyes,' the old woman said, fussing about, plaiting her hair and coiling it first one way then another, standing back from her to view the effect. Rian began to see that this woman had once been handsome. There was something graceful in how she held herself and her pudgy face was lit by blue eyes, bright as a May sky. After the woman rubbed oil into her hair to make it shine and painted her face with coloured pastes, Rian felt like a woman for the first time. She wasn't sure if she liked it or not.

Ussa had got Og and Li to lay out her wares on a sheet of sail cloth and she was strutting about, trying to draw people's attention to the glinting weaponry and gems. She added a bronze necklace and bangles to Rian's outfit and made her stand in the centre of her display. 'Smile, you ungrateful little bitch, you might never get another chance to be tarted up like this.' Whenever Ussa noticed that her smile had faded, a finger nail pressed into one of the welts on her back brought the grimace back to her face.

She drew plenty of admiring glances and Ussa encouraged

anyone who showed any interest to look closely. One of the leather traders, a man with piggy eyes and a too-tight jerkin came and poked at her, making her open her mouth so he could look at her teeth, squeezing her arms between his fat fingers, complaining about how thin she was.

Ussa stood watching, hands on hips. 'We've been at sea, and she can't hold her food on the water. She's no use to me. She'll fatten up no problem, if that's what you want. I lost one of the crew at sea so we lack muscle on the oars. I'm needing a straight swap for a man who can row, ideally, or a good offer.'

'She looks like she's fading away.' He kept his hands on her longer than he needed to, but he wasn't interested in buying her.

After she had been standing in the sun for what felt like hours, the tailor woman came over. With a cheery smile, as if delivering the best news of the day, she said, 'The Chieftain's asked for a slave display shortly over at the broch, you should take her there.' Then she whispered something in Ussa's ear that made them both cackle.

Ussa clapped an iron shackle around Rian's ankle, with a sub-stantial chain attached, and walked her clanking up to the broch as if she were a cow. Just to the left of the entrance was a line of five people: three men, one older woman and a boy. They were all chained to a large metal hoop set into the wall of the building. Ussa stood Rian at the end of the line, ran the chain through the hoop and back to the shackle around her leg.

Rian looked at the other slaves. The boy and the youngest man looked frightened but the older woman and men seemed indiffer-ent to everything around them, their faces showing no emotion at all.

'Don't look at them. Look at him.' Ussa pinched her arm, and pointed at the man stepping out from the door of the broch.

The Black Chieftain was huge, a fortress in human form, dressed like a battlement in black leather studded with stones. Everything about him was big and dark: his beard, his eyes, his hairy hands. There was no mistaking why he was the Black Chieftain. Rian shrank at the thought of what being his slave might mean. He had first choice of the captives.

He said something to a tall, grey-haired man to his left, then turned to the line of slaves, stepping a little to his left to stand directly in front of each of them in turn and looking them up and down. Rian was last. He looked her up and down a second time and leered at her as if he wanted to eat her. He turned to the grey man at his side. 'That one.' He gestured towards the middle of her chest with a finger. 'And those.' He made a tiny downwards flick with the digit towards the boy and the biggest of the three men, then turned away and strode off towards the market. The grey man turned to Ussa and the other traders and set about negotiating the sale.

Ussa stood, legs apart, her eyebrows raised at her small triumph. 'I'll take him.' She pointed at the second biggest man. His face was misshapen but his arms and legs were thick with muscle.

The grey man waved one of the other traders across, who unlocked the slave Ussa wanted and gave her the chain. She tugged at the slave like a dog and walked away without looking back at Rian.

'There's a feast tonight,' the grey man called after her, 'you'll be welcome.'

She turned and nodded acknowledgement, then strode off sharply, keeping the chain so tight the slave had to skip after her.

After the grey man had made arrangements with the traders he took Rian and the boy slave into the broch. An old woman led Rian into a side chamber and set her to work with a quern.

BLACK CHIEFTAIN

A team of people were cooking at a central fire pit watched by the Chieftain who sat on lavish furs. Behind him was a wooden carving like those on the prows of some of the boats in the harbour, demonic animals with wide eyes and bared teeth. The place seemed to be seething with monsters: two improbably large and malicious looking dogs sat on each side of the big man. They too scrutinised the activities at the fire: a roasting boar on a spit and several smaller spits of fish and fowl, bread cooking on flat stones and a cauldron of something green.

Rian was surprised to see Ussa and Pytheas on a bench to the left of the Chieftain. To his right were two younger versions of himself, neither quite so large nor quite so black. To their right was a woman wearing a colourful gown, fat gold torcs and bangles on both arms. She got up when she saw the new slaves enter and spoke to them in the guttural dialect they used. Rian's companion scuttled off obediently to the other end of the room.

'You don't speak our tongue.' The woman spoke Keltic. Rian shook her head. 'Serve ale – see.' She pointed to a bald servant with a barrel.

Rian hurried to obey but could not fail to see the woman's frown. This was the Chieftain's wife, she assumed from her age and dress.

The bald barrel-master confirmed that this was indeed Maadu. Rian took a jug and proceeded towards the Chieftain. He reached around her waist and she flinched at the touch. Another servant brought him a dish of the prize cut of boar and this mercifully required the attention of both of his hands. She filled his drinking horn and stood holding it where he indicated. Ussa ignored her, speaking in the local tongue with rapid fluency to the Chieftain who nodded along.

Beside Ussa, Pytheas sat wearing a waistcoat of fine fur that Rian hadn't seen before. His hair was clean and tied back neatly and his eyes darted about with curiosity. When she had stepped up he had nodded to acknowledge her presence but no more, but when the Chieftain addressed him he responded in Keltic and glanced in Rian's direction, speaking slowly as if he wanted her attention.

'See this?' Pytheas thrust up his sleeve to reveal a bracelet of beads the colour of autumn leaves. 'Amber! I want to learn where it comes from. I met a man today in the market who told me you may be able to take me to where it is found.' He looked expectantly at the Chieftain.

'It's no mystery where it comes from,' snapped Ussa.

'The Amber Coast.' The Chieftain nodded. 'They say it washes up on the beaches.'

'I would like to know this place,' said Pytheas.

'Did you get to know this little kitten?' The Chieftain pawed at Rian with one greasy hand while waving for his drinking horn with the other. Maadu was frowning at her. She tried to step back out of reach but his stretch was long and he grabbed her skirt and tugged her towards him. As he pulled, the dress fabric forced her to shuffle his way. His hand rode the material up. He groped around the back of her leg. She couldn't restrain an 'ow!' as his fingers scratched one of the belt-wounds on her thigh, and he looked round in surprise.

'Well, did you?'

Pytheas failed to look embarrassed and said simply, 'What do you think?'

'I think you probably prefer boys.'

Pytheas looked at Rian and the Chieftain followed his gaze, reaching again up her skirt and once again producing a wince.

'What's the matter with you?' He tugged her closer. He emptied his drinking horn in one gulp then tossed it aside and used both hands to lift up her dress and the under-slip.

Rian wanted to disappear into the floor as her thighs and buttocks were displayed to the room. There was a wolf-whistle and then another but the Chieftain silenced them with one hand. Seeing her wounds, he kept on lifting the material which snagged around her waist.

'Strip her!' he shouted to the old steward who had brought her in and was now standing behind them. 'What's this?' He kept her skirt raised with one hand, poking at the welts.

His fingers were rough. The wounds stung and Rian's eyes welled with tears of shame.

'Damaged goods, that's what this looks like. A good slave, my arse.'

He was shouting, presumably at Ussa and Pytheas, although by now Rian could see nothing as her clothes were being tugged unceremoniously over her head.

She stood naked, her bare back with its lattice of strap marks revealed for all to see. There were titters and murmurs around the hall.

'It's revolting. I can't look at it,' said the Chieftain. Rian turned her head and saw the disgust on his face, his nose crinkling as if she had a foul smell.

'Get rid of her. She is soiled. Soiled and bloody. You didn't tell me that when you sold her.' He was shouting at Ussa.

The steward was bundling her out of the Chieftain's view towards the stairs. He thrust her crumpled dress at her and she clutched it in front of her, wanting only to get out.

As she shuffled up the staircase in the dark, she heard Ussa. 'It's only a whip wound. It will heal in no time. She needed to be disciplined.'

And the Chieftain's wife's voice. 'I need an extra hand on the farm. I'll take her with me.'

MOUSA

Immediately after the meal, the Chieftain's wife, Maadu, took charge of Rian. She had put her dress back on and was sitting at the top of the staircase listening to what she could catch of the mealtime banter that went on below.

Maadu's big form loomed. She was carrying a lamp. Rian backed against the wall to let her pass but she stopped. Her eyes gleamed in the flickering light, scrutinising her.

'Off with that.' She gave a tug at Rian's dress, pulling her into the landing beside the stairs.

Rian breathed in the shame and pulled the garment once more over her head.

Maadu put the lamp on a shelf and rummaged in a trunk. She pulled out a jerkin and a skirt made of a thin, dirty brown cloth. She tossed them at Rian. 'That'll do for now. It's summer. And you'll need that.' A rough blanket followed. 'Now, up again.' She pointed back to the staircase.

Rian climbed the final flight, clutching the rags to her, aware of the big woman following her and of her naked back.

The top floor of the building was nothing more than some woven sticks under the roof. It was smoky and stuffy and the wickerwork was uneven with plenty of gaps. There were three other bundles of rags, indicating other people would be here later. Maadu put the lamp on a shelf again and pointed to a space. 'Sleep there tonight. Tomorrow morning I'm going to Mousa, early. You'd better be ready. Let me see that back.'

She twisted Rian round with a pincerlike hand on her shoulder and poked at the wounds, then went away again without saying anything.

Rian folded the blanket and, groping around in the dark, identified the flattest bit of floor in the section she had been allocated. She was about to put on the jerkin when Maadu reappeared with her lamp. She brusquely smeared something fatty with a resinous smell onto her wounds. It stung so much Rian struggled not to cry out.

'That'll do.' The woman took in where Rian had put her blanket and nodded, then stomped away down the stairs.

Rian dressed. The clothes smelled of mice. Then she lay down, curled up on her side and allowed the tears to flow.

She woke often in the night, when other people came and took up their sleeping places, and after that, startled by the scuffles of bats or mice in the roof. It was like trying to sleep in a rickety basket. The hazel and willow sticks were hard and knobbly and uncomfortable, but she was tired and somehow the night passed.

When she woke to greyness, she got up, took her blanket and crept downstairs, hoping to go all the way out to see the dawn and maybe get away. But on the ground floor she was stopped by the grey steward who gave her a succession of tasks: sweeping up, clearing and washing dishes and feeding the scraps to the Chieftain's scary dogs. Eventually, when she confessed to needing the toilet, he shackled her ankles, attached a chain, made her pick up a bucket of slops and showed her out and round the back of the building to a filthy latrine next to the midden. When she came out and tried to wipe her feet, he grabbed the bucket, filled it from a horse trough and sloshed it in the direction of her legs, soaking her skirt and the bottom half of the blanket she had wrapped around herself against the morning cold. He laughed, tugged the chain and led her back inside. She was hungry and thirsty but did not dare ask for any sustenance.

When Maadu came downstairs there was a frenzy of activity culminating in a rowdy departure. The boys were staying with their father to go whaling, while Maadu would manage the farm-work at Mousa. The biggest son and two other young men headed off down to the harbour and Maadu supervised the packing of baskets and bundles. Rian became a pack animal, chained to two other women and marched with heavy loads repeatedly down to the shore and back, until eventually Maadu seemed to be ready to go. She and her daughter, who everyone called Cuckoo, as well as the three slaves, clambered aboard a sturdy, hide-hulled open fishing boat, not quite as big as Ròn. Maadu's son and his two friends set sail.

Once they were under way, Maadu handed water and oatcakes out to the slaves. Rian was so thirsty and hungry she could easily have consumed the whole ration for the three of them. Her portion was the smallest. As she chewed she watched the other two women, one grey-haired and wrinkled as a dried apple, the other dark and haggard and perhaps in her mid-twenties. Both had dull eyes and a total lack of interest in everything around them. They did not speak unless directly asked a question that a grunt or a gesture could not answer.

On arrival at Mousa, Rian began to understand why. Their work regime was brutal.

The broch was perched on the shore at the south side of a bay, looking out across the sea to the mainland far beyond. Behind it, the farm stretched across the island, with fields sheltered by a hill where cattle grazed. It was a beautiful place but there was little chance to appreciate it.

The three women were put immediately to work, carrying the baggage from the boat, which set off back to the mainland as soon as it was unloaded. The older woman, Gurda, was given cleaning tasks inside the broch, while the dark woman, Fi, was sent to catch and milk a cow. Maadu led Rian round the back of the broch, pointed out the latrine, the midden and the tool store and told her to dig out the pit and make it clean and ready for use. For the second time that day, Rian was barefoot in filth and there she remained until the work was done, last summer's rotten effluent dug out and deposited in the midden. By the time the sun was low in the sky she was caked in mud. She stank, and although she managed to rinse her arms and legs in the sea, it was too cold to wash her clothes. They would have to stay dirty until another day.

At least there was plentiful water here; a stream chuckled down into the sea nearby. However the only food the slaves were given was a meagre, watery porridge. The cows were half wild and protective of their calves and Fi had failed to catch one, so there was no milk and Maadu was in a filthy temper, even though she and Cuckoo had fish to eat with a heap of bread and something else to follow that smelled of honey. The porridge didn't satisfy Rian's hunger.

When she was told she would sleep up on the top floor she was so weary she did not hesitate. The floor was even more makeshift than the one in the Chieftain's broch. It was made mostly of willow, not like the sturdy hazel hurdles they used at home, but she was too tired to care and sank rapidly away into sleep.

She dreamed of Pytheas cutting off her toes, frying and eating them. She woke in a sweat. It was dark. She had no idea where she was. She slept again. This time Pytheas was not only chewing on her toe, he was trying to make her eat one too, forcing her mouth open and shoving it between her teeth. She tried and failed to resist. Then, worse still, he was separating her legs and probing her with her own big toe.

She woke wailing and struggling. The old woman, Gurda, was bent over her, ugly as a gargoyle, whiskery and wrinkled. 'Be quiet.' There was no sympathy in her face. 'Go back to sleep.'

Too soon, far too soon, she was woken again by Gurda and told to empty chamber pots then carry in buckets of water. After more watery porridge, Maadu sent the three of them to weed the fields of bere and oats that had been sown earlier in the year.

Gurda made it plain that, as the newest slave, it was Rian's job to cart the baskets of weeds to the heap, so at the shout of 'basket' or 'full', she must stop her own work and go to them, strap the burden across her forehead and lug it up to the corner of the field, then back again, empty.

The second time she returned Gurda's basket, she said, 'Can you call me before it's so full, so it's not so heavy?'

Gurda did not even raise her head in acknowledgement of the request. It was drizzling and as noon came and passed, it got wetter. The baskets of weeds dribbled mud all down her back as she carried them and they didn't get any less full despite her pleading. Her legs were smeared with the peaty soil and her hands soon stung with its acid. The wounds on her back smarted. The day was long.

SUMMER

As the summer wore on, the days grew longer.

One calm day, the midges were driving Rian almost demented in the field. Gurda shouted 'Basket,' from where she was weeding and Rian stood, wearily, slapping her neck where an insect was biting. A weird pulsing tone made her pause and look up. She couldn't see the bird but knew what it was: a snipe, drumming. For some reason it reminded her of Buia, and that made her think of the times they had spent out on the hills together collecting herbs. Many of the weeds they were pulling up from the field were useful. It was a shame simply to dump them. They should be drying them, or at least letting the cattle have the benefit, not just tossing them out in the corner of the field to rot.

She lifted her head and took Gurda's basket, replacing it with her own. 'I'm going to give some of these to the cows. They're good for milk.'

'That's not our job.'

'I don't care.'

She heaved the basket onto her back. It was always awkward to do it without someone helping, but neither Gurda nor Fi were willing to offer a hand. Holding the strap with both hands, one on each side of her forehead to take the strain, she lugged it up to the weed heap. There, instead of simply tipping it out, she separated out the palatable herbs. The docks and thistles and bracken could stay but the sweet grass and tender herbs, like dandelion, tormentil, violets and skullcap, would be appreciated by a suckling cow, so she tore the roots of them and knocked the earth off. Did they like creeping buttercup? She would find out. The groundsel was so useful it was a shame to waste it even on cattle. As for sorrel, well, she'd eat it herself, right there and then. She chewed a tangy mouthful and set off with the lighter basket to befriend a cow.

It didn't take her long. She had watched Fi do everything wrong: getting too close too quickly, so they took off at a run, then waving her arms and shouting, frightening them with her own fear. Rian liked cows. She knew how to be with them. She wandered up to the nearest cow, a black, hairy creature with a calf in tow. As she got close the cow stopped grazing to stare at her. The calf was curious. She talked to them in simple language and a low voice.

'Hello cow. I've got some tasty green stuff. You might like it.'

She put the basket down and lifted a handful of grass out. It was longer and lusher than the thin blades growing among the heather. The cow was interested. Rian guessed she had probably been fed from a basket in previous years. If she wasn't made afraid she might be biddable.

She was. She came close, snuffling at the grass in this stranger's hand, then accepting it. Her big grey tongue rasped Rian's fingers. The calf explored the intoxicating smells in the basket, then allowed itself to be scratched between the ears. Rian took care not to get between the mother and her child. The cow butted its offspring aside to stick her own, basket-filling head in among the treats Rian had brought her. She lifted out with a big clump of groundsell in her mouth, and Rian, having let her understand what delicacies were inside the creel, hoisted it on her shoulder and turned towards the broch.

'Come on.' She started to step away, glancing over her shoulder. 'Come along.'

The cow followed the basket and the calf followed its mother.

'Good girl. Come along.' Rian strolled and the cow paced along behind. They stopped every now and again so that the big animal could enjoy a reward for her co-operation, chewing into the grass and herbs in the basket.

They were soon at the broch. It took Rian a bit more effort to persuade the cow to pass through the gate into the walled yard behind the building but she persisted and eventually the big beast was trusting enough to cross the threshold.

Rian shut the gate behind her and wondered what to do next.

The broch door was half open. She stood beside it and coughed. 'Maadu? I've brought the cow.'

The woman filled the doorway. She was chewing. 'Who said you could leave the field? Get back to work.' She pointed out to the bent backs of Gurda and Fi, virtue being shown to the sinner.

Rian retreated. As she passed the gate to the yard, she gave the remainder of the basket's contents to the cow, who was standing waiting to be milked, her calf suckling.

Maadu called after her. 'Bring some more grass when you come in.'

Was there a hint of approval in her tone of voice?

No approval whatsoever was forthcoming from Fi and Gurda, who treated Rian as a traitor. Porridge was 'not good enough' for her on account of her eating 'grass'. Her small portion was withheld. Slops were her duty. All dirty jobs fell to her. Her blanket was no longer in her sleeping place. The water butt was out of bounds. 'Keep your filthy hands out of there,' Gurda said. She must drink direct from the peaty stream, trying not to disturb the sediment where creatures squirmed and wriggled in the mud.

For the first few nights, Maadu made her strip and smeared more fat on her welts but after they began to heal there was no further attention paid to her. Both Cuckoo and her mother wrinkled their noses when she was in their proximity and Gurda gave her no opportunity to sneak away to wash her ragged clothes. Sometimes Rian caught a whiff of her own stench. She often felt sick, and found it hard to hold down the meagre food they let her have.

So be it. If she must be dirty, she would be dirty. Her hands were rough and sore from weeding in the acid soil. It didn't matter. She retreated to the high-up place she had discovered when Ussa beat her.

One evening, feeding the cow from the basket of weeds she had brought, which was the closest she felt to having a friend, Rian noticed among the herbs some scallop-shaped leaves and a delicate spray of lady's mantle flowers. It occurred to her that she had not needed it since the Seal Isles. Normally it was what eased her period pains, but she had not bled for how long now? Weeks and weeks. Being thin and hungry could make your bleeding stop. She should try to eat more somehow, despite Gurda and Fi's desire to starve her into submission. She took to devouring the pig nuts, silverweed roots and anything else edible she dug up while weeding, munching with her back turned.

But still she didn't bleed.

Weeks went by.

She made herself think back to what Pytheas had done to her.

It wasn't just hunger.

She was carrying a child.

His child.

She tried to push the thought away but it was a burden she could not put down once it had occurred to her. She had to lug it around while she worked in the field or carried water or scrubbed floors. It made everything heavier. At night it lay on her chest while she tried to sleep, smothering her.

The nights were so light, it had been ages since she had seen the moon. It was impossible to keep track of time. Days blurred into one another.

When the mornings were fine, warm and breezy, Maadu would want to go outside, so she would set Rian and sometimes either Fi or Gurda, to cleaning duties indoors. On wet days, or times when it was still and midges were biting, Maadu would stay in and the slaves were given work outside in the fields or yard.

More weeks went by. Some mornings when Rian woke up she understood the blank look in Fi's eyes, the bitterness in Gurda's tongue. Then the realisation that this was where she was headed filled her with anger.

She learned to cry at times and in places when nobody could see her and slap her for self-pity. She also learned opportunities for filching food and made a dry hiding place in between some stones at the bottom of a dyke behind a patch of bracken. Not that she had anything to hide in it, except for the occasional broken oatcake or piece of cheese, but she had a plan, and bringing it to fruition would require a secret place to stash things in.

The plan began with a damselfly. Maadu had sent her up the hill to bring back some more cows. Her success with getting one of the beasts to co-operate had been noted, or perhaps Gurda and Fi had both refused the task.

The cattle were out on the headland grazing and Rian couldn't believe her luck to be sent to get them. This was almost freedom: an almost dry day, an almost open-ended task which could take the entire morning, the chance to walk alone and talk to cows.

They were skittish and nervous of her, having spent a while together on the hill without people bothering them, and they took fright and galloped away when she got too close, so she waited for a while to let their curiosity bring them back to her. It was beautiful on the headland: the sea spread out to the east, the morning sun splicing through flat clouds, light spilling across the surface.

She crouched by a pool fringed by sundews, noticing their tiny white flowers. Rubbing sweet gale between her fingers she released its fragrance, then wiped it on her exposed skin to keep the midges from the worst of their biting.

Bog bean flowers struck frilly white poses and turquoise water lobelias jewelled the water on delicate spikes. A movement on a rush drew Rian's attention and she watched, enthralled, a creature haul itself up the stem. She reached towards it, wanting to catch it to see what it was, but her disturbance only served to knock it off its stem, or perhaps it jumped to save itself from her. The sediments from the pond floor swirled and in the murk she couldn't see the creature. She sat back on her heels and waited. Before long the little animal was clambering up the same stem again. This time she would leave it alone. Up and up it climbed, eventually breaking the surface, continuing up until it was entirely above the water, its eyes huge for the size of its head, staring as if astonished at this airy world above the waterline. Then it began to shrug itself out of its skin like a seedling tree emerging from soil, breaking out of a nut, discarding its shell. Lacy fronds like skeleton leaves unfurled from the grub. It clung with its new wings outstretched, drying them, its body the same iridescent blue as the lobelias, thin as the stem and as long as a little finger. Its wings, two pairs on each side, were a lattice of threads, more delicate than any person could spin, a filigree of spider yarns. Testing them, it rattled. Its body pulsed, bouncing on the stem and then without warning it flung itself into the sky and darted over the lochen, a blue spark of life. Part of Rian went with it, jinking and free, and when it alighted quivering on another rush, she was filled with a clarity of purpose as vivid as its sheen, as pure as the blue air.

A heavy huff of breath behind her startled her, then she saw the reflection in the pool of black shaggy forms. The cows had come to her. One was nosing in her basket. She got to her feet and shoved the big animal's head out of the herbs. There were a dozen or so of them, a mix of cows and calves, heifers and bullocks, no bull, but enough of them to need to be careful. All except the calves were horned and they were all half-wild. She started up a one-way conversation with them in a low sing-song voice and set off to cajole them back to the broch with her.

Along the way she picked some club moss and fingered it absently, then tucked it away in her pocket. She might or might not use it; she did not know if she wanted the baby inside her to be allowed to grow. That was a decision she could make once she was free, but at least with the moss in hand the option was open to her.

Later on, lower down towards the broch, yarrow leaves and plantain presented themselves and she gathered them in case of wounds and sores. After the cattle had been persuaded to amble and jostle into the yard, and the gate was closed behind them, she laid the herbs out to dry in her secret place in the wall behind the midden, thinking of how she might contrive a pouch for them to travel in and where the makings for fire could be acquired. Tinder was easy: cotton grass and heather stalks were everywhere and there was no difficulty in gathering them in her pocket while she walked to the field and back. But flint and blade were a different matter. She would need her wits about her to lay her hands upon such things, and the risk was high of them being missed and searched for.

'What're you looking so smug about?' Maadu was sitting in the sunshine outside the broch.

The shout broke Rian out of her reverie. She waved her hand at the cows and said nothing.

'The pails aren't scalded and the yearlings will be a menace. I don't know what you were thinking of bringing them. And unless you bring the cows some more to eat they'll be breaking out before you've milked them.' The fat woman had clearly not had anyone to complain to for hours.

Rian dimmed the damselfly sparks in her eyes and began the mental climb to the high crag where she was safe from verbal wounding.

'May the Goddess preserve me from stupid slaves. Stupid and lazy. What have I done to be cursed like this? Get a move on, or I'll have to take the whip to you.'

Rian tried to hold onto the satisfaction of having brought the cows in from the hill, for which there would be no other thanks. She made a plan: water on the fire to heat for scalding pails, then a basket of grass to tempt the heifers and bullock away from the others. By the time she brought another basket of grass for the mothers the water would be boiling. Then the milking could begin. There were worse tasks. She would look bored and take her time, ignore the threats of violence and watch out for herbs to gather.

Inside, rekindling the fire, she looked at the flint hanging on its hook and wondered.

At midsummer Maadu was collected by one of her sons and she and Cuckoo went off to Clickimin for the solstice festivities, leaving the three slaves to fend for themselves. Gurda attempted to be in charge but although Fi and Rian made a token gesture of obedience towards the older woman, in reality anarchy prevailed and for two blissful days they did more or less what they desired. They gorged on milk until they were sick of it and sat revelling in Maadu and Cuckoo's absence, putting more fuel on the fire than was necessary, doing nothing.

Escape was, of course, what Rian most wanted but there was no boat. The coracle that she had been eyeing had been towed away behind the ship when Maadu left and it was too far to attempt to swim the channel to the mainland, although she considered it long and hard. She tried to content herself with gathering more herbs, but the weather was wet and drying them by the fire was not the best way of treating them. Mostly she kept away from Gurda and Fi and allowed her thoughts to play at the puzzle of captivity, exploring hypotheticals, mostly centred on the coracle. Now that it had gone, she was furious that she had not seen it for the lifeline that it was. When it returned she would use it, wait for a night-time when she was last to bed and sneak out and away in it across the Sound. And then what? Then she would need to find a way to avoid recapture.

The two days were soon over. Rian was sitting at the broch door when a slim sailing boat approached from the north, a coracle bobbing in its wake. It anchored in the bay. People and goods were lowered into the little vessel and it was skulled ashore and emptied. The operation was repeated and a straggle of people made its way towards the stone tower. Maadu was first, huffing with the weight of a basket.

Rian retreated around the back, taking refuge with the cows, but Gurda's voice reached her there.

'Carry, carry!'

Rian fought the urge to hide. She was vaguely curious about what might have been brought that required carrying. She dragged her feet down to the boat where she was given a huge basket of cloth. On her next trip she helped to lug up one of a pair of low benches. Maadu wrapped them in skins and set them up proudly in her preferred spot inside with a commanding view of the door, close enough for easy reach of the fire, her back towards her bedroom between the walls of the building. There were also three piglets which were installed behind a willow hurdle barrier in a corner of the broch.

Cuckoo was sulking and went straight to her room with a bundle of clothes. Presumably she had found life in Clickimin much more exciting than being stuck on the island with only her mother and slaves for company.

Two men from the boat came onshore. One was another of Maadu's sons. He was younger than the others she had seen, perhaps seventeen years old.

The other was a man she recognised but could not place immediately. He was strolling up towards the broch when she passed him on her way down for more baggage and he showed no sign whatsoever of knowing her, but she looked sideways at him through her hair and remembered.

He was the man who had thrown her to the ground when they had arrived at the Seal Isles, the cousin of the bronze smith and of Ussa.

This was who Ussa was seeking, the one she claimed had stolen some precious stone from her.

The one Badger called the Walrus Mutterer.

Maadu's son was ranting to him, pointing out the broch, the fields, as if trying to impress him. He was looking about in an affable way. There was a loose fluidity about his movements that made Rian want to straighten her back and instead of stomping, to glide. The men's voices faded as they walked away. There were heavy loads of firewood to carry. The next time she passed him, when he was taking a look at the cows behind the broch, she was stooped under a back basket so heavy she could barely shuffle. After that, the pain of the burdens reduced her to a beetle-pushing-a-ball-of-dung emptiness. There were only footsteps and the basket on her back and her shrieking mistress complaining that she did not carry it quickly enough and its contents were being ruined by the rain.

When it came time for preparation of food, Rian was given a quern and told to grind grain.

Gurda was full of herself. She had been given a threadbare blanket, a cast-off from Cuckoo's old bedding, but she wore it around her shoulders as if it was a new cloak of fine wool. 'The boy Leven is off to hunt for walrus. This will be his last meal before goodness only knows how long at sea. A month, the man says, maybe, and no sight of land except for the place wherever it is they find those great beasts. Have you ground the oats yet? They're hungry.'

Rian increased the rate of the turning stone and watched the young man and his guest. They had taken up their positions on the new benches, one side each of a stone block, on which two cups of mead and a flask stood. The hunter held his cup close to the rim, lifted it to his lips, tipped his head back, tossed the remains of its contents into his mouth and swallowed. Leven refilled both beakers.

Rian kept the rhythm of the grinding stone even, and the hunter raised his voice so everyone could hear him, even Cuckoo in her room.

'This reminds me of the time I was in the broch of King Ban.' He spoke with a sing-song lilt, in time with Rian's turning stone. 'I was told a story from long, long ago.' His voice had an accent that was familiar to her, with soft 's' sounds and rolling 'r's. Although it was the accent of one of the southern isles, it was still softer than the northern dialect, and it reminded her of home. She poured more grain into the quern and the story unwound out of him as if she was spinning it out by turning the stone.

Maadu stopped rummaging in her baskets of cloth and turfed her son off his bench. He perched on a stool. All eyes were on the Walrus Mutterer as he spun his yarn.

'A couple took over the living on one of the islands. There was a cow there who was docile and a good milker and she became part of their lives. She bore calves that were black and hairy and strong, and they in their turn bore young. The couple worked hard, making hay for the winter and tending the beasts. They ended up with a fine herd.

'Well, the original cow didn't get any younger, and one autumn night after a wet summer without much of a harvest, the man said that he doubted she would get through another winter so perhaps they should try to sell her on. His wife wouldn't hear of that, so he suggested they might as well eat her as have to feed her from their meagre supply of fodder.

'They sat by the fire and discussed what they would have to arrange. Killing and butchering a cow is not something you do lightly. Eventually they had a plan. The man said he would get up early in the morning and do the deed, and then they would have the whole day to preserve the meat with salt and smoke. They laughed together at the thought of the good meals they could look forward to over the winter.

'But when he got up in the morning, the cow was nowhere to be seen. She was a good animal and normally she would lead the other cows in for milking. But as if she had heard what was planned she had made herself scarce, along with every single one of rest of the herd. He went looking and followed their fresh hoofprints out of the open gate of the inbye, down across the machair grass by the shore, onto the beach and into the sea.

'They told an old neighbour what had happened.

'"Well," said she, "you know where that cow came from now. She wasn't going to wait to get what you had planned for her. And when a cow from the sea returns to her homeland, she takes all of her offspring with her. You'll not see any of them again."

'And they did not.'

Manigan shook his head and smiled at his audience.

'That's a good one.' Maadu turned to Rian. 'Have you not done the milking yet?'

Rain was teeming down outside. Rian stopped grinding and emptied the meal into a bowl, which she handed to Gurda. She stood up, making sure she didn't look at Manigan and, holding his story inside her so its magic would not be broken, she took it out with her to the cows.

The yard was slippery with dung and the cattle were grumpy and reluctant to be tethered under the shelter for milking. She fell down trying to catch one of them, bruising herself and getting filthy as well as wet. Fortunately, the milk pail stayed upright but she was soaked and miserable by the time the job was done and she could return indoors.

Maadu and her guests were eating. The smell of fish was mouth-watering but Rian had no reason to suppose any of it would be left for them. She winced as she noticed the Walrus Mutterer wrinkle his nose at her dung-splattered state.

Gurda gathered the plates and put the leftovers by the three slaves' bowls. Rian was given the dishes to wash before she could eat and when she finally got the chance there was nothing left but a meagre scraping of green vegetables and the scorched end of a bannock. She retreated to a corner with her bowl as Maadu carved a big cake into four generous portions for herself, Cuckoo, Leven and their guest. Rian tried to listen in to the discussion of the hunting plan, but soon bored of Leven's boasting about a fishing adventure earlier in the year.

When Manigan made signs that it was time for him and Leven to leave, Cuckoo got up and tossed the remaining chunk of her cake to the pigs which jostled each other for possession until one scoffed it. Maadu tore her cake in half, pushed herself to her feet and more deliberately fed it to the piglets.

'Won't you stay the night?'

'No, thank you. The boys are waiting and the tidal race should be helpful now.' Manigan slapped Leven on the shoulder. 'Do you have everything you need?'

Leven pointed to the bag of bread and cheese Maadu had offered them, and his sleeping roll wrapped in cow hide.

'Blade?' Manigan asked.

Leven patted the sheath on his belt.

'The makings for fire?'

'What? Like a flint, you mean?'

Manigan nodded. 'Aye, you never know when you'll need to make a fire.'

Maadu settled herself back down in her chair. 'Have a look in that toolbox in the corner.'

Leven rummaged and unearthed a leather packet in which there were some flints.

'They were your grandfather's,' Maadu said. 'You're welcome to take one.'

Manigan was waiting by the door. 'Are you fit? Time to put some water under us.'

The young man grinned like a puppy.

Then Manigan turned to Maadu. 'You treat your pigs better than your people.'

As if he were a stupid child, she replied, 'They're only slaves.'

'They're people.' He shook his head. 'That one there?' He gestured at Rian with a frown but no apparent recognition. 'Even under that filth there's a person.'

Maadu gave a short, scoffing laugh. 'Stick to hunting, Manigan. And stories. You're good at stories. And I know what I'm doing with my slaves.' She turned to her son. 'Are you ready? You'd better not keep your bleeding heart captain waiting.'

Manigan had gone, but the person he had pointed at was left with the knowledge that there was at least a possibility that a sailor might be an ally. And so Rian's plan took shape.

COMMODITY

Fragrant orchids came into flower with their impossibly sweet scent. Cuckoo picked every one she found and her corner of the broch was so full of the perfume it became cloying. Terns raised their chicks and flew training flights en masse, shrieking in long, racing formation down the shore then turning and hurtling back the other way. It was exhausting to watch. Rian knew that soon they would be gone and wished she could do more in the way of her own preparation for escape. She could not take to her wings, but when the opportunity presented itself to board a boat and fly away with sails for wings, she wanted to be ready.

The first sunny day that Maadu and Cuckoo spent outdoors, and she was set to cleaning duties in the broch, she waited for a moment when Gurda and Fi weren't watching and took the chance to find the flints that Leven had left in the toolbox. She took one and put it in amongst some kindling by the hearth, then waited to see if it would be missed. It wasn't. A few days later, she moved it again out of the broch and into her hiding place in the wall beside the milking shelter.

The days and weeks passed, an endless round of milking, weeding and drudgery. Every so often a passing boat would call in, but few stayed more than a mealtime, mostly pausing for the tide to take them favourably north or south, avoiding the roiling water of the Roost off the southern tip of the mainland. Rian heard several sailors speak of the tumult and everyone seemed scared of it.

One day, a brisk easterly wind was blowing and the women were out in the field doing the last pass through the barley before it was harvested, taking out what few weeds remained. The wind had been mounting all day and it whistled and rattled through the tall corn which scratched Rian's bare arms. Emerging at the end of a row she saw two boats in the Sound, one heading in towards the bay, having rounded the cape at the north end of the island. The other was sailing north making good speed. The first boat was setting an anchor.

'Boat.'

Gurda came to watch, then threw down her basket and marched off to the broch to tell Maadu.

Rian watched the second boat reach the water beyond the shelter of the island where the waves were white topped, and then turn and beat its way into the bay. By the time the first boat had lowered and loaded a coracle, the second was preparing to anchor. Rian recognised it as Ròn, not least because of the white-coated figure at the prow. Her stomach churned and she retreated into the perfect invisibility provided by the barley.

To remain unseen was only possible for a while because Maadu needed provision to be made for the visitors and Fi and Rian were shouted in from the field. Rian was sent to milk the cows and could be partly hidden behind a big hairy animal while she watched the new arrivals.

The wind remained strong and the skippers of both boats had decided to ride out what may well prove to be a gale getting up. They would stay at anchor overnight. Both boats had passengers or crew who preferred to sit it out in the comfort of the broch rather than afloat. The first boat was a whaler. Three men, all relatives of Maadu or the Chieftain, came ashore from it. From Ròn, five people made their way to the broch. Ussa had clearly acquired more crew as there were still several people on board.

As the shore party approached, Rian recognised, along with the trader, the striding form of Pytheas with his staff and box, and the heavily loaded frame of Og. Still by the shore two figures, one large and one small, were organising a large amount of baggage. Cuckoo ran down and made an animated welcome. As they turned to greet her, Rian realised it was Gruach the bronze smith, and Fraoch. A buzz of hope in her chest was soon swallowed by the shame of her dirty state and she shifted around to hide herself behind the hairy anonymity of the cow.

She managed to avoid going into the broch where she could hear the voices of Ussa and Pytheas, but Cuckoo sought her out and fold her she must carry water to the smith.

Cuckoo had some hot pancakes to offer them and set off ahead of Rian down to the shore. When Rian appeared with two pails of water, Cuckoo looked most surprised when Fraoch shouted 'Rian!' Her arms reached out to hug her in delight. Rian hung back but as Cuckoo chatted on, she met Fraoch's gaze.

The bronze smith's daughter seemed older somehow. Questions flowed silently, a long frown and a sigh that Rian heard as compassion but might just have been the natural sound of someone taking a rest from work. Gruach stood up from the fire he had lit, hands on his waist and looked at her, then interrupted Cuckoo.

'Well, Rian. How are you?'

She tried to give him a smile, but couldn't speak.

'You look…' Fraoch paused, as if thinking what to say, and settled on, 'thin.'

Rian wasn't sure how to respond.

'Do you live here now?'

Rian gave a little nod and glanced at Cuckoo, who seemed to be relaxed about her speaking, even interested.

'Ussa sold me to the Chieftain.'

Fraoch looked blank.

'The Chieftain. This is his wife's house.'

'My mother's house,' said Cuckoo.

The fire was crackling and spitting.

'I want to hear all about everything.' Fraoch gave Rian a

squeeze of her arm and turned back to the forge.

Cuckoo said, 'How does a nobody like you know them? They're famous.'

Rian glowed a little inside. It was the only glimmer of something better than scorn that Cuckoo had ever showed her.

'They came to my home before I was...' She couldn't bring herself to say the words. 'We travelled together on the first part of my journey.' *My journey.* She heard herself. Was that what it was?

'You must have stories you haven't told us.'

'You haven't asked.' It came out sounding rude, but Cuckoo seemed unperturbed.

'True. I didn't think there was any point asking a slave for a story. Do you have lots of stories?'

'I don't know.'

'Well if you don't know...'

They fell silent and stood a little distance away watching as Gruach and Fraoch continued setting up, preparing for the evening when the performance of the forge would really get under way, especially if the wind continued rising, when sparks would fly, metal would melt and flow and the smith would work his magic. For now, as if building a stage, they were arranging shields around the fire, stacking wood into an elaborate-looking lattice for show or some other function as yet unclear, unpacking tools and laying them out with ceremony. There was music too: Gruach made tongs and hammers ring out as he tapped them on his great anvil, shaped like a dragon.

Rian and Cuckoo looked on for a while, then Cuckoo said they had better go back to the broch. She pointed to a bundle that looked like one of Ussa's bags of trade goods. 'Carry that.'

Rian arrived back with aching shoulders and was put to work on the butter. Ussa was lying down in her designated bedroom. Pytheas had gone up a hill with his gnomon, accompanied by two of the sailors from the other boat, no doubt taking one of his measurements of the height of the sun.

For a while it was tolerable. As long as she was left alone with her thoughts, the rhythm of the churn brought back songs of Danuta's hearth and she could allow her mind to wander where it would and follow the stream of consciousness wherever it flowed. But after a while Cuckoo and Maadu got themselves into a squabbling disagreement and Rian found her thoughts being interrupted. The guests required feeding and Maadu had both hands in a bowl and was squeezing balls of dough as if she intended damage. Cuckoo had a long list of things she wanted to get from Ussa to enable her to prepare for her brother's wedding at the end of the summer. 'She has good cloth, so I could make a new dress.'

'You've plenty of cloth,' Maadu said.

'I'll need ribbons and some bangles. I need to look my best, you know, this might be the best chance I get to find my own husband.'

Eventually Cuckoo left off and the women worked in silence for a while, and once the smell of the baking dumplings filled the room there was at least the illusion of peace.

Late afternoon a soft knock came on the door. Cuckoo opened it and Fraoch said, 'I've come to visit Rian. Is that all right?'

Rian kept churning and felt a smile spreading up from her chest until it burst out all over her face.

'Hello.' Fraoch stepped inside and curtseyed to Maadu as if in the presence of a queen. 'Are you Maadu? I am very proud to meet you. My father Gruach the Smith sends you his greetings and hopes you will visit his forge later.'

Maadu nodded wisely. 'Welcome, Gruach's daughter. Your name?'

'I'm Fraoch. I'm the daughter of Ranu, granddaughter of Raanvaa the Wise.'

'I knew Raanvaa well. She taught me the art of the drum.'

Rian was intrigued.

'It smells gorgeous in here. Herb dumplings!' Fraoch smiled at the rows of dough baking on hot stones by the fire, nodding as if greeting them.

Maadu cackled. 'You have all of Gruach's charm, I see, and if you've your grandmother's wisdom you'll be a wise one yourself one day.'

'If that's a prediction, I am honoured.'

Maadu gestured to a stool beside her.

'So you said you've come to see Rian. How's that?' She spoke as if no-one else were in the room except her and Fraoch.

'She's my friend. She's a wise one too, you know.'

Maadu laughed out loud and shook her head. 'She's a dumb slave and not much good at anything except the cows.'

'No, really. She has the herb lore. Her foster mother taught her.'

Maadu looked at her, brow ruffled. 'She is just a slave now. Tell me, how is your mother?'

Rian's smile of friendship was burned away by shame. She kept churning. Buttery lumps were forming now. Much deference was being shown between Fraoch and Maadu. As Fraoch explained how her mother had died while she was still a child and she had travelled ever since with her father, the butter formed and Rian could stop the paddle and lift the pats of gold out onto a big wooden trencher.

'You make the butter magic look so easy, Rian.' Fraoch beamed at her, eyes twinkling. Then, to Maadu, 'You know, their house has herbs hanging from every inch of the rafters.'

Rian knew Fraoch was making this up, because she had only been, to her knowledge, in Danuta's broch once or twice and that was in early spring, when all the herbs were long packaged away and stored for safekeeping.

'In summer, you can't stand up without getting something leafy tangled in your hair.'

Rian smiled and her belly twisted with homesickness, as if she could smell the herbs of home.

Maadu turned to her. 'So what would you do for a broken bone?'

Rian chanted the early lesson for splinting an arm. 'Golden rod and Brigid's yellowstone, a poultice of these will mend a broken bone.'

'And a sword wound?'

Another easy one. 'Leaf of yarrow clots the blood flow, leaf of plantain makes it heal again.'

'Fever?' There were several to choose from. 'Violets in whey cools the frey. Meadowsweet drops the heat. Far too hot? Crab apple tot.'

'And a baby not willing to be born?'

Rian stopped. 'It is not permitted for me to say.' She chose her words carefully, not wanting to refuse or to look as if she didn't know.

Cuckoo had been listening carefully all along. 'I bet she doesn't know.'

Maadu didn't take her eyes off Rian's face. 'Cuckoo, you can take this butter to cool outside in the shade now. Mind you don't drop it. And then go and ask Gruach if there's anything else he would like to eat or drink.'

A whine began. 'But Rian's supposed to ...'

'No buts. Take it now please.' There was a stony sound to Maadu's voice that Rian had not heard before.

Cuckoo picked up the butter and left.

Gurda and Fi watched from the corner, the old woman peeling silverweed roots, the younger at the quern stone.

'So you know the moon magic? What can be done for bleeding pains?'

Rian took a breath. It was one of the most well known remedies, hardly a secret at all. 'When the womb cramps with the moon, shilasdair roots and mead, and soon.'

'Why on earth did your foster mother allow you to be enslaved?' Maadu asked.

Rian shook her head and tried to stop tears welling up at the kindness in Maadu's voice. She had wondered the same thing so many times in the preceding months.

'I don't know.'

Fraoch said. 'Danuta's son is an idiot.'

Maadu and Rian both looked at her, waiting to see what else she might say.

Cuckoo burst in. 'He needs water. Buckets of it.' She was carrying two empty pails.

Maadu turned to Rian. 'Fetch it.' Any trace of respect or kindness in her face had gone.

Fraoch waited while she filled the buckets from the stream and they strolled down to where Gruach was hunched by his fire, bellows pumping.

After they had dropped the water off they went to sit on some rocks by the shore, out of eyeshot of the broch.

Rian said, 'How long are you here?'

'The usual.' Fraoch shrugged noncommittally.

'And where will you go next?'

'Wherever. We've been invited to the big wedding do in Clickimin at the next full moon. You should try to get to the feast too.'

Rian nodded, and the two girls smiled. Rian had no doubt it would be impossible, she a slave, Fraoch free, but it was enough for her to have mentioned it for the feeling of being wanted to warm her, like a dandelion flower in sunshine.

'Seriously, will you not be going to the feast?'

Rian shrugged. 'I don't suppose so.'

'I'll get Ussa to tell Maadu you should go. She'd love to see you there.' Fraoch's eyes twinkled.

'Get lost.'

'She knows you're beautiful and will remind the Chieftain of her.'

Rian raised her eyebrows. 'Is she…?'

'No. Not the Chieftain. Just his gold. She lusts after his money, that's all.' She paused, then leaned towards Rian. 'And possibly one of his sons.'

Rian snorted. 'She's old enough to be their mother.'

Fraoch nodded. 'That's what she likes best.'

Rian rolled her eyes and they laughed. She felt as if she was alive for the first time since she had been at Mousa.

'Where did you go after I last saw you?'

Fraoch gestured everywhere with her arms. 'Around the islands.'

'We went to Thule,' said Rian.

Fraoch gawped at her. 'Thule?'

Rian began, in a quiet voice, to relate the story of the journey and Fraoch listened, bathing her in attention. Rian talked softly, trying not to bog down in details. She desperately wanted to tell Fraoch about what Pytheas had done. Surely Fraoch would understand? She knew so much about the world, and seemed so fearless.

She spilled it all out, her lack of monthly bleeding, the certainty that she was carrying his child. After a while she realised she had spoken more than to anyone for weeks.

'What'll you do?' Fraoch was staring at her, looking horrified. 'Can you stop it? With the moon magic?'

'I've got a herb to kill it. It'll be horrible, but…'

Fraoch finished her sentence. 'Not as horrible as having a baby. I can't think of anything worse.'

Rian put her hand on her thigh, feeling the brand, the taut soreness that might always be there. Unless she got away, her child would be a slave too. It would not be right to bring a baby into the world to meet that fate. She would do anything to avoid that. Anything.

Fraoch picked up Rian's hand. 'You're very brave.'

Rian was surprised at herself for not crying. She felt unburdened, light as a bird.

There was clapping from the broch and Maadu's voice, shouting over the wind.

Rian got to her feet and gave Fraoch a little grin. 'Maybe I won't be here for ever.'

Fraoch's face was all smiling curves.

*

In the broch, Pytheas and Ussa were on the new benches, treated as guests of honour. As Rian carried two pails of water past them to the tank in the floor, Pytheas drew his feet in under his knees, disgust on his face, even though there was no possibility of her touching him. Shortly after, they went to watch Gruach's preparations and Maadu joined them to make her requests to the bronze smith who she wanted to make some kitchen pieces as gifts for her son's wedding.

There seemed to be a never-ending stream of things to fetch and carry: peats for the fire, water, buckets of slops for the fly-infested midden. Gurda made sure Rian had no rest, although she took the opportunity of Maadu's absence to sit and do nothing. Ussa's loud laughter signalled the end of the reprieve.

Maadu blocked the light from the doorway. She pointed at Rian. 'You. Out here.'

As she stepped over the threshold, the big woman grasped her lower arm. 'What's this about you being pregnant?'

Ussa was chuckling. Pytheas was pale and holding himself very straight.

'Does Fraoch speak the truth?' He spoke in Greek.

'*Alithi.*' She remembered it. The truth. '*Alithi Fraoch legei?*'

'She didn't waste any time, the little slut. I should've charged extra.' Ussa had her hands on her hips. 'Two for the price of one, eh?'

'How far gone are you?' Maadu lifted Rian's tatty jerkin and poked at her belly. 'It's not showing, is it?'

'She's skin and bone,' Ussa said. 'She'll not show for months. Best feed her up if you want it, although it might be better to get rid of it if you want to keep her working.'

'From what Fraoch was saying earlier she could do that herself. She knows a thing or two about herbs.' Maadu pulled Rian's skirt down and made her turn to the side. 'No, no sign yet. Tits?' She wrenched the jerkin up around Rian's neck and prodded her breast. 'Aye, I could just about believe it. They're bigger than they were. What do you think?'

Ussa added a few pokes. Pytheas looked on, wide-eyed.

Rian wanted to die. A heifer would be treated more gently in a market. But more excruciating even than the nosy fingers was the knowledge that Fraoch had told them. She had thought Fraoch was her friend, had treated her as a confidante. She had trusted her. It was a loss Rian couldn't bear. Tears wanted to flow, but she bit them back.

'She'll be an utter waste of space with a brat. That's all I need.' Maadu let go of her arm.

Ussa took it upon herself to advise. 'Tell her to dose herself with something to get rid of it.'

'I'll do it myself. What's the stuff they use? It's one of the hill mosses, isn't it? Something weird like that.'

Ussa shook her head. 'Better make sure it's done carefully though. You don't want it going wrong. A breeder might be useful sometime, even if you don't want her pregnant just now. You don't want to damage that.'

Maadu continued poking, thoughtfully. Rian might as well have been a kitchen implement. She looked her in the eye, tugging the jerkin down over her breasts. 'Do you know what to do? Do you know which moss to use?'

Rian just stared back. The clubmoss she had hidden away could stay exactly where it was. If she chose to use it, it would be her decision, not Maadu's.

Maadu, however, was not satisfied. A ringing slap sent Rian's head sideways and the jerk made her almost black out. She brought her hand up to the piercing pain below her right jaw, half-closing her eyes.

'Well. Do you or don't you?'

She made a short nod.

Pytheas was looking calm again.

Ussa hooked her arm through his. 'There were no doubt others took their chance on her. I shouldn't have any great expectation it was your doing. Goodness, though, on the boat! I marvel that you found the space. And to think I never noticed!' She turned to Maadu. 'Men, eh? There's only ever one thing on their minds. They never miss a chance.'

Rian seethed with hatred for Ussa. Was there no end to the lies she would tell? Ussa knew exactly what Pytheas had done to her.

Maadu spun Rian around by twisting her arm and giving her a shove. 'Away and milk the beasts. And get what you need, and deal with it. You'll not be in sight of this fellow. I thank heavens I've not had any of the men here. You have to watch their every move if you mix the sexes, you know.'

DAMSELFLY

Rian needed no further encouragement to get away. The tears were spilling by the time she reached the yard and even the cows were insufficient comfort. She put the pail down and kept walking. She didn't care if anyone saw her. She needed to be alone, to digest what had happened, to let her fury at Fraoch express itself, to pull herself together after the shame of Maadu's treatment of her. She stomped away up the hill past the pool where she had watched the damselfly hatching, and on to a bigger lochen over the brow of the hill looking east into open sea.

The initial wave of tears had calmed and rage took over. She still felt sorry for herself, of course, but the anger was hot and full of energy and she let it course through her. That bronze smith's daughter, she was Ussa's cousin, or niece or something; the same blood, the loyalty always to kin. That's how it was. She saw that clearly, as clear as the rain clouds on the eastern horizon. The wind was up even more strongly now, but Rian welcomed it. The elemental power was at least impartial and uninterested in the people that got in its way. Let it blow. Let it rage on her behalf.

She felt dirty. Maadu's fingers seemed to have left smears on her that she couldn't bear. She stripped naked and left her clothes on a rock, then grabbed some soapwort leaves and waded into the shallows. The water was cold and splashy in the wind, and the smooth stones on the bottom were slippery with algae. Rian didn't care. She washed swiftly, rubbing the leaves into a pulpy mass that foamed then spreading it over her skin, scrubbing herself clean. Then she dipped herself in the water, gasping, to rinse. She was all goosepimples and shivering, but it felt miraculous to have washed the filth off. She dunked her hair in the water again and waded back to where she could reach more soapwort leaves. A good lathering and a struggle with her fingers to tease out the matted tangles from her hair as much as she could, and then another dunking in the loch and she was clean all over, cleaner than she had been since she left home.

Shivering hard now, she dried herself on the relatively clean lining of her skirt. She dressed and then set off back over the hill. The rain clouds had reached the island. She would be rain-soaked by the time she got back. But as soon as the wind was on her back and she was moving, she warmed up. As she marched along, she plotted revenge, poisoning them all with foxgloves. But then she heard Danuta's voice in her head, dire warnings about evil thoughts, and abandoned that plan. She needed to focus on escape. She was clean now, she could look after herself. She must be ready for the first opportunity.

Back at the yard, she checked her hiding place in the wall. The herbs she had tried to dry were mostly mouldy. It was a useless place for keeping that sort of thing. But there were herbs everywhere. The fire-starter was more important. She sorted the bare minimum she would need into a tidy pile: cotton grass, heather buds and stalks, the flint. She needed something to carry them in.

The cows still needed to be milked and they seemed to sense her new resolve, standing calmly while she pushed their calves away to take a share of their milk. With the milk pail full, she returned to the broch where salvation waited. Maadu and Cuckoo, Pytheas and Cuckoo were all out watching Gruach at work.

Fi took the pail from her. 'You're all wet. What've you been at?'

'Nothing.' Rian sat down on a stool by the fire, tipped her hair forward and combed out her hair with her fingers.

Gurda set a tray of risen bannocks beside her and tapped her on the shoulder with a griddle pan. 'You can bake those while you dry off.'

She pulled up another stool and sat making more dough patties, as Rian cooked the ones on the tray.

'Maadu's been talking plans for the wedding. We're all getting to go.'

'When?'

'I don't know.'

Fi shook some carrageen into a pan of milk. 'Full moon, whenever that is.'

Rian turned the bannocks over in the pan. The moon was half now, and shrinking. 'Twenty days or so.' Could she wait that long?

Gurda and Fi had stopped what they were doing and were staring at her. What had she said out loud?

Fi stirred the milk. 'Fancy yourself as a witch?'

'I do not.'

Gurda pointed over to a heap of old clothes on a chest. 'We've to get new clothes ready for the feast.'

Rian got up to look. They were castoffs from Cuckoo and Maadu, both far fatter than any of the three of them. 'Is there needle and thread for taking them in?'

'Over in that basket.' Gurda pointed towards a pretty wicker sewing case at Maadu's bedroom entrance.

Rian peeked in. It had all she needed for making herself a pouch for her fire-starter kit and some herbs. Her adjustments to one of Cuckoo's dresses would include a little extra preparation.

That evening she claimed a headache and went upstairs to her bed to avoid seeing any more of Ussa, Pytheas or, especially, Fraoch. Miraculously, Maadu left her alone. She didn't come down until she had heard them depart the next morning. Maadu asked if she had taken the herb necessary for getting rid of her 'little problem' and Rian allowed her silence to be interpreted as assent.

In just over two week's time, when the moon was rising earlier every night, Rian had made a tidy little bag for her fire-making tools, which she carried everywhere with her in her pocket. She had dried some herbs, brazenly, in the broch, pretending she was doing it for Maadu, then filched some for herself. Maadu made it clear that her food portions should be increased and Rian's confidence grew with them.

She even took the chance of moving a little pocket knife from the toolbox out to her hiding place in the wall out in the yard. It was a bit rusty but better than no blade at all, and once it didn't seem to be missed, she added a snug sleeve for it in her fire pouch.

There was a flurry of activity when they scythed the barley crop down, winnowed it and stacked the straw. It was back-breaking work, but it meant fresh grain.

One evening, Rian sat with the quern between her knees, grinding. She had always enjoyed the feel of seeds under stone, the rotary motion, and the songs that Danuta used to sing came back to her. She moistened the stone a little with tears, feeling sorry for herself in the hush of the room, her back smarting as the movements stretched her wounds. Her mind turned to how she might escape.

Time flowed with the spindle, the loom and the quern stone turning. Rian thought back over all that had happened to her over the past months. She felt it had been a lifetime. She was no longer the innocent girl that had been branded that awful day. The hearth was no longer a place of comfort and safety. She was friendless. Sold, sold on, sold back, sold on again into deeper and deeper servitude, into blacker and blacker emptiness, until she no longer knew where she was, who she was, or what she was doing there.

She turned the stone. She ground down the memories of Ussa and of Pytheas. She ground to remember poor Callum and Faradh, their bodies thrown to the fish and the monsters of the sea.

The thought of sea monsters brought back the memory of the giant spirit of the sea and she heard again the strange song that Toma had sung to it. Toma had never been her enemy. Perhaps, while they were in Clickimin, if she could find Ròn could she persuade him to sail her away to freedom? She hummed the tune to herself, having to slow the quern stone rhythm which did not fit the lilt of the song like a boat's motion did.

Maadu's hands halted their kneading. 'What was that song?' She was staring at Rian, who went silent.

Some instinct told her not to volunteer too much. 'It's from the sea.'

Maadu was not satisfied with this but Rian would not let herself be pressed into saying more. She didn't rightly know herself what it was. But she did know she wanted to see Toma again, although she didn't know clearly why. It was just that sense of their bond when singing those mournful notes, the feeling of a comrade who understood that the great forces of the earth are amenable to a will if that will is pitched true. Toma knew songs of the sea spirits, a song that could find a safe way out of pack ice. That, surely, was enough of a reason?

Maadu's youngest and middle sons came to collect their mother and sister in the Chieftain's boat, and there was a frantic rush to load up all their summer gleanings and Maadu and Cuckoo's wedding gifts in time to catch the returning tide up the Sound. But Rian was willing, and hauled basket after basket down to the shore. Once off the island, she was never coming back. That big harbour would give her the means to escape, somehow or other. It had to. She was determined.

The night of the wedding, they got to wear their new clothes. Rian brushed her hair and plaited it carefully. She gathered from the looks she got that her dark green dress suited her well.

FEAST

The feast was noisy. An awning made of sails had been rigged up over the forecourt of the broch, creating an atmosphere of a huge tented hall, with torches and candles lighting the space. The three slaves were told to help the cooks distribute food and drink among the throng, work at the cooking fire, clear away empty dishes, and generally be useful in ensuring the smooth sense of abundance the Chieftain wanted to convey to his friends. They must lavish his guests with all the best dishes and fob off starving gatecrashers with simple fare. Rian was told to serve drink to the throng and was given a jug to go around filling drinking horns. Some men grabbed at her buttocks or breasts, others bellowed at her for refills. She got better at keeping out of reach. Each time she returned to the broch, where the cooking fire blazed and smoked, she wished someone else would take the jug.

Overlooking the crowd, the Chieftain, black as ever, sat on his great seat like a throne, which had been carried out and placed beside the doorway.

Ussa was among those close by the Chieftain. She was, just as Fraoch had suggested, inveigling herself into favour with one of the unmarried sons, caressing him with her eyes, whispering in his ear and laughing at his remarks. Pytheas was by her other side, watching everything. Rian caught him looking her up and down and he pursed his mouth approvingly. She made sure not to look at him again.

To her surprise, sitting among the poor men at the far side of the yard, with his back to the Chieftain's family, was Manigan. As Rian took her jug towards that end of the party, trying to satisfy the thirst of all the drinking horns and mugs thrust at her, whilst also trying not to incur the wrath of the steward by being what he considered profligate, he winked at her. What was he doing there, especially among the beggars? She caught his eye a second time and he put his finger across his lips to signal secrecy. She nodded, though she thought it unlikely that he could somehow manage to remain incognito.

After a while the steward decided she was being far too generous with the drink and sent her to help the cooks, but they were all busy, so she was set to cleaning empty dishes. The water tank was running low so the grey steward told her to fetch more from the well. 'And be quick about it.'

She hurried off out of the door and down the alley, a pail in each hand. It was almost dark and quiet away from the crowd. Was this her chance for escape? The well was down the hill, on the way towards the harbour. The sudden opportunity made her breathless, giddy. Where should she go?

Before she could decide, half way down the first narrow passage between huts, a figure emerged from a doorway. Rian backed into a gap between buildings and slunk into the shadows.

The man closed the door behind him. The bolt slid home with a dull thump and he winced and looked about nervously, a knife held out in front of him following his turning head. Rian cowered. In the other arm, the man was holding a large, unwieldy cloth bag and, by the look of his hunched shoulder, it contained something heavy.

As he turned in her direction, scanning, Rian held her breath, glad of the shadows. Then she almost shouted out in recognition: she would know those round, flat features anywhere! Only the look on his face stopped her. It was a mixture of guilt and glee, as wicked an expression as she had ever seen on Li's face. So rather than let herself be known to him she remained, shrinking into the hiding place, while he satisfied himself he was unseen, sheathed his knife and set off down the alleyway away from the broch. He passed close by, but she didn't move a muscle. She got a clearer view of his face as he strode past. It really was her former fellow slave. Hugging the bag to his chest with both hands, he headed for the shore, no doubt to stash whatever loot was in it on board Ròn.

Rian guessed she had witnessed Ussa's quest being achieved. If Li had the stone head in that bag, and if she told Manigan, he might be willing to help her.

Then again, he might not. He was part of that family. Why should she embroil herself any more with them? But he had a boat. She needed someone to help her sail away. She crouched for a while longer in the shadows, wondering what to do, then got to her feet. She filled her buckets at the well then headed back to the noisy gathering.

Back in the broch, she was berated for taking so long, given an apron and set to work washing serving dishes so they could be refilled with good things for the guests. She sat by the fire, rinsing and scrubbing pig fat off bronze platters and wiping earthenware bowls, cursing herself for missing what might be her only opportunity to run away.

Another huge dish was thrust at her by the steward. 'Wash that, quick. We need it for the venison.' The dish was smeared and greasy with meat fat.

The steward returned, took the clean dish, and told her to take off her apron and get ready to serve again. The venison was the highlight of the feast and everyone would need ale or wine to toast the hunters. Rian was put to work pouring little beakers of wine on a big tray. Once it was full, she was sent off to distribute its contents.

'Mind you don't drop it.' The steward held the door for her.

She minded, treading carefully, and people were more than happy to lighten her load. It was empty by the time she neared the far side of the throng and she had to return for more beakers. But she had seen that Manigan was still there. The second tray took her to the bench where he sat and she made a point of stopping behind him and saying, 'Wine, and some news for you,' as she passed him. He half-turned to her, presumably unwilling to turn his head where he might be recognised. Rian leaned across in front of him, asking those near him to clear a space on a bench for the tray, then set the drinks down. As she had hoped, everyone began helping themselves to beakers and passing them around. Her arms ached.

She put her mouth as close to his ear as she dared and spoke in a murmur. 'Ussa's slave has just stolen something heavy from a hut down that alley.' Rian gestured over to the left.

He put his hand on her arm. She looked down at his long fingers. Then he let her go and reached for a wine cup, as if what she had said meant nothing to him. She picked up the now empty tray and returned to the broch.

On her way past him, the Chieftain caught hold of her dress and pulled her in. He asked if everyone now had a toasting glass.

Rian nodded.

He leered back, drawing her face down to his, so she could smell his beery breath. 'You can expect to hear from me later. I think it's time I got to know you better.' He slid a hand up her skirt. 'Is your arse healed?'

She tugged away.

Maadu was watching unamused, her arms folded.

Ussa leaned across the Chieftain's son and plucked at Rian's new dress. 'You're looking a bit better than the last time we saw you. Isn't she?' The question was addressed to Pytheas, who was seated next to Ussa on the other side. 'A pretty little thing when she brushes up.'

Pytheas' eyes were black and he had the slack mouth that Rian recognised meant he had drunk plenty of everything that had been offered to the guests. He was licking his lips and flaring his nostrils, his face flushed. 'Yes. Before, you looked a peerie tired, but now you look a peerie beautiful.' 'Peerie' was the word for little in the local dialect.

The Chieftain smiled indulgence at his effort to ingratiate himself. Ussa stroked his arm as if he was a pet.

Rian caught Ussa sharing a conspiratorial wink with Maadu, then she took them all by surprise.

'If the Chieftain will sell her back to me, I will offer a handsome price: a piece of amber, the colour of her hair.'

The Chieftain pulled at Rian's hair, which was plaited down her back and her head jerked backwards and round as he examined it, as if to test its value. 'We'll talk about it tomorrow.'

Ussa blinked like a lizard. 'I may not offer again tomorrow.'

The Chieftain smiled with one side of his mouth. 'Add in a piece of ivory, and she's yours. I know you like trading with the Mutterer.'

'How appropriate, exactly the colour of her skin,' Ussa said smoothly.

Maadu was nudging the Chieftain and pointing to the crowd, whose drinks were waiting.

'It's a deal.' He let Rian go, and gave Ussa's outstretched hand a cursory shake. 'But now, it's time to toast the happy couple.'

Pytheas caught Rian's hand. 'Welcome back.' His smile was like a cat's, his eyes glazed.

She tugged away, tears of fury blurring her vision. Was she no more than a trinket, to be passed from one person to another in exchange for baubles?

The Chieftain banged his drinking horn with his knife handle and stood, signalling to a young page behind him who leaped to his feet, put the mouthpiece of the carnix to his lips and gave a blast like a rutting stag. Throughout the place heads turned and conversations stopped. The Chieftain began to make a speech praising the hunters and the gods who blessed their hunt. The smell of venison filled the air now as the cooks teased flesh from the roasted carcasses, piling it up on bronze platters. The steward waved Rian over and gave her a plate of meat to distribute.

The Chieftain drew his speech to conclusion with a toast. As everyone except the slaves raised their cups and drank, Rian looked around. Manigan had gone.

The meat was devoured, the noise level dropping for a while as all mouths, except those of the slaves, were occupied with chewing. Then everyone seemed to be talking at once and a kind of crazy exuberance took the place over. A plate of venison was passed back half-full from the Chieftain's family to circulate among the cooks and skivvies, and the steward rushed over to supervise and control this largesse. Rian seized the moment, grabbed the water buckets again and slipped from the broch, skirting the crowd and heading for the well.

She set the buckets down there and looked about her, waiting for her eyes to adjust. It was fully dark now. There was no-one in the alley as far as she could tell, but the shadows were deep. There was something creepy about the hush away from the broch. She began to creep along a passage between the buildings. There was an eerie glow that made her want to tread even more quietly, as if each step might take her into the net of some demon. She reached the end of the first building and at the corner she stopped, trying to control her pounding heart. She needed to find Manigan. Would he be in the hut she had seen Li leave?

She looked up and stopped breathing. The sky was green, the colour of bright wood moss, and rippling. Fear rose in her like a snake. What world was this that she had stepped out into? What spirits had gathered for the feast? What powerful wizard had conjured them? Was this something she should warn someone about? But who?

She stood, gazing up, as the spirits moved in the sky. She had seen them once before as a child. One night Danuta had woken her up and led her out of the broch at Clachtol, to stand on the headland and watch the dance. Buia had already been there, and had taken her hand. Danuta explained that they were spirits trapped in a livid sea of green that oozed out of the north. Their pain was clear as they writhed within the mesh of light, like fish caught in a river-mouth net. Watching them now, Rian understood what they were suffering.

The sky to the west was obscured by the hut. She crouched down and peered around the corner to look up at the lights. The green faded, then surged. Into her left ear a voice said, 'The dancing ladies are splendid tonight.'

She jerked away but something had hold of her dress. She tugged but a hand clamped over her face and she was bundled into a hollow, bumping against a stone step and down into dampness.

'Tell what you saw.' The voice in her ear, a ghostly whisper.

She was lying on her back. Something cold was oozing up into her dress. She didn't dare speak to the ghost-voiced demon, but it insisted.

'I need to hear what you saw. Please.'

'Green light,' she found herself saying. 'Beautiful but sad.'

'Shhh…'

She felt breath on her neck. It stank of seal blubber. Could it be him?

A sound of footsteps: the hurried tramping of a single person going up the alley. Then nothing. The distant hubbub from the broch. A sound of music and voices raised in a chorus. Darkness and cold damp soaking into her buttocks, shoulder, thigh, where something clamped her to the ground. It shifted when she tried to push at it.

'The green lights are the lost souls, the spirits of all those people who didn't try, who failed to struggle.' The voice was like the fur of an animal. Was it inside her head? She gathered herself and writhed out of its grasp, but it seemed to be many-tentacled and only pinned her more firmly by both calves and one shoulder to the ground.

'Good. You struggle. You'll not wither in the sky like them, will you? Now tell me what you saw. Who did you see stealing something earlier on?'

Nothing would have induced her to speak. Nothing. What if it wasn't him?

'You are frightened. Of course you are. It's not surprising. But I don't intend to hurt you, unless…' The voice stopped. 'Just tell me what you saw and I'll let you go, probably. Ah. Too honest for my own good. I may not promise something I cannot be sure of. It's my curse, and some say my greatest virtue, this incorrigible honesty. I'll make a story of this yet, I can see that already. I know you must think I'm a brute and a cur holding you here like this. It's a terrible thing to do to a kitten like you, like putting a fox cub into a seal fat barrel, pretty little thing in a smelly hole like this. If only you knew I'm not half, not even one tenth, of the demon they say I am. They make out I'm a pirate. But I'm just a hunter with a boatload of stories, and on a good day some ivory to swap for iron, and enough skin to mend my ship and shields, blubber in the lamps and fresh meat in the pan.'

His voice wound on. She was drawn along it like a rope held out in the darkness. It was soft but firm, flexible but strong. It had the rhythm of the sea in it and the texture of years.

'This ground is wet. You'll be getting cold. I'm sorry. But if you tell me what you saw, then maybe we can move somewhere a little less uncomfortable.'

She wondered if she should cry out for help but there was little point and she didn't seem to have a voice of her own any more. This dark voice beside her was more than enough of a voice for the whole world.

'You're a brave one, I see. I can feel your courage. You're frightened, but you're like a bear cub. You don't show your fear. You're waiting for your moment to escape, which is good. Do you know who I am? Of course you do. What do you know of me, I wonder? More than I know of you, I'm sure. All I know of you is that you're a beautiful slave girl and that you speak the tongue of the west of Alba and you have sea eyes, and for some reason you told me you saw one of Ussa's other slaves stealing something from my quarters. That was what you said, wasn't it?'

Of course it was Manigan. Yet she couldn't begin to tell him what she knew of him. She couldn't speak at all. But something in her body must have seemed to reply to his question with assent, because he continued.

'Each time I've met you, you belong to someone different. I can't pretend to imagine what that's like, to belong to someone, to be a slave. And Ussa always seems to be close by when I see you so although it's men who buy you I guess it's Ussa who is at the heart of your enslavement, so either you hate her and want to help me because of that, or you're her spy, her tool. How do I tell which? If you're acting for her, trying to trick me, I shall have to kill you. Unfortunately even if you hate her, which I think you do...' He had loosened his grip on her slightly. Did her body give so much away? 'Even then, she may still be using you. I know Ussa. I know her tricks. I wouldn't trust her not to play tricks with her own daughter, let alone a slave.'

His voice was just a murmur, a whisper. 'Can I trust you, even though you are a slave? I want to. You are as beautiful as a flower and I want to believe you are as true. The primrose never lies about the springtime but sometimes snow comes, even after the first flowers have led us to believe we were safe from winter. Even the most innocent things cannot protect us from the treachery of people like Ussa.'

He fell silent and Rian felt a shiver shudder through her and something in him tautened.

'So. Nothing. I need to know what you saw but... Ach I'm going. This is pointless.'

The grip on her leg was suddenly lifted and she heard him roll away from her. She was free to move. Like a bird freed from the clutch of a hawk, she scrabbled out from the hollow and broke into a run down the alley towards the well.

But as she reached it, she no longer knew why she was there. The knowledge of where Li had gone was in her, and she had to

183

follow this knowledge. It was her only chance. She resumed the same hell-for-leather running pace down to the shore, slithering where it was wet, but her balance was good and she didn't fall. It was strangely quiet, presumably as so many people were at the feast.

Now to find Ròn. It wasn't hard. Out in the open it didn't seem so dark. The green and white lights in the sky reflected on the water. The beamy trading currach stood out among the narrow boats the sailors here preferred, like a bull among a field of ponies.

Having spotted the boat, Rian ground to a halt. What now? There was no option but to continue now she was this near, so she edged her way down to the pier. Some boats stood high and dry where the tide had abandoned them. Ròn was in the water, rafted off another vessel roped to the end of the jetty.

Toma was sitting silhouetted at the bow, looking out to sea. He turned and saw her, waved as if he was expecting her, then got up and gestured in greeting, sweeping his hand towards him to show she should cross the boat hanging off the pier. She stepped down into it, clinging to a stay, then Toma handed her in with one hand on her lower arm, her own hand grabbing his sleeve as she jumped into the vessel. He seemed to be excited to see her. He spoke rapidly to her in his own tongue, which she had never understood, holding his head in a mime of agony but then the next minute smiling widely at her and stroking her hair. She had no clue what he was so animatedly communicating to her, but he was clearly the only person on board.

'Li?' she asked. She needed to know if he had brought the stolen article here.

He tugged her to Ussa's side of the shelter at the bow and pointed inside to a mound of boxes and packages, ushering her to go in. She hesitated. It was all shadows and hard to make much out. He bent down and pointed with one poking finger at a bundle on the top of the heap in the far corner, then holding his head in both hands and shaking it, rolling his eyes as if in pain, whining.

Once more he gestured to her, pushing her into the shelter, clearly indicating she should go in and get whatever it was. 'Take it away,' he moaned, in Keltic. At least this she understood.

The bundle did look as if it could be what Li had been carrying. She took a breath as if diving underwater, stepped into the cabin, reached for the bag and retreated with it. It was extraordinarily heavy.

Toma backed away from her as if she was now capable of inflicting a poisonous bite and pointed back off the boat. 'Go.'

She gestured with the bundle as if to throw it overboard and the look of panic on his face and terrified shaking of his head made clear what he thought of that idea.

She paused. She had to ask him. 'Can you help me escape?'

He shook his head, sadly. Then he spoke again. He seemed to have forgotten that she didn't understand his language, but then he pointed to the bag. 'Manigan.'

'Manigan?'

He raised his eyebrows and held his hand out, palm up, seeking confirmation of something.

'Manigan,' she murmured, nodding.

He closed his hand into a fist and knocked on something invisible to signal he was satisfied.

She wasn't exactly sure she knew what deal she had made. Did he simply mean that the stolen property was to be returned to its owner? Or was he suggesting that Manigan might help her? She clambered out of the boat and onto the vessel it was tied to.

As she hit the deck, encumbered by the bundle, Toma said her name.

She turned.

He was leaning over the side of his boat. He mimed opening the bag up, and looking at it, then he slid his flat hand under his chin and across his neck in a slicing motion. His meaning was clear: looking inside meant death. Once again he held his hand out in a question of comprehension, and when she nodded, raised his fist to denote their pact. Then he winked at her and gave a sly smile. 'Bless you.'

She clambered across the second boat and up onto the jetty, then wondered where to go and how to find Manigan. Where would he have gone? How could she find him? More importantly, how could she hide the stone?

She didn't even have to begin looking. As she crept off the pier she saw him. He was standing by a wooden post, waiting for her. Within three steps she was close enough to see his white-toothed smile and disbelieving shake of the head. He was wearing a big coat made of thick leather. She momentarily doubted it was him. Was she being tricked?

But then he spoke. 'If you aren't a goddess, you are the Mother's own child, bless you if you aren't. Give me that here before it corrupts your primrose soul.'

That voice again, the flowing poetry of his praise of her. She bathed in it. She handed him the bag and he tucked it into his coat and clutched it under his elbow.

'However will I thank you for this?'

'Buy me,' she said on impulse, surprising herself.

She looked up at him but couldn't make out his expression in the shadow. He said nothing. In embarrassment, she dropped her gaze and stood, not daring to move.

Their silence became strained. She tried to listen to the creaking of timbers against floats, the lapping of water against the jetty, the sighing songs of rigging. But Manigan's speechlessness was the loudest sound. After all his effusiveness, no words.

She had nothing else to say and she could not look up at him. That would be too awful.

His feet were in big boots. One turned slightly out.

She shifted her weight onto her right leg trying to edge herself away.

This silence was so obviously a refusal, she could hardly bear to breathe. Was there a way to escape him? He was not holding her and yet she was frozen to the spot. She didn't know who else to ask. Perhaps she should have simply pleaded with him to help her?

She turned her head towards the boats. Above them the green spirits still writhed in the sky, but lower towards the horizon now. She watched their struggle. Stars gleamed through them like holes in the sky. She could feel him standing beside her, his presence huge, bovine. A shudder of cold went through her, as the sweat from running drew chill air onto her body.

And still he did not speak.

Her own two words seemed to echo out to the livid sky-dance and back again.

Buy.

Me.

The strange ghost-forms rubbed themselves against the impassive stars, their pain shimmering and streaking the sky.

Buy me. Her request was an impossible demand. How could a hunter buy a slave? Why should he? What made her think being owned by him would be any better than being owned by Pytheas, or the Chieftain, or Ussa? Why did she think he would be kind? What did she know of kindness? What did she know of him? Nothing. And yet also everything. She knew his whole life, one long adventure on the ocean. She knew there was nothing in his life that would fit her and yet she would do anything to accustom herself to it. She could become a hunter. She could live on the ocean. She could learn the ways of the sea. She could learn to be like Toma. She could learn. Perhaps she should explain this to him, tell him that although he thought his life was not suitable for her she could adapt to it. She would find ways to be useful. But as the words tried to formulate themselves in her head, he spoke.

What he said was worse than a slap.

'I don't pay for women.'

CHOICE

The words broke the enchantment. She looked up at Manigan and saw the face of a hunter, scarred and weather-beaten, rugged in the dimness, stubbly with unkempt hair. A whiff of fish and bilge water washed over them from the boats as a breeze picked up, and here was his own smell. It was like standing beside a seal man. Perhaps that's what he was, one of the selkie folk.

She had hoped he might help her. Now that she understood he wouldn't, she had never felt so unwanted. Abject misery filled her.

He shifted the bag to under his other arm and put the one nearest her around her shoulder, pulling her towards his chest. She resisted, but he was so much stronger than her it made no difference. He turned her to look out to sea.

'Do you know Bradan, my boat?'

She said nothing but pointed at the unmistakable vessel, its mast taller than any other, its sleek shape and long bow unlike the beamy trading boats with their big holds for cargo, or the whaling boats of the Chieftain's fleet, or the slender little inshore fishing boats. As if it knew they were looking, the pennant at the top of the mast fluttered.

'The wind's changed.' He released her shoulder. 'Take this.'

He was proffering the bag. 'Don't look inside it. Hide yourself and it on Bradan. Get under the sail. I'll not be long.'

She took the hessian bundle which seemed even heavier than before. She almost staggered with it.

He must have seen her confusion. 'Are you ready? Do you need anything for the journey?'

'Journey?'

He laughed and his face crumpled and stretched like clouds opening to let the moon shine through. She saw his eyes gleaming. He seemed more demon than human. 'I am going to steal you.'

She grinned.

'Are you still the Greek's?'

She shook her head. 'Ussa's.'

'Good. She owes me plenty.'

'She bought me back off the Chieftain tonight.'

'Off the Chieftain? Even better, he owes me more.' He patted her on the shoulder. 'Away and hide.'

She should ask a thousand questions. What she was about to do was more dangerous than anything that she had ever done. She was on a precipitous ridge. To turn back, to return to the feast, undoubtedly meant punishment for her absence, and worse: Pytheas' bed, most likely, or Ussa's whip. To go on, to do as Manigan said, was madness.

But to go back was slavery. There was no real choice. Madness was the only option.

Rian put one foot forward and stepped into the future. Another step, the bag heavy in her arms. A third. She looked back and Manigan was standing watching her. He inclined his head and though she couldn't see it she knew he was smiling at her and all the demon had evaporated. 'Hide like a mouse.' His soft voice followed her and it was warm and she trusted it, even though she had no reason to. She took another step, and another, and adjusted her hold on the hessian bundle and set off down the soggy bank towards the jetty, her eye on Bradan, its mast-top signal flag beckoning her. The lights in the sky were green again, a great rippling curtain across the north. In the west, two columns of white rose up and wavered and sank again. Under such heavens anything was possible. If the very star spirits could dance this way, there was nothing that might not be dreamed and yet come true.

There seemed to be nobody on any of the boats as she stepped carefully along the slippery wooden jetty, although there must have been some, presumably sleeping or spellbound. She crept along past Ròn. There was no sign of Toma now. Bradan was out off the other side where the boats were tied three deep. She clambered carefully down into the first. It was awkward with the stone. On the second boat a bundled figure was snoring, rolled up under a hide shelter between the mast and the prow. Rian held her breath, motionless, but the snoring was deep and even. She tiptoed across the open deck and then heaved the bag over onto Bradan, at the point where she was lashed on. It was more difficult to climb aboard this time, as the boats were so different in shape. Bradan stood higher in the water, so she had to reach up and pull herself up and over the gunnel. But once she was over and into the vessel she was hidden from view. She made a space between two rolls of sail and tucked herself in, pulling it over her. Inside was dry and dark. She thought of what it was like to be a mouse and made herself smaller, snuggling deeper in.

Water lapped against the keel, the boat's struts and sheets and sinews replied to every touch and the stone seemed to magnify the murmur, as if it too was involved in a conversation with the ocean depth. Perhaps this was what made Toma's head hurt. She had never been able to understand the sea's words, try as she might to listen to its babble.

ESCAPE

CHASE

The next morning, Manigan stood at the helm, glancing behind him northwards towards Ròn. They still had a good lead but could not shake their pursuer. Rian knew exactly what it would be like on that boat, oars going, the slaves driven on by oaths and goading, their fur-clad mistress chanting the rhythm of 'pull and thrust and pull and thrust' at them like a sorceress, so that even the wooden spars would bend in frenzy to impress the waves and defy the currents and winds that should have been resisting them. She was a crazy-woman and when she wanted something she could overcome any other force of nature. Rian knew it to be true. She still felt it, branded into her shoulder and thigh.

Anyone seeing Manigan's boat in harbour would have said it could not survive the ocean, it was so narrow and slight. Yet on the sea it flowed with the waves, it flew rather than ploughed. It seemed a little puffin of a thing pursued by a skua. The hulking trading boat with its great powering sails took advantage of every wind, and when the breeze dropped, the oars carried it on and it bore down on them.

Rian still sat by the mast where she had woken to the frenzy of Manigan and his two friends rigging the sail and casting off into the dawn, laughing and half-cut. One of them was Badger, who had been on board Ussa's boat. The other had been introduced to her as his brother, Kino. He was tall, thin and sickly, with tangled fair hair and a short, boyish beard. One of his eyes was clouded, its lid not fully open, which gave him a questioning look.

Now the two of them were asleep on their benches, coats over their faces, snoring. Manigan had given her a big man's coat and leggings. She had rolled up the sleeves and ankles and felt like a child dressing up in adult's clothes. Manigan kept the helm, looking tired but unworried, one eye on the boat behind. He kept the sails taut, their speed just enough to keep ahead.

He yawned. Then he caught her watching him and winked, lifted his chin towards their pursuers and grinned. 'Will they catch us, do you think? Eh, little green-eyed witch? What do you think?'

She found it hard to pull away from his scrutiny, but she wanted to watch him dance with his boat and she couldn't do that with his gaze burning into her. So she made her eyes fall to the coil of rope she had made beautiful at her feet. Then she let them creep slowly to his leather-boots, skin-clad shins and thighs, his body bundled up against the wind yet moving freely and paying constant attention to ropes and sail and rudder, loosening, freeing or taking in slack, giving the boat what it seemed to want to keep moving. He was humming and swaying with the motion of the sea. She dared to look again at his face for the expression of devotion that seemed to be there. His face reminded her of Danuta at her ceremonies with herbs. But when he caught Rian watching she had to glance away, because he looked at her so differently from how he looked at the sea. To her, he presented a smile so disarming she wanted to throw herself open to him, yet the sense that he could see right to the back of her was terrifying. His presence made her suspect that she was made of fire, when she had always thought she was made of stone.

And so she tried to keep her eyes from his, and they sailed on, dogged by Ussa.

'You don't say much, do you?' he said.

She shook her head and shared his smile.

'I'm a talker, me. I like to talk. It gets me into trouble sometimes, but it gets me out more often. A happy dog will wag his tail, my mother used to say, and that's how it is with me. And you, you're a puppy with your tail between your legs and I'm not surprised. You've probably still got blisters on your hands from rowing that Queen Bitch whenever the wind dropped.'

He threw her the question with his eyebrows and she lifted her hands in demonstration of her answer. She still had callouses from her time on board Ròn and plenty more scars from the summer at Mousa.

'Aye. Oh yes, that'll do nicely.' He shifted a rope and the main sail seemed to loosen, then stretch, the boat leaned over and the murmur under the keel filled to a trickle.

Rian kept watching the boat behind. She wasn't sure but it seemed to have gained on them. It seemed bigger than before.

They were out of sight of land now. The sea rolled away towards the east, a ruffled blue-grey sheet under the dull, silvery grey sky. The horizon was far, far away and nothing more than a blurred line where the sea merged with cloud. It was the same all around. An even light from the high, hidden sun made the ocean seem vast and empty. There was just Bradan and Ròn. A guillemot flew by heading north, low over the water, swerving towards them and up to survey the strangers from on high, then dropping back close to sea level and flapping onwards.

The main sail began to flutter and loosen. Manigan cursed. The wind had dropped away as quietly as it had risen as if a hand had smoothed the fabric of the sea.

'That bird stole my breeze. Ach well, it's no better for them.'

Looking back Rian saw that indeed their hunters were wallowing without any sign of life in the sails.

Manigan turned to face backwards, watching Ròn. 'The oars are slow to come out this time. The slaves must be sleeping or rebelling.'

But then the boat sprouted appendages and began to crawl like some kind of insect towards them across the silken surface of the ocean.

'I'm damned if I'm rowing.' Manigan scratched his head. 'Come on wind, come on! Do you know any wind spells, little witch? You are a witch, aren't you? With eyes like that and such quietness. The stone says you must be. Only a magician could have found it and carried it and hidden it without suffering for it, and you don't seem to be suffering as far as I can see, except for being mute. Were you always this quiet, or has the stone struck you dumb?'

Rian shrugged. Maybe she was under some kind of spell. It seemed completely plausible to her.

He sat tapping his foot and looking anxiously at the sails, and she wasn't sure why, but the song came to her that Toma sang when they were out in the misty northern ocean. Its eerie notes seemed to come from her without her opening her mouth, a humming that seemed to come from the boat itself or perhaps even through its hide, from the sea.

Manigan's foot stilled.

She looked up and saw that he was staring at her wide-eyed. She paused.

'No, don't stop,' he whispered.

And so she continued, allowing the sounds of the song to follow the tune, moving her lips and mouth to the words she had learned, the meaning of which she had no idea, but their sound was beautiful and sad.

Badger sat up on his chest, bleary-eyed, staring at her in amazement. He kicked the other man, who stirred and pulled the coat off his face and half-raised himself with a look of drowsy wonder, rubbing his eyes. She sang on and then from behind them at the stern, Manigan joined in. It was like someone lifting her bodily out of herself, his voice deep and rich below hers, in unison, unwavering. Together they stepped along the tune, note by eerie note, the three falling intervals, each subtly wider than the previous one, returning repeatedly to the tonic. Sometimes he met that note with another, its harmony so sweet it made Rian look at him in wonder. She could see from the way he sang that the words had meaning for him, and although she didn't know them she felt it full of loneliness, yet those moments of harmony gave it hope, like glints of starlight in a clouded night sky. The song ended on that note, and as it faded, Badger called softly as she had heard once before from Toma, when the sea spirit had risen from the ocean as they were fogbound in the north.

'Blow!'

He was pointing out to the south-west ahead. Rian turned and strained to see anything on the calm surface. Her gaze scoured. Nothing. But Badger kept his arm outstretched and there, as far ahead of them as Ussa's boat was behind them, a spurt of spume like a puff of smoke. A dark shape rose out of the sea: a fin rolling in a curve, slicing back into the water. And then it was gone. Stare as she might there was nothing but the smooth surface of the ocean, with no sign of where the spirit blade had cut it.

'Blow!' The call was from Manigan this time. She looked back. He was pointing further west. Following his arm she just caught the same curving motion. Then it was gone.

First a shimmer on the water, a blurring, and then a flap in the sail. A trickle under the keel. A breeze.

The song had worked its miracle.

Badger got up and helped Manigan raise a top sail. Kino joined them and together they rigged a third sail, thin cloth out in front of the boat. Bradan began to course along again. Now all awake, the crew needed sustenance. Badger passed Rian a battered bronze cup of water, bread from a bag and some leathery fruit. She didn't recognise it but it tasted sweet and satisfying.

'Have you met my wee brother?' Badger asked her.

She looked at him. Kino, his one good eye bloodshot, his face a thin, haggard version of the big man, dipped his head to her, barely hiding his indifference. He pulled a pottery jar out of the wooden box he had slept on, took a swig, then replaced it.

'You'd be better eating this.' Badger proffered bread.

The younger man shrugged and took it, looking as if he had only accepted it to avoid an argument. He took one bite then put it in his pocket.

'If you're not eating it, I will,' said Badger. 'Or give it to the girl, she looks ravenous.'

Kino tossed it at her as if to a dog, and she only just managed to catch it, saving it from the bilges. Badger was right. She was hungry.

'You can helm for a bit if you're awake now, Badger. I want to relax and find out what my new cargo is like.' Manigan shuffled Rian along the bench and she was forced to sit up close to him. 'So tell me.' He leaned back against the gunnel. 'Who are your people?'

Her tongue froze in her head. The thought of Danuta made her utterly homesick, but other than her, who could she tell of? Even Danuta was not truly her own. 'I don't have any.'

'What? No kin? But who taught you to speak the language of the west? Is that not an island voice? Are you from the Long Island?'

'No. I've been there, but I lived across the Minch from there.'

'Assynt? You're from Assynt?'

She gave a tilt of her head in agreement and smiled at his delight.

'Oh, that's a wonderful land to be from. Those mountains! They are the children of the Goddess. And those people are strong. So whose family do you belong to? I stayed in the house of Tormaid once, and I met many people.' He reeled off a list of people from Ardbhar, the broch in the north, and its nearby hamlets.

Rian marvelled that he could know so many of the folk and recall their names. They sounded so incongruous here on the ocean, as if he was conjuring the land out of the water.

'So are those your people?'

She shook her head. 'I lived in Drost's broch, at Clachtoll, but I am not from there.'

'Clachtoll, aye, I know where that is. I don't think I've met Drost, but I know the name. I've heard he's a hard man.'

She wasn't surprised that was his reputation, but the next question took her aback.

'So why did he sell you? I can see why he bought you, but not why he'd move you on.'

Indignation flared in her. Was that all he saw? A chattel to be traded, or in his case, simply stolen? 'I wasn't bought by him. He was supposed to be my foster father. But Ussa had a sword he wanted more than me.' The bitterness in her mouth was like a rotten tooth, an ache that she could not ease.

'Ah, Green Eyes. What's your name again? Rian?'

She nodded.

'Green Rian, aye. You've been treated badly. It's a crying shame for someone so lovely, such a pretty bird, clipped and caged when she ought to be flitting about singing and being beautiful.' He brushed her cheek with the back of a finger. 'Ach those broch men, they have no idea of what wealth and goodness lies all around them. If they can't count it or fight with it or watch it glitter, if it isn't stone or metal or...'

His voice tailed off and he looked back at Ròn, shrinking on the horizon behind them.

'We're losing them. It's Sedna to thank. I think you must be able to speak to her, to call a breeze like that. You can sail with me whenever you wish, Rian.' He looked her full in the face as if drinking her in, but did not touch her again. His gaze was like his voice, soft and salty. 'You remind me of someone else. You're not at all like the Assynt people, now I look at you. Are you an elf's daughter?'

He paused, but she didn't answer.

'How did you come to be there?'

She was surprised that she didn't find his curiosity annoying. She found herself wanting to unburden herself of her story, but the words would not come. She had nothing to say, and tears welled in her eyes, remembering Danuta and the few frustrating times she had enquired, fruitlessly, into her origins. 'I don't know,' was all she could muster.

'I imagine life was hard.'

She could see he was making his way around something in his mind as he talked. 'I am trying to work out what it means to have you with us, or where to take you, if it comes to that. Who else is in his family? Did you have any friends there? There must be someone who might shelter you. I live a dangerous life. I don't think I should take you hunting. You're so...' He paused. 'So delicate. There are no butterflies in the Arctic.' He rubbed his head thoughtfully. 'Or not many. We might have to leave you somewhere before we head north again.'

Rian wanted to ask him questions but dared not.

'Is there not a medicine woman at Clachtoll? Are there none of her kin alive?'

'Danuta.' Speaking the name felt to Rian like an invocation. 'She was my... she was like my grandmother. My foster mother died. I never knew her. Danuta took care of me. She is a healer.' She stopped, uncertain as ever about how much she could say of the secret matters she had been taught.

'One of the sisterhood, eh?' He frowned. 'So are you ...?' He seemed to have to think of the right phrase. 'Are you a moon-dancer?'

She stared at him, then quickly looked away, but he had seen her recognition of the name. Only very few girls were given the chance to become moon-dancers, to learn the sacred rituals associated with the waxing and waning of the moon, the secret medicines of fertility, how to bring a child into the world or to bring back menstrual bleeding if it ceased. Rian was sure it was taboo for a man to speak the name. But Danuta and the sisters had talked to her of these things when she had been to the winter festival and the next Beltane fire she had hoped she might be chosen. But here she was. No chance now of being the virgin at the sacred fire. Anger welled in her and she shook her head, suddenly furious at him and tired of his endless questions. He must have sensed he had pushed her as far as he could because he fell quiet.

The breeze had dropped away again and their advance had slowed. Behind them, Ussa's boat, never quite out of view, was gaining on them, growing perceptibly bigger and close enough for them to see the oars out. When it came to the race, Ussa would clearly always win in the calm with her slaves rowing while they drifted.

'She's catching us.' Manigan did not seem too concerned. 'Fancy a bit of rowing, Badger?'

Badger threw him a hand gesture that made it quite clear what he thought of that idea.

'Kino, grab a sweep. There'll be drink for it. I want to keep my distance from Queen Bitch out there.'

Kino swore at him in the Keltic tongue but shrugged and joined Manigan, helping him to lift two oars into their slots. They took a chest-seat each and began to pull, Manigan chanting the rhythm in a guttural, two-note song of utter lewdness.

'Foreskin, rawskin, fuck her out, fuck her in.' Over and over.

Badger joined in the chant from the helm but Kino kept quiet, his jaw clenched with the strain of rowing. Manigan, fluidly stretching back then reaching forward, singing at full pelt, seemed to be enjoying himself. The boat started to crawl across the water.

Kino kept in rhythm for about a dozen strokes, then started to falter.

'Keep it together, rawskin,' Manigan chanted, but Kino missed a stroke then caught the oar in the water on the return of the next one. The oar belted him in the chest and he bent over, coughing. Manigan halted.

'Is that it? Is that all you can manage? Kino man, think of the last woman you had. Close your ears, Rian. Get into the rhythm.'

Kino coughed again, a loose hacking that racked him, then straightened up.

'One more time.' Manigan leaned forward, Kino followed and they set off again. They managed a few more strokes until Kino was breathless once more.

'Fuck it. Badger, what's your price?'

'I'm not rowing, mate. I told you. No oars. My rowing days are over.' He shook his head implacably. Rian looked beyond him. The boat was so close now she could see Ussa in her white coat at the prow.

'I'll row.' She pushed herself to her feet and clambered across to the chest that Kino was sitting on, hacking. She touched his shoulder and he heaved himself up to let her in. She seized the oar and looked across at Manigan, rowing in rhythm with him. 'Ocean, motion, ocean, motion,' she chanted.

Manigan almost lost his oar laughing.

Then there was a howl and a clatter. Manigan leaped to his feet and Rian turned to see Kino toppling onto the gunnel and almost overboard. A spear was lodged in his back. Manigan tugged it out without ceremony and reached for the knife at his waist.

'Fire. We need fire. Rian, Badger, get a fucking flame going, quick. Quick!'

He was sawing at the rope attached to the spear, the other end of which was being pulled by Li on Ussa's boat. They were so close Rian could see the grim expression on his face and hear Ussa barking 'pull, you wimp,' at him.

'Fire, by the Goddess, Rian!' Manigan had almost sawn through the rope. She reached for her pouch, pulled the tinder box out, glad she had taken the time to fit herself up to make a fire.

'Where?' She unwrapped the flint and kindling. Manigan cut the rope and flung it into the sea. Badger was rummaging in his chest.

'There.' Manigan pointed to a chunky thwart at the stern.

Badger tossed her a metal plate. She arranged some cotton grass loosely surrounded by some dry heather tops. Rian murmured the word of ritual honouring, took a breath and struck the flints together. A spark pounced on the fluff, sputtered, and she breathed onto it, coaxing it into flame. She fed it more heather and it crackled the fierce birth greeting as she breathed on it too. The heather caught hold of the flame and chuckled. She gave it more and it flared. She breathed again, looking for something else to burn. 'I need sticks to keep it alive.'

Manigan had his chest open and was pulling things out like a dog after a mouse.

Badger tossed her some birch twigs from a bundle he was holding, grinning at her. 'Quite the fire devil, aren't you!' He nodded as she snapped the twigs and fed her flames with them.

'Bless you.' Manigan had found what he was looking for and was unwrapping from a stinking cloth a round, sticky object. He pulled on a thick glove, took the ball in his hand, and brought it close to Rian's fire. It sputtered and the flame licked up it appreciatively, flickering over the surface. Manigan rolled it lightly across his gloved palm. It was about the size of his clenched fist. A foul, resinous smell came off it, as well as black smoke, but the flames danced over it and there was the smell of leather charring from his glove.

He turned, steadied himself, looked over to Ròn, then lobbed the ball towards it, just catching the prow. It tumbled into the boat. There was a shout from Toma, scuffling from the oarsmen and a lot of smoke. But the rowing continued and the boat advanced.

Now Manigan was sliding another, smaller ball onto a light spear and squashing it into a sausage shape along the shaft. He handed it to Badger

'Go for the sail, throw high.' He reached for another ball like the first.

Badger lit his spear and threw. It dipped steeply, just catching the edge of the sail but failing to pierce it, then fell onto the boat. More smoke belched from it.

Another ball from Manigan caught one of the oarsmen and rolled into the middle of the boat. Ussa had moved from her

viewpoint on the prow. The rowing stopped and there was chaotic shouting. Another spear thrown by Badger hit its target and
pierced the sail, and fire guttered down it as the oily substance
melted, flaming. But a well-aimed bucket of water soon put it out
again.

Rian's fire was dwindling. 'Badger, more sticks!'

He kicked his bundle towards her and she fed the flames.

Manigan tossed another fireball among their pursuers and
Badger attempted a second hit on the sail. It fell short, hissing
into the sea, so he reached for another and this time it hit its mark
and the big sail began to burn.

Rian kept feeding her fire, carefully containing it in the dish at
the stern, but worrying that the wood under it was smouldering.

'Wind, damn it, come on,' Manigan muttered. 'Rian, cast
another wind spell. Badger, if you don't take the freaking sweep
now I'll throw you overboard.'

'No need,' Badger calmly gestured east where the water was
ruffling.

The breeze reached them, the main sail tensioned and Manigan leapt for the sheet to let the sail take its fill of the motion.

Badger brought the boat round to allow more wind to push
at the sails and Manigan darted about, loosening and tugging at
ropes as if feeding them with the invisible food of air. There was
that comforting trickle under the keel and the distance to Ròn
lengthened. Her crew were still too busy with buckets of water,
staunching flames, to take advantage of the wind. If anything the
breeze was making their job harder as it encouraged the blaze in
the sail.

'Fly Bradan, fly my darling.' Manigan stood looking back. 'If
this breeze keeps up we'll leave them well behind.'

Rian wasn't sure if he was addressing the boat or the crew in
general.

Badger said, 'They might catch us in a calm but that old tub is
no match for Bradan with a wind. Any wind at all.'

Manigan nodded.

Kino was slumped against his chest, whimpering.

Rian captured some glowing embers in the fire pan, then Manigan grabbed a bucket and doused the smoking mast step with an excessive splash that left Rian wet all down one side. She only just managed to keep the pan dry.

'Sorry!' He laughed, as gleeful as his sails.

She took the smoking embers back to the shelter at the bow where they might be coaxed back to life later, then she turned her attention to Kino.

He was shivering and sweating. Rian touched his shoulder and he flinched. 'A drink,' he murmured, then, rousing himself, hurled a string of abuse at Manigan. 'If I don't get a drink I'm going to die.' He seemed to be oblivious to the hole in his back where the spear had lodged.

Rian thought of Drost. How often had she heard the same from him?

Manigan shrugged and pointed to the chest behind the mast. She opened it. Inside, among a clutter of ropes and tools, were some bladders and flasks. She took out a wooden jug with a narrow spout, uncorked it and sniffed. It was rough, but it would do to calm Kino while she examined his wound. She handed it to him and watched him glug, then took it back. He shuddered as the brew hit his stomach, demanded more. She gave him a second slug and asked to see his shoulder.

'Ach, it's nothing.'

'You're bleeding,' she insisted.

He let her help him off with his leather coat. It was massively thick and heavy.

'Auroch,' he said, proudly. The spear had buried through, but the coat had absorbed most of the power of the weapon. 'As good as armour.'

Inside the coat, all there was to Kino was a scrawny, wasted body. The thick gansey and woollen undershirt had clearly never left his body in recent memory. Rian rolled the fabric up his back, asked him to take his right arm out of the sleeve and examined the wound. It wasn't deep.

'You'll not die of this. But you look to me like you need to eat more, if you can.'

'I just need to drink more.' He reached for the flask. She stopped him.

She dipped a cloth overboard and washed the wound with seawater, then dried it and smeared a little yarrow butter into the cut. 'Do you have a clean shirt?'

He laughed at her and shouted to Manigan, 'Did you hear that, Man? Do I have a clean shirt?' Finding this a hilarious idea, he chuckled away while she contrived a bandage of wool pulled from the fleece she had stuffed into her boots and a bit of rope tied around his chest to keep it in place.

'If you can keep that clean it'll heal no problem,' she said. 'Your right shoulder will be stiff, but you're lucky, your coat saved your life.'

'Proper little healer, aren't you?' Kino grabbed the flask and took a third, glugging swallow.

'That's enough,' Manigan shouted. 'If you let him he'll drink the boat dry.'

She couldn't imagine how he could pour so much of the drink down his throat. His eyes were already glazed, and before long his head was drooping with sleep.

FAIR ISLE

The sun was dipping into a bank of cloud on the western horizon, a glowing fireball turning a stripe of sea the colour of blood and scattering fish scales of pink across the sky. A fresh breeze blew now and the boat coursed over the swell. A group of dolphins emerged abreast and ahead of them, leaping from the sea in graceful curves.

Ròn shrank further and further into the distance behind them as Manigan and Badger gave Bradan full sail and let her fly. Badger handed around some bread. Manigan was watching the sky and scanning the horizon.

'See that.' He pointed to the uppermost pink streaks across the sky. 'They're travelling north, fast. Some big weather out there is my guess. I'd rather not get caught up in it. Once we're out of sight of Queen Bitch we'll bear south a bit while we've got the chance, try to make landfall before the big one hits.'

'You can read the sky.' Rian had heard stories about great sea-farers who could find their way across oceans by understanding stars and clouds.

'None better than Manigan.' Badger offered some more bread. 'That's why I'm here.'

'It's obvious if you know what you're looking for, and I've been looking all my life. The sea is home to me. I know her moods and I know how to tell if she is building up to a tantrum. My grandfather taught me well.'

'He was the Walrus Mutterer before him. Do you remember I

told you? Eat man, I'll take the tiller.' Badger pushed Manigan off his perch at the stern.

'You told me about Great Aunty Onn. I don't remember a grandfather.'

Manigan smiled. 'She was the one who taught my grandfather, her little brother, the muttering. And if you've heard her story you know everything there is to know about me.' He shuffled Rian along the chest and sat beside her. 'But I still don't know nearly enough about you.'

To steer his curiosity away, Rian said, 'Ussa told me you are her cousin. So is she granddaughter of the Mutterer?'

'No.' Manigan settled himself, hands on thighs, right shin touching her left shin. She felt the intimacy of his body as if they were magnets drawn together. 'Ussa is the bastard daughter of the bastard son of Don Sevenheads, so called because of how he ringed his house with the skulls of his seven most recent murders. Except he didn't call them murders. He called them honour killings, though there was never any honour in them. He was a legendary monster and she has his ruthlessness in her blood. No. We're kin through our grandmother, Amoa, the daughter of a druid in Belerion. Do you know where that is? I should take you there, deep south, loads of places to hide out. Anyway, he was appointed Merlin, chief druid, and he was always out and about, so my granny was raised and educated by the Keepers. You know who they are? The women who keep the spirits. I guess her mother was one of them, though she said she felt she had many mothers and they were all in service to the One Mother. More mothers than she knew what to do with. What were you asking? Oh yes, Ussa.

'The way she came to exist is a story of violence from start to finish. Our granny was raped by Sevenheads when she was thirteen and she was so ashamed she ran away and had the child alone in hiding. But when the Spirit Keepers found her it all came out about the rape, and when Sevenheads discovered it was a boy he took the child and raised him in his own household, though from what I ever knew of him my uncle Donnie had a brutal childhood. I never saw him smile and I never knew a greedier person, except for Ussa herself, who was Donnal's only child, by Sevenhead's housekeeper.'

'And your grandmother?'

'She stayed with the Spirit Keepers, and the next son she bore was fathered by the Walrus Mutterer, my grandfather. He was a mild man, and must have been young and handsome then. I think they loved each other but she trusted no man after what Sevenheads had done and he was mostly away on the northern ocean. I think they were handfasted, but she never left the Spirit Keepers and my father and his younger sister Fraoch were brought up among them, as was I, until my grandfather took me to sea.'

'So your mother was a Spirit Keeper too?'

'No. My mother was from the Island of Wings.' He noted her surprise. 'That's how I know your language. I have kin there and on some of the small islands south of there. My father went to sea with my grandfather and one time when they were sheltering from bad weather, he met a beautiful blue-eyed island girl. Well, he was smitten and she was smitten back and when they set off back to sea she joined them in the boat and sailed with them. They had a couple of winters on her island home. My father adored her people and we were always made welcome by them. I never knew her but she was as tough as any man they say, though not tough enough to survive giving birth to me. I was taken to the Spirit Keepers and Fraoch brought me up alongside her son, Gruach, who you've met, and his wee girl.'

There was pain in his face, a tightening around his eyes, though he seemed to be trying to contain it.

'Gruach the smith?'

'Aye. His daughter was named after her grandmother, my aunt, blessings be on her.'

'Fraoch is your niece, then? Nearly. Your cousin's daughter.'

'Aye. She's a bonny lass, a bundle of fun if you catch her right, though she's too much under her aunty Ussa's influence for my liking.'

Rian reflected on all this information. It made sense of a lot, not least why Gruach travelled with Ussa so readily. They were all part of one family. And it helped her see why Fraoch had betrayed her to Ussa, although she didn't want to think about that. Besides, she wanted Manigan to keep talking.

'What was it like to be brought up by the Spirit Keepers?'

'Awful. I ran away. You see, I know how you feel. I took off on my Grandfather's boat after...' He stalled and turned his face away but not before she had seen pain in his eyes. 'It wasn't a safe place. I mean, it was supposed to be safe, but nothing can stop a greed like Ussa's.'

'I don't understand.'

'You must remember that.' He turned to her and his blue eyes bored into hers. 'One day maybe I can tell you everything. I trust you, I don't know why. Bronze and amber, and now me. It feels portentous.'

She frowned. He wasn't making any sense all of a sudden, after having drawn her into his story. Badger had warned her about him. Was this how he spellbound people, carrying them along with lucid words, then bamboozling them in a fog of phrases that didn't make sense? She didn't know which question to pursue, and the moment to ask was gone.

He pointed off to the south west ahead of them. 'Land, thank the Goddess. We'll reach the Fair Isle by night time.'

She could only make out clouds, but they were careering along, the wake of the boat hissing behind them.

'See the birds?' He pointed to the south. Sure enough, there were more birds than before, especially ahead of the boat. Guillemots in rafts of four or five birds were floating in the water. As a gannet soared across the bow, its eggy eye caught Rian's and she followed its flight. Its black-tipped wings tilted, and she wished that she could stretch out her arms and glide with it, up and away. It stalled, tilted towards the sea, tucked its wings into its body and plummeted like a spear, hitting the water with a splash and emerging with a fish in its mouth.

Manigan twisted around and swivelled off the seat, tugging at a rope as he went, calling to Badger to adjust the course to the still invisible landmass. The boat turned towards the cloudbank and Manigan and Kino took in the two extra sails, then swung the yard so it was on the other side of the boat. As they hauled the sail taut, Bradan heeled over with the force of the wind. Rian clung to her seat, staring ahead into the distance, watching as the wheeling bird throngs gradually materialised into the shadows of a solid mass and before long, into discernable cliffs.

'The Fair Isle.' Manigan was standing with his back to the mast, scrutinising the approaching island. 'We'll get a safe anchorage here and let the storm go through.'

'But what if Ussa lands here too?' Rian asked.

'I'll worry about that if and when.'

There was no opportunity to worry anyway. At this moment, Kino sprawled across his wooden chest and vomited over the side of the boat.

'Thanks for getting it overboard,' Manigan called cheerfully. 'You're learning.'

Rian rushed over to him, ready to help if she could, but he shook his head and demanded to be left in peace to die.

'You'll not die on my boat, Kino,' Manigan said. 'We'll hit land soon, then you'll be fine.'

He was true to his word. Bradan cruised into a geo between rocky cliffs. Badger jumped off and pulled her into the shore. A smaller boat was moored just off a stony beach on a running mooring.

Manigan threw Badger another rope and they made the boat secure, then set about rolling the sails into neat bundles and coiling ropes, discussing the tide. They concluded that it would soon be on its way out and would leave them high and dry until the morning.

An old man appeared as if from nowhere and Manigan jumped ashore. Rian watched from the boat as they exchanged a few slow phrases with the occasional nod and hand gesture. Then the man turned and headed away up towards the cliff and soon seemed to disappear into it.

Manigan returned. 'The old boy's happy for us to be here overnight and reckons we'll be sheltered enough. It's a slack tide just now, so it's not going to give us too much trouble.'

'Will he give us a roof over our head?' Rian asked.

'Aye, if you want. I'd as soon pitch up on that patch of grass and keep an eye on Bradan but if you're wanting a night with the cows he says we're welcome. I'll go up there and see what the craic is once we're done here.'

Kino heaved himself ashore and began hobbling away in pursuit of the old man. Badger said he would stay with the boat, tilting his head at the cliff with a wry smile.

'Are you coming?' Manigan offered Rian a hand out of the boat. She was still wearing the bulky man's coat and it was awkward. She followed him across the slippery rocks. There was not really a path but worn stones and the occasional built step made the clamber up the side of the geo relatively easy.

Before long they were strolling on springy grass, rich in bedstraw and knapweed, much like the machair of home. Rian felt as if goodness was flowing up out of the ground beneath her with every bouncing step. She stopped, knelt, and put her cheek against a tuft of thrift. Some of the flowers were still pink, mostly dried out. She breathed in the sweet breath of the island, and wanted never to leave.

'Look!' Manigan pointed out holes at the edge of the grass at the top of the cliff.

'Puffin burrows!' Rian was delighted,

'The whole island is riddled. Have you seen them?'

'Yes, we have them at home.' She grinned. 'They make me laugh. They waddle like chubby little people.'

'They are. They're the wisest sea birds. They hold all the knowledge of how to subdue a wicked sea spirit called Drøgha. When you kill them, so the northern folks say, you have to suffer a winter storm in penance.' They walked on. 'Of course, they're tasty and plenty of folk are hungry enough to eat them and so that's why the sea sends Drøgha to kick up trouble for all of us.'

'Just for eating puffins?' Rian was incredulous. Eating puffins couldn't possibly cause a storm.

'I don't know. It's a good story though, isn't it?'

They caught Kino up, and the three of them soon arrived at a little hovel that was the old man's home. They dipped inside and crouched among the wet straw and cow dung. Fish hung drying from the rafters and a peat fire smoked in the centre of the hut floor, in a ring of stones barely functioning as a hearth.

Manigan produced a flask from his pocket and handed it to the old man, who sat on a block of driftwood, two briny eyes in a bundle of rags. He slugged and shuddered and the tide rose in his eyes. He handed the flask back to Manigan who lifted it to his mouth, drank, shook his head like a dog and grunted, then passed it to Rian. She shook her head, so he passed it over to Kino and began talking to the old man in a dialect Rian found hard to follow. It was full of words from the Cat Isles and as she tuned in she found it made some sort of sense.

The talk was of storm and fish, the sea animals and spirits, the weather of the short summer, when the puffins departed their nests, the stranding of a whale last winter, the difficulty of finding enough driftwood to keep a fire burning, the labour of peat cutting. The old man pointed proudly to some iron tools in the rafters, then got to his feet and indicated Manigan should go outside. Rian followed. Round the back of the hut was a pile of peat turfs and Manigan was encouraged to help himself to several. He handed a few to Rian. 'Unless you want to sleep with the old boy?'

She shook her head.

Manigan ducked back into the hut and exchanged a few words with Kino, then thanked the old man who returned indoors to enjoy the rest of the flask, no doubt.

Manigan and Rian set off back down to the shore. They chose a spot that was sheltered among the rocks, then set about making it comfortable with a sail and some fleeces and blankets from the boat. There was little in the way of driftwood but up the cliff and over into a west-facing bay they found enough for a blaze. The old man's peats would keep them warm through the night. Manigan produced oatmeal and a cooking pot, and as night came in they sat with full bellies by a warm fire, listening to the sea's dialogue with the rocks.

STONE

Badger's head was soon drooping. He curled up under the sail, snoring like a well-contented dog. From time to time, Manigan would go to check to see how Bradan was lying as the tide dropped away. Once he came back with the bag that had caused all the stramash and sat down by the fire with it. He pulled a flask out of his pocket and offered it to Rian.

'What is it?' she said.

'Honey wine.'

She took a swig. It was delicious.

'Did you look at the stone?' he asked her.

She shook her head.

'You really didn't take a peek?'

'Toma made out it was making him ill.'

'The stone gives what its holder asks of it, mostly. Toma's a wise old boy. He'd not want it.'

'He was holding his head as if it was killing him.'

'Aye, he could probably hear it whispering to him, threatening him. It wouldn't like to be on Ussa's boat, poor thing. Anyway, it's safe again now.'

'You talk about it as if it's alive.'

'You must. It has lived far longer than any mere mortal. When you see it you'll understand. Are you ready? Do you want to see it? I'd like to introduce you.'

'Is it dangerous?'

'That all depends what you ask of it.'

'I don't want to ask it anything.'

'Just wait till you see it.'

He opened the top of the bag and pulled a blanket-wrapped bundle out. He was sitting cross-legged and placed it gently down on his ankles, braced between his knees. Then he opened the plaid. Rian gasped.

A bright-eyed man with long black moustaches was staring at her from Manigan's lap.

Manigan dribbled a few drops of his wine from his cup into a dimple on top of the stone then made a formal introduction in Keltic. 'Master, meet Rian, runaway slave who rescued you from the thieves. Rian, meet the Master Stone.'

'I am honoured,' she said, and bowed her head, trembling.

'You may ask the Master what you will.'

She glanced up, but the strange stone face had knowing eyes like a pig and she had to look away. She shook her head.

'You are wise.' Manigan was smiling gently at her, his face amber in the firelight, his hair gleaming. He was ceremonially still, but not stiff. 'The Master would be happy if you would touch him.'

'No.' Rian recoiled.

'Why not?'

'I can't.'

'Of course you can. The Master requests it.'

'I do not know who he is. I can't.'

'Just touch him. Then you'll know.'

'I can't.'

He shrugged and pulled the cloth around the neck of the stone which stared at her with an expression shadowed and flecked with firelight, all possible moods crossing the face.

'That's all right. The Master understands. I don't, but the Master always does.'

'Why do you call it the Master?'

'That's who this face is called.'

'I'm scared of it.'

'Him.'

He bent his head down to look at the stare. 'She's scared of you.' He turned the face towards him. A pinched, smiley little boy was now beaming at her from the stone.

She gasped again.

'Who's that?'

'The Boy. He's not scary, is he?'

She pulled her knees up to her chin. 'How can it be a boy as well?'

'He is triple. Like the Goddess.'

Then he turned the stone again, and the boy was replaced by a wizened visage, lined and full of gentleness, with penetrating eyes. She was spellbound by it and could not move her gaze.

'The Sage. It is rare to see all three faces, but you're special. It is conventional to greet this one.'

'I am honoured to meet you.'

The lines on the old face seemed to move in the firelight, as if it was smiling with an expression of deep peace. There was something about it that reminded Rian of Danuta, and she felt the terrible longing for her that she had had all the time when she was first captured. The pain of missing her was just as sharp as ever. She had simply found ways of shoving it aside, ignoring it, avoiding any thought of her. But here she was. The love in the old face before her was sharp as a dagger.

'You have asked him something difficult,' Manigan murmured.

'I didn't realise I was asking anything.'

'Your eyes are always full of questions.'

'I must go home. Danuta needs me.' She didn't understand where this came from, but looking into that old face she was certain of it. 'And I have more to learn from her that no-one else can learn.' It was as if someone else was speaking for her, a part of herself that had been silent since her capture, cowed and angry.

'Well, you're on your way.'

He said it in such a matter of fact manner that Rian was

surprised. He looked relaxed there, cross-legged, leaning his back slightly against the rock behind him, as if he sat out on shores beside fires all the time. Perhaps he did.

'Do you have anything else to ask him?'

Her mind was full of questions but she shook her head. The stone was alien to her again, after its brief moment of kinship. Would home ever be the same again after what Drost had done?

Manigan smoothed the plaid out, thanked the stone head formally but simply in the Keltic manner, with the 'you' reserved for an elder. Rian repeated it. He nodded, wiped dry the dimple in its crown, folded the blanket over it and slid it into the bag.

Now it was hidden again, she could relax. 'Why do you have the stone?'

He put the bag down on his right side and stretched his legs out. It started to rain, spitting into the fire.

'It's a long story. You want to hear it?'

By way of an answer, Rian put another piece of driftwood onto the fire, another bigger piece across it, and then a third diagonally across the two.

'Sit here.' He indicated she should sit beside him. He arranged the sail to cover them from the rain. It flapped in the rising wind but they were mostly sheltered by the rocks.

'It was put into my grandmother's safekeeping. The one I told you about, the granny I share with Ussa.'

The fire was lapping around the wood, greedy and warm, and as the flames danced, his soft voice unravelled the story of the stone.

'My Aunt Fraoch told me that her mother Amoa was given the stone by her father, the Merlin, after he had a dream that came true. It was a dream of destruction, of the death of the old king, the king's son and heir, and the baby grandson, all on one night. They were the Bear Clan, although they never called themselves that as they had a superstition about never using the name of the animal. It's a bit like us and the walrus: when we are hunting, it is considered disrespectful to call him that. Imagine if someone said to you, 'Hey, human.' It's not nice, is it?'

'What do you call them?'

'Oh anything polite. Whiskery One, or Mister Tusker, or just Old Gentleman. Anyway, back to the Clan of the Furry Paws. The bloodline of the kings and queens ran back to the earliest days when bears and humans shared the land and some women chose to live with the great bears of the forest. They bore children who had the strength and the bravery of mighty animals and grew up to be hunters and heroes, protectors of the people. They were a wild clan. They lived in timber halls in the woods and in caves in the mountains. They had no slaves and no farmland. They lived only on the wild foods of the forests and hills, the lakes and rivers and seashore, and their livestock grazed in the woods and were as wild and dangerous as the folk: huge hairy cattle and goats, tough little ponies and bristly pigs with great tusks.

'Now these people held many secrets. They might have been wild but they were clever too and they found treasure in the mountains. They protected the little people who mined gems and who sifted gold out of the water flowing in streams, and the little people paid them for that protection. So the bear people were wealthy as well as powerful. They kept hoards of riches in caves watched over by dragons. No-one had ever been rich like that before.

'For many generations, as well as gold and silver, the cleverest of the bear people worked with copper and tin, and fostered their children with dwarves in the mountains to learn their skills in weapon-making and bronze-working. These smiths were a mighty tribe within the clan and the kings always made sure to be fair to them, granting them the land they needed to mine their minerals and woods sufficient to fire their forges. They encouraged the charcoal burners to work with them and they always rewarded them for their crafty skills with feast and gifts of cattle. So the smiths were content with the bear kings and accepted them as patrons and protectors.

'It was a grand alliance of hunters, herders, fishers, foresters, miners and smiths that the bear kings ruled over, and there was peace in the land. Everyone shared in the plenty.

'Now, the greatest of the kings was Ban, and that sounds like it must be a good thing, to be the greatest. But the thing about greatness is that it has a tendency to try to increase itself. It's in its nature. The great want to be greater. Every tree wants to grow, but one day a storm comes to every great tree and blows it down.

'That's what happened to Ban,' said Manigan. 'Put another stick on the fire.'

Rian did so and put over it the two ends of one of the bigger sticks that had burned through in the middle, so once again a triad of wood was burning. She sat back and he passed her the wine. She took a swig and passed it back.

'You tend the fire just like my Aunt Fraoch used to do. Three sticks at a time.'

'That's the only way I know. That's how the fire spirit likes it.'

'What happens if you give it four? Or two?'

'Two leaves it hungry and grumpy and four makes it work too hard and get upset.'

'Is that so?'

The rain was getting heavier, spitting in the fire, and the sea outside the geo was roaring, but in their sheltered spot only a breeze tugged at the smoke and swirled it about, sometimes in their faces, sometimes away.

Badger stirred in his sleep.

Rian asked, 'Did what happened to Ban have something to do with the stone?'

Manigan chuckled. 'Sorry. My stories take a while sometimes. I'll get to the stone eventually. Where were we? Oh aye, Ban and the troubles. Do you not know all about this?'

'No. I've never heard of Ban.'

'I'm surprised. I thought all the old women told that legend. I'd expect your granny, what was her name?'

'Danuta.'

'Aye, I'd have thought she'd tell it.'

'Is it just a story then? I thought you were telling something about your great-grandfather, the Merlin, not just an old legend.'

'What do you mean, just an old legend?' He elbowed her in the side in mock outrage. 'Anyway, this happens to be what my old granddad Mutterer called a true legend. If you still want to hear it, of course.'

He pouted.

'I'm sorry. Put me out of my misery. What happened to Ban?'

'Is it annoying you that it goes on so long?'

'No. I like it.'

'Really?'

'Yes. It's like being with the women at a ceremony. I love long stories.'

'Oh, I remember the women's ceremonies. When I was a boy I sat by the fire with the Keepers. I loved it. Then they said I had to stop being there and go with the druids, but they never told such good tales, I didn't think.'

'The druids are supposed to be full of good stories.'

'Aye, well. Some of them, maybe. Aye, right enough. There was the old Merlin, they called him Riabach, he could yarn all night long, and there's Uill Tabar, only one arm and hairy as a horse, but he tells a tale well, and he makes me laugh, he makes us all laugh, and he rhymes. It's the rhymes that are the funniest, to be honest. Are you all right?'

Rian turned and was looking at him as if he had struck her.

'What did you call him? The funny one?'

'Uill Tabar. Why?'

'Nothing.'

'Come on. You look like I've offended you.'

'No. No, you haven't.'

'You're sure?'

She struggled inside herself, wanting to tell him. She felt instinctively she could trust him with her life, that there would never be anyone whom she could trust more deeply, but this was the one big secret she possessed. The name Danuta had told her was like a secret talisman, an unspoken mantra. If she said it, would she unwittingly destroy its magic? But if she never shared it with anyone, how could she use its power? And Manigan knew the man whose name it was. Until now Uill Tabar had been a fiction, no more than a label. It could have been no more than the name of a character in a made-up story, but Manigan knew him as a man, hairy and one-armed and funny. He was vivid to her and she knew suddenly it might be possible to meet him, to talk to him, to listen to him, to find out her own story, to discover who she really was, where she had come from. It seemed a possible end to the horror of slavery and the fear of endless running away.

'Are you all right?' He nudged her arm.

'I want to meet him.'

'Who, Uill Tabar? Why?'

She turned and stared at him. 'He knows who I am.'

He returned her wide-eyed gaze. 'Fancy you knowing him.'

'I don't. He's just a name. I wasn't really sure if he was real, to be honest.'

'Oh, he's very real.'

'Don't tell anyone.'

'You can trust me.' He patted her thigh. 'Thank you for sharing your secret.'

She wondered what she had told him. Perhaps he thought Uill Tabar was her father. Perhaps he was. She tried to picture a hairy one-armed comedian druid as her father and was dismayed. If the name had meant anything to her it had been of a noble, dignified keeper of lore, not some ugly figure of fun. And the secret that he was holding was supposed to unlock a mystery about her people and her role in the world, not merely be a grubby declaration of paternity by some drunken druid.

'I'll look forward to your meeting. There'll no doubt be a good story in it, knowing Uill. If he's keeping it for you, you can be sure of that.'

She wasn't sure she wanted to know anymore. 'What about Ban? And the stone.'

'You really want to hear that old tale? It's late. We should sleep.'

'No, I want to know first, about the stone, then sleep.'

'You'll sleep no easier once you know.'

'I'll not sleep at all if I don't.'

He waggled his foot towards the fire. 'Three more?'

She chose another stick. Another of the big branches had burned through and its two ends could be placed onto the centre of the fire. The three-way cross complete, she sat back.

'The stone was made by King Ban's smith, whose name I can't remember now so we'll call her Red. She had made a great discovery: she had learned how to make iron, to take a brown ore found in the bogs and smelt it with all her magic to create a metal harder than any we had ever known. It was such a powerful new magic that the chief druids knew it had to be dangerous. Something needed to be brought into the world to counter that danger. And so they gave Red a stone and told her to use tools made from the new magic metal and see what came from the block, then listen to it until it spoke to her and whatever it said would be the right thing to do.

'But the King was greedy and he said to Red, you can do what you like with that stone. But I want you to make me the greatest sword you can out of that new metal and if you don't, be sure I'll know about it and you'll meet the sharp end of my armoury.

'So Red was frightened and went away back to her forge. She worked first on the tools for working the stone: a chisel, a hammer and a spike. She made the spike as strong as she could, the chisel as sharp as she could, and the hammer as heavy as she could. Then, sitting beside the forge, she began to shape the block of granite they had given her. It was spherical and roughly the size of a head, so she thought perhaps a face might come, and she began working above a bit of a bulge on one side. Soon it was clear to her that this was a nose, with two eyes above it. Once they were looking at her, she set about a little smiling mouth and before long it was a boy's face.

'It said to her, "Red, I'd like dimples in my cheeks, then turn me round so I can watch the fire, and you'll find my Master."

'She did just this, and sure enough, around the side of the stone was another likely bulge, so she ground away above it until eyes appeared. They glared at her until she'd chiselled out the mouth, so the stone Master could speak.

'"Red, I would like two fine moustaches, then turn me round so I can watch the door. Your work's not yet done."

'So she did as she was told and on the remaining side of unworked stone she saw the trace of a dint, where a mouth might be. She took the chisel to it and the mouth spoke.

'"Red, I am old and tired, be gentle with my eyes."

'Red very carefully chipped away above the mouth, shaping a nose and digging out the curves around the eyes, all the while having to endure the stone mouth moaning as if she was taking the tools to real flesh. The mouth spat out flakes of stone that fell down onto the lips. Eventually an old man looked out from the stone at her and said, "Thank you Red. You have done well. I am the Sage. Now sit yourself down with a dram, and we'll talk."

'And Red said to him, "I was told to make you so I would understand what to do with this new metal I have discovered how to make. It is hard and strong and easy to shape."

'And this was when the Sage made the first of the Stone's prophecies.' Manigan pressed his hands down on his thighs, then bent his legs up, pulling his knees to his chin. 'But I think the rest of the tale must wait for another day. There's someone coming.'

Rian looked away from the fire and tried to make out any sign of a person. 'Where?'

He gestured up the geo, but she couldn't see anything beyond the flames except stars and the gloom of the cliff. 'I can't see anything.'

'Nor me. But smell him!'

She wasn't conscious of any smell except the woodsmoke and, when she thought about it, the tang of seaweed. But Manigan was right, and soon even over the roar of the sea she heard a crunch of footsteps on pebbles and a figure appeared among the rocks beside them.

A deep voice spoke in the strange dialect that the old man had used earlier. 'Are you the one that knows how to deal with tooth-walkers?'

'I am. Have a seat by the fire. We're glad of your island's shelter.'

Standing just outside the light of the fire, an odd flicker illuminating parts of him, the figure was more ghost than man. A dark gleam of a sealskin coat, a bulk of a body, a hairy head. Rian wondered if he was selkie or human.

'There was a heap of them on the island of scales. Two days ago and for ten days before that, and we couldn't catch one of them.'

'They're wily enough.' Manigan scratched his head, peering out at the man.

'There's a drunk up at the Old One's bothy who says you can cast a spell on them.'

'I know the muttering.'

'How's that?'

'I was taught by my grandfather, Alrith.'

'Alrith.' He spoke the name as if it was not just familiar, but awe-inspiring. 'My father sailed with him once. Said it was the most dangerous sea voyage he ever did. They went up to where the sea freezes.'

'Aye.'

Rian could see Manigan tensing, as if to spring up or fight. 'And you are?'

The man remained just outside of the fire's light. Manigan's hand was on the knife at his belt.

'I'm Jan. They call me the Bonxie. If you're willing to help us catch some of the sea-beasts we'll be going as soon as the wind eases.'

'It's already easing.'

'Aye. Are you on?'

Manigan kept his hand firmly gripping his weapon. 'Will you sit by the fire?'

'I will not. I came here to ask you a question and I'll go when I've heard your answer.'

'What's in it for me?'

'The ivory of any animal you kill.'

'You know it is an offence to the Goddess to kill more than one.'

'We'll kill them all if we can.'

'Then you're not only greedy but stupid.'

There was a glint of metal from the shadows, but the dark man said nothing.

Manigan took a deep breath. 'I will come. But you must know only one of our toothy friends will die; I will do it in the correct way. If you kill others the curse of Sedna will be on you and you will drown. I will take his tusks, the heart, the penis and the belly skin. You can have the rest. Do you understand?'

'We'll go at first light if the wind lets us get our boats out of the geo.'

'Do you understand my conditions?'

'I heard you.' The man melted away into the night, his feet audible on stones for a little way then drowned out by sea roar.

Manigan shuddered. 'Better get some shut eye.' He turned to Rian. 'I'm sorry about the story. I think the time isn't right now to carry on. There'll be another time.' He reached over and touched her cheek with his finger tips, looking intently at her, then pulled one end of the sail around him and curled himself into a sleeping ball.

Rian sat staring at the fire, wondering what she was going to do next, then yawned and made the fire safe by pushing all the unburned ends in among the embers and piling on the peats. It glowed and the peat smoke made her eyes smart with homesickness as she settled herself down to sleep under the other corner of the sail.

But sleep would not come easily. The dark man haunted her, and Manigan's matter of fact talk of killing the sea monster. What did that mean? Questions torrented over her. How was she going to get home? Was there anywhere else she could go? And Ussa and Pytheas, where were they? Had they given up the chase or were they still on their tail? Of course, because of the stone, Ussa would never give up. She still didn't know why Manigan had the stone and Ussa wanted it so badly. In fact, all of Manigan's story-telling had left her with nothing but loose ends, threads half unravelled and tangled, with no conclusions. From what Badger had said she had expected Manigan to be a great teller of tales, but instead she'd heard only a jumble of half-told histories and some bits of myth.

HUNT

'Porridge?' Rian was nudged awake by Manigan. It was still dark and the fire was low. 'We need to eat before we go.'

He tugged the sail away from the rock, her only shelter from the rain, and folded it. It was calmer now, though the sea's roar had barely muted. She woke up the fire while he fetched fresh water. He cooked up some oatmeal and although the fire warmed her up a bit, the hot food made her feel sick.

Bradan was almost afloat again. The three of them heaved her back down into the water and as they did so, Kino and the old man appeared down the cliff. Kino stumbled groggily aboard and the old man helped with ropes, pushing the boat off.

They rowed out slowly to the mouth of the geo. Dawn was breaking over the ocean to the east. There were breaks in the clouds. A gull escorted them out to sea then soared away as if bored by their slow progress. The boat's rocking made Rian nauseous.

Around the headland they saw two other boats, lolling in the waves. Rian's guts tensed in fear that one of them was Ròn. But Manigan seemed relaxed, raising an arm in greeting to them. With gestures it became clear that they would head south, and they raised and tightened the sail. The wind was north-westerly now and they made easy progress.

Rian wasn't the only one feeling sick. Kino was the first to hang over the side of the boat, but only just. After she had thrown up, she felt a bit better, but then had to endure endless jokes from Badger about her drinking habits.

Within half a day they sighted islands ahead. The front boat headed past the first of the archipelago and into the calmer water between two islands. Soon a long spit of lower land emerged. On a beach, a clump of dark bodies could easily have been taken for boulders, but all the pointing from the men on the other boats made it clear that these were the target animals.

The boats grouped together and dropped sails. Manigan took an oar, and with Kino on the other, they brought Bradan alongside one of the other boats. Jan Bonxie, the dark man from the other night, was on board.

Manigan called to him. 'Best stay out here. Don't get any closer or you'll spook them. I'll go around the back of the spit to land. See the big guy a bit apart? That's my gentleman. The rest will hit the water at some pace, don't worry about it, just stay back and let them go.'

'We'll do what we'll do,' said Jan.

Rian felt sick. It seemed obvious to her that he had no intention of following the instructions but Manigan seemed to think Jan hadn't understood.

'The guard, he's my target. If he heads for the water, I should've wounded him, and if I have then I'll signal to you. Go after him and take him out by spear. Otherwise you shouldn't need your weapons. Is that clear?'

Jan shrugged and Manigan took this as assent. As far as Rian could tell he didn't seem to doubt the man, but the two boats were bristling with ferocious-looking spears. Jan himself had a vicious hook with a barb at the point. There was no way she could see them floating off-shore, keeping this armoury idle while Manigan took all the glory of the kill.

Nonetheless, Manigan seemed focused on his plan and pushed off, allowing the current to drag them along the length of the spit. He set Kino and Badger, with surprisingly few complaints, to the oars. While they manoeuvred down the shore and pulled up onto the beach, Manigan rummaged in his chest, pulling out two knives in scabbards, an ugly spike with a catching barb at the end and a small, round, walrus-skin shield. One knife went down his sock, the other he tucked into his belt. He slung the spike on its strap across his back. Finally, he sheathed his long dagger and strapped its belt around his hips so it hung down his left thigh.

He indicated where they should hold the boat and wait for him. The tide was dropping, so they would need to be careful she didn't get grounded on the sand.

As the boat nudged the shore, Manigan grabbed his shield and jumped down from the bow onto the beach. He splashed the few steps up to dry ground then fell to his knees. At first he seemed to be paralysed with fear. He remained on his knees and hands, head down. One hand went to his dagger, then back to the ground. Then he sat up and rocked back on his heels and made hand gestures – open palm up to the sky, out in front, back down to his weapons. Rian guessed he was chanting some kind of ritual prayer and wished she could hear the words. He turned to the boat and signalled for them to shift away to the end of the spit where he had told them to wait for him.

Badger and Kino rowed the boat a few strokes out into the current, then allowed it to drift along until it was where Manigan had indicated they should wait at the end of the spit. From here, beyond a low rocky outcrop, they could see the heap of bodies, slumped in sleep. They looked just like big seals, except Rian had never seen seals in such a cluster. It was hard to make out one animal from the others, they seemed to be lying on top of each other. It was impossible to tell how many of them there might be from this distance; a dozen at least. One animal was a little apart from the rest and it kept lifting its head, looking around. As their boat scrunched up onto the beach and Badger jumped out to hold it against the current, the big creature seemed, for a while, to stare right at them.

From here they could see Manigan crawling towards the walruses and the two other boats watching from just off the end of the spit, drifting on the current and pushed out by the wind, then using oars to return to where they had a better view.

Everyone was watching Manigan's progress towards the herd of animals. It was painful. As slow as the tide. He edged his way across the spit to approach them from downwind so they would not be able to hear or smell him. The sound of the waves would disguise his footsteps. How close he could get undetected would all depend on how sharp-eyed their guard was.

For what felt like ages Manigan did not move at all. Then he took a creeping step forwards. This was followed by another long pause.

After a while, Rian tuned into what he was doing. He froze as the guard lifted its head, scouting around, watching the boats or listening or sniffing for a scent of danger. It knew there was something happening, that was clear. Rian could see its fearsome white tusks jutting out. But eventually, the creature relaxed, allowing its head and fangs to slump forward onto the sand, and Manigan would move tentatively towards it until it stirred again.

The breeze was fickle. One minute they were being pushed into the spit and the next, Badger was struggling to keep the boat from drifting away. The shifting air carried the walruses' smell, like winter cattle mixed with fish, which reminded Rian of the scent of early spring fields when they spread dung among the sea wrack gathered from the beach and lugged up over the winter to fertilise the ground. When the wind turned, Rian worried that the walruses would be able to smell them too.

Manigan crept nearer to the guard and some of the heap of animals stirred. Flippers lifted. Then they, too, slumped back into relaxation. Manigan eased closer. He was moving now like a walrus himself, hugging the ground, so close he must almost be able to touch the guard.

Rian saw that Badger on the shore was intent on the scene as well. Kino was sitting, elbows on knees, hands propping up his head. He gave a yawn of utter boredom.

Rian looked back to Manigan but he had vanished.

Panic seized her. Had he been crushed? She couldn't breathe. Don't let him be a corpse lying squashed under a stinking sea-beast. He was the only man she had ever liked to sit close and listen to, the only one who had ever treated her with respect. He had rescued her. And now he might be dead on a beach!

She forced herself to scour the land for some sign of him. He couldn't just vanish. It wasn't possible, not now that everything depended on him.

She convinced herself she could see him lying flattened among tangled seaweed beside the guard. She looked for a long time and absolutely nothing happened. One of the other walruses waved a flipper in the air, twisting it as if wringing out a cloth, then flopping it back onto its chest.

The boat wallowed in the shallows. Rian's stomach churned and she fought the nausea.

But Manigan was not dead. A thud of tusks against a shield wrested Rian from her thoughts, and there, where everything had been as still as an engraving, was commotion. The guard reared up and the floppy heap of walruses was transformed into a storm of heavy bodies charging towards the sea, sand flying. The guard bellowed. Rian saw a blade and Manigan on his feet, dancing out of reach of the roaring monster.

At the far end of the beach, sand sprayed from flippers, then the crush of grunting animals hit the water with an explosion of splashing smacks and spray. Waves jabbled out from the foaming confusion.

Badger was soon battling Bradan, which seemed to be trying to escape too, tugging into the baffled sea. The two other boats rocked and danced, their oars in the water, ploughing towards the frightened walruses whose heads bobbed like barrels, stretching themselves up to see what was happening on the spit.

Rian was intent on Manigan, though Bradan's rocking made it hard to get a clear view. She saw a weapon lifted high – the spike, perhaps – and then the boat lurched and she couldn't tell if it had struck. She saw him bend to pick something up then defend himself from the huge white tusks with his shield, staggering backwards with the impact. Another wave slapped Bradan and she nearly toppled, grabbing onto the mast.

She looked back. Manigan was running down the beach but not towards them. He was shouting and gesticulating with both arms, his shield and his hand gesturing a halt, his head shaking. She saw the open mouth and over the waves she heard his voice in a bellow of rage. 'Don't kill them!' She remembered the curse he had laid and a shudder went through her.

The walrus was not following Manigan. It lay, motionless. She did not know how, but he must have overcome it.

The men on the two boats were intent on slaughter. Spears hit the water, splashing, and were hauled back in on their ropes to be tried again. Then one struck and stuck and stayed, and the men on that boat, the smaller of the two, went at the kill with spikes and blades. The sea turned red with gore.

The bigger boat soon did the same. Two spears hit almost simultaneously. Jan Bonxie hollered instructions as he hauled the rope in and a great body rose, thrashing, beside the bow. At the stern another harpoonist struggled to fasten his line as it pulled through his hands with the strength of the harpooned animal, diving away to escape capture.

The activity galvanised Kino into speech. 'They shouldn't do that. The curse'll be on them. It's sacrilege. He told them. He told them clear as daylight. Barbarians. Who are they anyway? Do you know?' He tossed the question at Rian and stared at her furiously as if they might be something to do with her.

She shrugged. 'No idea.'

'The old boy said they're not Fair Islers. Bunch of pirates.'

She looked for Manigan. He had turned his back on the water and returned to the guard, kneeling beside it in what looked like prayer. She couldn't take her eyes off him. The contrast between the mayhem on the water and his still figure was mesmerising.

There was shouting and splashing from the water, thumps of something making contact with wood, more shouting, but she ignored it. Manigan's head was bowed.

For a long moment she watched him, then he lifted himself to standing in one smooth action and turned to face them. He gave a signal, a 'come' gesture, that seemed to switch Kino into a well-rehearsed drill. He started gathering things from chests and around the boat – a hank of rope, an iron saw, two big hessian sacks and some other metal tools with blades at odd angles. 'You'd better get ready,' he said to Rian. 'Get a knife.'

Badger pulled the boat in and tied a rope around a huge driftwood trunk. He was trying to hold the bow steady. 'What are they doing? The curse'll be on them. Idiots.'

'Bastards.' Kino had the rope around his shoulder, the tools bundled with the sacks.

Rian found a big knife and showed it to him.

'And fire,' he said. 'He might want a fire.'

She found some kindling in Badger's chest and stuffed it into a pocket with her fire pouch.

Rian looked quickly towards the other boats. Around them, walruses bobbed about, looking startled, as if trying to make sense of the water-borne threat. One big, noble head pushed up from the surface, showing its great fangs, and turned its bemused gaze on the smaller of the two boats. A spear landed, digging into the flesh at the base of its head. The big creature's mouth opened in a roar of pain and outrage. It smacked its head down into the water and drove its body full tilt into the boat, then dived. The huge curve of its back thumped the hull. With a twisting hand-wave of its flippers, it was below. The vessel tipped and the harpoonist fell overboard, shrieking and flailing. The boat lurched, heeling dangerously onto its side, men toppling. It righted again, but for now their attack on the walruses was thwarted by a scramble to bail water.

The bigger boat was bucking as the men in two groups

struggled with thrashing walruses at each end of the vessel.

'Let's go!' Kino was clambering over the bow with his equipment.

Badger steadied the boat while Rian bundled up her big coat and jumped down into the shallows. Hitting the cold water up to her knees, and a splash of a wave up her thigh, she shuddered.

Badger put a hand on her shoulder. 'Try not to be scared.'

She looked up at him, aware she must be wide-eyed and pale, desperately wanting to get back onto what felt like the safety of the boat but also pulled to be with Manigan, helping him to do whatever it was they needed to do.

She said nothing, just tried a smile.

'Do exactly what he says,' said Badger. 'No questions.'

Kino was watching the stramash. 'Manigan's going to kill them. Sacrilegious bastards.'

'He'll not fight unless he has to.' Badger allowed a wave to lift the boat. 'It's the walruses they've got to worry about.'

'Serves them right if they drown,' said Kino, marching off up the beach.

Rian carried herself carefully up onto dry land, trying to avoid the kindling getting wet and ignore the ruckus around the two boats. She kept her eyes on Manigan. Kino had rushed up and dumped his tools and was talking animatedly.

As Rian arrived, Manigan lifted his hand and cut Kino off mid-expletive. 'Mother Earth, Father Sea and all the spirits are watching. We must make clear our separation from those people. We'll have to try to do the Old Gentleman the honour he deserves as swiftly as we can and go. I have said the sacred words. There's more ceremony to be done but we can't do it here with that going on.' He gestured behind him to the sea. 'I'll not leave the body to be wasted. Some of it can stay for the birds and crabs but we'll take what we can.' He turned to Rian. 'It'll be hard work. I would normally spend three days here and work with a fire, but we cannot. Not now.'

Rian took in the carcass. It was huge, far bigger than a cow. Its monstrous body was covered in thick leather which appeared cured. It was latticed with scars, a record of the old warrior's life: warts and parasites, injuries and battles. It lay half on its side. A gaping wound in its neck pooled blood. Manigan had already made a slit down one side of its body.

'Can you skin an animal?' he asked her. 'It's like a cow, only with more fat.'

She nodded.

'Don't worry if it's not well done. Do the best you can.' He held one of the strange-shaped blades and showed her how to use it to prise the skin off, little by little.

She took the blade and tried it herself. 'It's like a pig.'

'Maybe, I've never skinned a pig.'

Kino had taken a saw and was attacking the base of the neck, cutting the huge head off. Manigan went around to the front of the animal and worked on the belly skin as Rian worked towards the spine. Blood was added to the fishy-cow smell; it was almost overpowering.

Her back was turned to the boats but she could hear them still splashing and swearing at the walruses. In front of her, Manigan looked out anxiously as he laboured.

She reached a flipper and before she could ask he said, 'Keep it on. Can you cut the bone?' He gestured to a knife and she tried but lacked the strength to cut it. He told her to stand back and took a short-handled axe and snapped the bone. She carried on skinning.

Once Manigan had peeled back the belly skin, he cut open the stomach which was filled with half-digested clams. He let the juices flow into the sand, then parcelled up the solids. Now the animal smelled of the deep ocean.

'For the ice people, this is the greatest delicacy.' He grinned at her as she grimaced, then went back to his butchery. Kino was still hacking at the neck. The tusks were bloody and half-buried in sand.

After removing the heart, Manigan set about the groin of the walrus and cut out the great penis. Rian found herself blushing as he handled it, her mind conjuring images of him naked. She had to force herself back to her task.

The hide was coming away from the body with what seemed remarkable ease as if the animal was willingly shrugging its skin off. Manigan cut through the bones above the rear flippers so they came attached to the skin, and as she pulled the skin away from the tail he cut chunks of meat off it, shoving them unceremoniously into a hessian sack.

With a grunt, Kino completed the severing of the head and fell back onto the sand.

'Take it to the boat,' Manigan said. 'Will you manage on your own?'

'Aye.' Kino got to his feet and hoisted the massive, gory head up by the tusks onto his back. He staggered off. Where he got the strength, Rian could not imagine. He was transformed from the bleary drunk of their earlier journey as if the walrus-killing woke a different man inside him, all wiry strength and passion.

Manigan saw Rian watching him with amazement. 'Kino lives only for the hunt and the drink. You get used to him.'

Before long, Badger was striding towards them, grumbling. 'Won't leave the head. Crazy man, that's what he is.'

'He's what he is,' Manigan gave him a benign smile. 'We need you anyway. Get your muscles over here, flop him over. Are you ready?'

Rian got out of the way so they could push the big body over. As the men rolled it, she punched away at the skin, which tore off with satisfying rips.

'You're good at that,' Manigan said. 'I should offer you a share. Make you one of the crew. Handy skills even if you are a bit of a weakling. We'd soon toughen her up, wouldn't we Badger?'

She couldn't understand how such a gruesome task as this could make him so cheerful.

As she pulled the hide free of the carcass there was a shout from the shore at the end of the spit. She looked round and saw a man gesturing. There was only one boat visible. She couldn't tell which it was, but it rocked as its crew struggled with ropes and a thrashing walrus almost as big as the vessel. Men were floundering in the water, which foamed red on the shore.

'Don't look,' Manigan chopped away at the flesh on the back. 'Roll the hide up.'

Badger eased the hide out from under the body and helped Rian to fold and roll it into a huge bundle, then tied a rope around and across it. He said not a word, but his frown was deep and anxious.

Manigan stopped chopping and a huge chunk of fatty meat slid from the body. He held the hessian sack open and deftly handled the slab of flesh into it, then slung it over his shoulder and stood up.

'Can you manage that?' He pointed to the other sack into which he'd put the stomach, heart and penis.

She nodded.

'And your tools.' He kicked the long knife towards her. It rattled against the skinning tool. 'Let's go.'

She grabbed the sack and knives.

Badger had pulled the hide bundle onto his back and was looking round.

There was another shout from the shore, this time a clear 'Help!'

Rian looked round at the man but Manigan's voice was fierce. 'Go.'

He put his back to the shore and bowed ceremoniously to the gutted, gory remains of the walrus. 'May the birds take your soul back to the ocean, my friend. We will try to make amends, and make you whole again.'

Rian was rooted to the spot. He shoved her forwards. 'Don't look at them, just go to Bradan.'

She tried to ignore that the boat was too low in the water and that there were men wailing in panic, men floundering in the cold sea, men drowning, surrounded by monster animals. She put one foot in front of the next beside Manigan, lugging the weighty sack, dripping blood. She stumbled across the spit to where Kino waited to help them on board the boat. Badger was ahead. He tossed the hide into Bradan and followed it on board. Kino gave her a shove up over the bow. Manigan and Kino were both in the boat with a single leap and they went straight for the oars, wordlessly turning the vessel and getting into rhythm, facing the sinking and wrecked boats with their frenzied sailors, but rowing determinedly away from them.

Rian sat on a trunk in the stern. She wanted to watch the struggling boat, the men splashing about, making for land, but Badger, who had the tiller, shoved her round so she was facing the two rowers. Kino snatched at each stroke with a brittle whip of his body while Manigan rowed with a rolling ease, yet despite their different builds and movements, the two oars rose and dipped and pulled in synchronicity.

Rage was building in her with each stroke. They were abandoning those men. Surely, no matter what they had done, they couldn't just let them drown?

'Don't be angry,' Manigan said. 'You think we should stay and help them, don't you?'

She looked him in the eye and nodded. How could he look so calm? What kind of man leaves his fellow sailors to drown?

'What if they drown?' Her voice sounded shrill to her. 'And we did nothing to help them?'

'They did not help themselves.'

They were out of the shelter of the spit now and the water was jabbly.

'Sail up.' Manigan abruptly ceased to row. Kino slumped forward over his oar, panting, then took up his position at the bow to help haul the sail. Manigan got to his feet and started untying ropes, then hoisted the sail with long, bouncing tugs on the halyard. He gestured to Rian. 'Here. Pull this.' She pulled and pulled and the small top sail began to inch its way up the rigging. They were under way.

She chanced a glance back. Already the spit was shrinking away. She could see no sign of either boat. There were several people on the land, but they were already too far away to see them clearly. Was that a boat on the shore, or a walrus? It was impossible to tell at this distance. There were sea gulls circling, drawn no doubt by the smell of blood.

She looked ahead. They were heading into the archipelago. Badger and Manigan discussed their course. Both seemed to be familiar with the place.

Kino was whistling a warbling tune as he tidied away the weapons and tools from the hunt, wiping them down and rinsing the blood off the decks with seawater. A well-aimed bucketful saw off a gull trying to investigate the potential for food.

Rian sat back down on the chest and allowed herself to feel sorry for Jan Bonxie and his men. The walrus head looked at her with baleful eyes. She was queasy again and hungry. Thirsty. She got up and without asking took a cup of water from the barrel. It was fresh from Fair Isle and it was cleansing after all that gore and violence. Kino took the cup from her and helped himself as she sat back down.

Where now? She was too angry to ask. Where was Ussa? No doubt she would not give up her pursuit of the stone, so she must be out there somewhere, trying to track them down. She had stupidly thought she would be safe with Manigan but as long as she stayed with him Ussa would be on their tail. Now Jan Bonxie would also be after him if he had survived. Was there no end to the running away?

WHALE ISLAND

They were close enough to an island to smell peat smoke. As they got nearer, a broch surrounded by a huddle of huts came into view. Around the point there was a sheltered shore. The sea calmed suddenly and they took the sail down. Kino consented to row. He and Manigan nudged the boat up to a shingly beach between low, flat rocks where Manigan jumped out, tugged the boat into the shallows then tied the rope around a boulder. He gave instructions for unloading, before leaving them and sprinting away towards the roundhouse.

Rian, grumpy with hunger and tiredness, didn't understand the purpose of this stop. She allowed herself to be ordered about by Badger and Kino but her frustration must have been obvious.

'What's the matter? Are you not feeling well?' Badger took a rope off her and stowed it.

'I'm fine. What are we doing here anyway? Where is this?'

'They call it Whale Island. We've still to thank the Old One so I suppose Manigan's checking out with the wise woman if he can do his ceremony at the temple. It's big power.' He held both hands in front of him as if at a blazing fire to signify some sacred force.

They finished unloading the boat, then sat in a line on the shore.

'You'll be hungry.' Badger took out a leather pouch. 'Emergency rations.' He grinned, handing Rian an oatcake. Kino took one too and they munched without speaking,

It was a warm evening and calmer now. A cormorant cruised

and dived just below them close to the boat, and a sandpiper peeped among the weeds on the rocks. The tide was falling. Soon the boat would be high and dry.

'Manigan'll be ages,' Badger said. 'We might as well have a hot drink. It could be a long night.'

He looked expectantly at Rian. It had become her role, fire-maker. She pulled out her fire pouch, gathered some driftwood and set about making a blaeberry tea, fuming.

Kino produced a flask of alcohol and offered to share it, but Rian refused.

Badger took a slug, and nudged Rian. 'What's getting to you? You don't need to worry on account of Bonxie and them. They got what was coming to them.'

She crossed her legs. 'But how many of them drowned? And we did nothing to help them.'

'Drop it.' Kino lay back on the beach, arms behind his head.

'Once the ceremony's done, you'll feel different.' Badger patted her on the knee and she jerked away.

'It's not right.' She said it under her breath and went to sit round the far side of the fire. Some midges came to bother them so she made the fire smoke until they left them alone.

Badger noticed some fish and put a line out to try to catch them and when one bit, he cooked it on the fire.

The evening grew softer. A curlew haunted a skerry off-shore, mewing, but there were no terns. Was it that time of the year already? Autumn. Away from her people Rian had not thought to keep track and honour the Earth Goddess for her summer gifts. What gifts? The walrus head caught her eye; it seemed to be looking at her, full of woe and misery. What gifts indeed? There were no hazelnuts or acorns forming on these windswept islands, probably no raspberries to gather or birch-slipper mushrooms or any of the good woodland herbs she should have collected for the next year's survival. She thought of what Danuta would be busy with and then heard her voice in her head. 'You keep your eyes open, wherever you are, there's always something useful to gather at this time of year.'

She opened her eyes and noticed the seaweeds on nearby rocks: dulse and sea lettuce, exposed now as the tide dropped. She got up, picked some and ate it raw. It was delicious, salty and crisp, tangy and fresh. She offered it to Badger and Kino. Badger ate some, but Kino screwed up his nose at it and took another drink. Then she laid more weeds out on a rock to dry and wandered up onto the shore to look for herbs.

So Manigan found her, with her hands full of lady's bedstraw, yarrow and clover, and the frown on his brow was erased by a smile.

'So, beautiful, green-eyed witch of the flowers! A bouquet to bless our ceremony to honour the old gentleman of the sea! That would be perfect. I'm sure he would like that.'

She tensed as he put an arm around her shoulder and said, brusquely, 'They're medicines, for drying.'

'Oh, then you must dry them.'

Was he mocking her?

'You're angry.'

'So?'

'Flowers and fury will add something to the ceremony, I'm sure, if you'd be willing to pick more.' His fingers brushed her head. 'And wear some in your hair as well, if you want. The old gentleman would like that. Bring your fire makings too.'

'I always carry it.'

'Of course you do.' He smiled at her as if she had said she carried the sun.

She frowned back.

He scampered off down to the boat and came back with a tough leather box on a belt, which he held out to her.

'I'd like you to have this. It's a firebox. It was my Great Aunty Onn's.'

She shook her head.

'Please. Do me the honour. Do the Old Gentleman the honour. Do yourself the honour.'

He thrust it into her hand and without waiting for a reply, strode over to where Kino and Badger were waiting. 'Right, we're on for the Whale House. Shadow is willing to help. Let's get the old gentleman along there.'

Kino hoisted the huge head onto his back, holding the tusks like handles one on each side of his chest. The whiskery creature seemed to be peering, if sightlessly, over his head.

Badger picked up the bundle of hide and Manigan fetched the three-faced stone in its bag from the boat. He slung the two sacks of meat and organs over his back, seemingly oblivious to their weight and to the dripping blood that smeared him.

Rian put the fire to sleep under stones and tidied up her drying seaweed, tied her bundles of herbs with rushes and set out after them, hanging back, reluctant to be part of it. But she couldn't stop herself from picking flowers as she walked.

Manigan stopped and waited for her. 'Flowers and fire and fury is a heavy load, I see.'

Her mouth was pursed. His acceptance of her anger was infuriating.

'Hopefully once the ceremony's done you'll find forgiveness too. I didn't like what we did today, but I am the Mutterer. I must obey its terms.'

He walked on, catching up Kino and Badger. The three men laboured along the coastal path with their heavy loads. She took a deep breath and followed.

Along the way she gathered a rainbow of autumn flowers: the round bonnets of the old blue man, purple knapweeds, yellow Bridie herbs and golden rods, white yarrows and bedstraws, eyebrights, heathers and clovers. She found meadowsweet still blossoming in a ditch and of course a clutch of her favourites, the bright yellow stars of asphodel from a bog.

Manigan halted them and waited for her again. They all put

down their bundles and stood looking out at the cliffs spattered with bird guano, and the sea pounding their base. Smoke curled from a hut nearby, in a hollow just in from the edge of the craggy shore. Further along the coast, a narrow peninsula was dominated by a turf and stone mound.

Badger wiped his brow and stretched his back.

Kino took a swig from his flask. 'So that's the whale house.'

Manigan nodded. 'Wrong was done today. By other men. Perhaps by us as well. Will you come and seek to make amends?' He turned to Badger.

'I'll come.'

'Kino?'

'We did nothing wrong. It was them.'

'Will you come?'

'Of course.'

'Rian?'

She paused. It was impossible to refuse. 'Yes. I'll come.' She felt power riding in from the sea to meet them. This place was right on the edge of the world.

When they set off again they were in step. Badger beat a rhythm with the handle of his blade on the walrus skin. Rian tentatively joined in with her knife handle on the firebox at her waist.

Manigan began a simple chant of four notes. 'Whale House hear us, Whale House see us, Whale House smell us, Whale House touch us, Whale House know us...' Kino started a counterpoint of 'Tooth-walker, tooth-walker,' which Rian shifted onto with her makeshift drum. And so they arrived in a ceremonial procession at the wall before the peninsula temple where a tall white-haired woman with an elaborate bone neck piece stood, barring the gate.

With a final shout of 'Whale House! Whale House! Whale House!' Manigan drew them to a halt in front of her. He put his sacks down on the ground, opened the smaller and drew out the heart of the animal.

Kino and Badger put down their loads and drew back. Rian retreated with them.

Manigan went up to the woman, knelt down, lowered his head, stretched his two hands out in front of him and offered her the bloody heart. 'Shadow, we bring this noble old gentleman to the Whale House to seek appeasement and to help him find his way back to the ocean cradle where he can be reborn. There has been wrong-doing. We seek to make amends. We bring our beating hearts and we return this one to the spirits. Will you let us in?'

The woman looked down at him with a stern face, staring hard at the three of them and saying nothing. Her eyes raked over them in turn, then returned to Rian.

Rian felt the woman's gaze exploring her like hands, a scrutiny more intense than anything she had experienced even as a slave for sale. This woman was not only sizing her up physically, she was rifling through her soul.

Rian felt she was teetering over a cliff and might fall over the edge. And then she was tumbling, tumbling, but the woman was nodding at her as if this was a good thing, a smile forming on her round face, and Rian found herself on her knees, her armful of flowers all in a scatter on the ground around her.

The woman spoke in a matter of fact voice. 'Come on in then.' Like someone welcoming them into her home, she unfastened the wicker door and opened it wide, and ushered them in through the mouth of the temple.

WHALE HOUSE

The smell was overwhelming: old bones, peat smoke and sweet flowers mixed into a suffocating fragrance. Rian reeled with it as she crossed the threshold and realised that she was the first, so magnetised by the woman she had simply stood up and stepped forward without thinking about it. They were in an antechamber. The woman held her hand out formally in welcome. They bowed to each other as if in a kind of dance.

'I am Shadow. And you are?'

'Rian.'

'Welcome Rian. This is the Temple of the Sea Spirits. We call it the Whale House. We are honoured by your presence. Please do not speak. Put your flowers here.' She gestured to a corner. 'Remove your boots. Any metal on your person, please leave it here.' She patted a chest beside her and watched while Rian removed her fire kit and knife from the pouch at her waist. Shadow touched the former lightly. 'Bring your firebox. If you like, we can use it in the ceremony.'

Rian stood aside to unlace her boots while Manigan was greeted, followed by Kino and Badger who each dragged in their bundles and piled their weapons on the chest. Shadow brought a big wooden trencher onto which Manigan emptied the sack of meat, and a tray on which he arranged the organs from the other sack – heart, stomach, kidneys, liver and penis. The fresh meat stench mingled with the general whiff of the place. Rian felt queasy. Shadow put the meat aside and indicated Manigan should carry the tray.

Shadow told the three men to move ahead further into the Whale House through a passage which they had to bend to enter. They lugged their burdens in. The walrus head seemed to resist Kino's efforts to heave it through the narrow space, so Manigan put down his platter and helped to shove the tusked creature inside, as if forcing it down the gullet into the belly of the whale.

Once they were in, Shadow closed the door. The darkness was almost total but Rian felt the priestess's hand on her shoulder. 'Do you know this ceremony?'

Rian shook her head, not knowing if she could be seen, but Shadow seemed to understand.

'Then I shall lead. Bring the flowers.'

Rian was pleased to be treated with such respect, as though she might know how to lead a ceremony, but she felt dirty. Whenever she had been into sacred spaces or involved in any of Danuta's rituals she had always been made to wash scrupulously beforehand. Yet Shadow didn't seem bothered by the filthy state the four of them were in. She bent down through the passage and shuffled into the space beyond.

As Rian's eyes adjusted she saw they were in a long, corbelled chamber. All down its length were stone stalls like the ribs of a great animal and between them were narrow booths, some curtained off, some open with shelves of vessels of wood, pottery, bark and bone. It was lit by a single tallow lamp beside a central fireplace. In the faint flicker the three men sat down next to each other on a low bench on the left of the hearth.

Almost without words, Shadow got the men to lay the walrus skin out, arranging its flippers and head so that it was like a deflated version of its former self lying on its side. Then she showed Rian a stool to sit on beside the hearth. She took the flowers and dressed the walrus head with them, then placed the internal organs roughly where they belonged inside the hide, lay the penis on the outside and lavished the creature with blossoms.

There were dry sticks beside the hearth and at Shadow's request,

Rian knelt down and began to make a fire. The men returned to their bench, Manigan closest to the walrus, then Kino, then Badger. Shadow lifted a drum down from a hook, placed it on the ground in front of her, took two beaters from around her waist and began to beat slow, deep thuds upon the skin, 'Pum-PUM, pum-PUM', like a heartbeat. Then in a high, haunting voice, she began a tune that flowed into all the crannies of the temple and set goose bumps on Rian's flesh. When Manigan's deep voice joined in, the harmony was exquisite, and the two lines of melody rolled and broke upon each other in mournful waves. Badger and Kino knew the chorus and Rian added her voice, timid at first, the vowels shaping themselves more clearly with each repetition.

The fire grew and flames danced with the song. Rian sat back on her stool and allowed tears to well up and flow. Such music could surely appease any wrong.

The space was open and huge. The song echoed around inside it. Rian noticed that her toes were taking her weight and her legs were crossed over them. She uncrossed them and pressed the whole flat of her foot into the earth, allowing her body to make contact with the ground and sitting upright as Danuta had taught her to do when using her voice. She breathed deeply, slowly, following the breaths of Shadow's singing. The music evoked the sea's motions, the sloshing of waves, the glide of a swimming creature, fluent in the dance of water. When it stopped, Rian leaned forwards, fed three more sticks to the fire and sat back.

Manigan got to his feet and went to stand beside the head of the walrus. 'It's time to bid farewell, old friend.' He touched the top of the wrinkled skin on the skull. 'Come and say goodbye.'

He gestured to Kino and Badger who got up and patted the giant creature, muttered under their breaths, then turned and strode, without instruction, out of the temple. They could be heard rattling belts and weapons in the ante-chamber, briefly, then the door banged. Their rapid exit made Rian see that they were happy to be out of there. Yet there was nothing she wanted less. Now the real ceremony would begin and neither Manigan nor Shadow seemed to be indicating she should leave, indeed Shadow looked relaxed on her bench in the centre of the space, directly facing the door, with Rian on her right, the walrus and Manigan on her left.

The firelight cast dancing shadows on the curved vault of the chamber and on the clutter of jars in the shelved booths: containers of the dead, no doubt, fragments, relics, memories. Other walruses? Perhaps. Forgotten people, almost certainly.

Manigan pulled the stone head out of its bag and set it on the bench beside him, with the Sage's face towards the walrus.

'Tell what happened.' Shadow's voice was so much deeper and more powerful than the singing sound she had made, Rian looked up at her. She was commanding, even though relaxed. 'Say everything the sea spirits need to hear.'

Manigan had his head bowed. 'I cannot.'

'You must.'

'I am the Mutterer. I cannot tell the muttering. It is secret.'

'If you do not tell us, it will die with you.'

'I can only tell the next Mutterer.'

'The secret is safe here. You must trust us. Do you trust Rian?'

'With my life.' He half turned towards her and Rian almost fell off her stool with the power his eyes directed at her. She felt naked. How could anyone look so beautiful? He gleamed in the firelight. 'But I cannot share the muttering with anyone except my successor.'

'Perhaps she is it.'

'No. It will be a boy of my blood. It is foretold.'

'You can tell us. It is safe.'

He shook his head and rubbed his hand over his hair as if his head hurt. 'I will tell all that I dare. May the sea spirits guide me.'

Then he put both hands on the head of the walrus and began.

'Old man, here is the story of your ending. May it not be the end of your story. May I not lie or tell half-truths. May the great spirit of the North bless this telling. May Mother Earth forgive me for my killing. May the sea spirits make your soul-journey as noble as it deserves to be. May I say all I can to help you find the safe passage to another life and may I say nothing that should not be said. May the dead here listen and help us to understand what we have done and how to heal the damage that we have been part of making. May the living hear and speak and learn and know how next to act. We seek only to appease and to prevent any further wrong-doing.' He paused.

'I am the Mutterer. I am duty bound to answer a request for help by those who seek to hunt a walrus. We were sheltering on Fair Isle. Jan Bonxie came and asked me to guide a hunt on one of the northern Seal Isles. We set out this morning at first light and found the walruses on a spit of sand. There were ten of them, guarded by this old gentleman. I had explained to Bonxie and his men how we would proceed, so I did as I always do.' This was not his normal story voice, not the rambling, striding locution Rian had learned to love to listen to. This was a formal report. He was choosing his words carefully, she could see, spelling out the events piece by piece in simple phrases, as if speaking to people who may not fully understand his first language, or speaking to a child. Or as if he was a boy.

'I landed and prayed. The old Gentleman was on guard, the others resting. I approached slowly and once I was within earshot I began the muttering. I told him the story and as I told, I crept nearer.'

'Tell us the story.' Shadow raised her beater and lowered it.

The drum spoke, 'Doom.'

Manigan shifted, his shoulders hunched. His voice shrank to a dark monotone.

'The story goes: This is a story about a walrus.'

Shadow gave a single beat and Manigan nodded.

'The story goes: Once upon a time there was a walrus.'

Again the deep voice of the drum responded as if pegging the story phrase into the earth.

'The story goes: The greatest walrus that ever was.'

The drum spoke again. *Doom.*

'The story goes: This is the tale of the walrus who saved the day.'

Doom.

'The story goes: He was your ancestor.'

Manigan paused. 'And then I said, "Are you listening to me? It's about a walrus. Open your eye and blink once if you understand."'

Shadow held the drumstick up. 'Did the walrus blink?'

'He blinked.'

'Go on.' She hit the drum. As the story went on, the drum gave an '*mm*' of understanding to each phrase, as if absorbing it into the stones.

Manigan laid both his hands flat on the walrus's head and took a deep breath.

'The story goes: The walrus needed a name.'

Dmm.

'The story goes: The walrus needed to be remembered.'

Dmm.

'The story goes: The walrus was old and knew that when he died he might be forgotten, and all his wise guardianship would be washed away, and wasted.'

Dmm.

'The story goes: The walrus knew that being forgotten was like a bright ice-wind, white and cold. By now the Old Gentleman was staring at me and I knew I had him mesmerised.'

Dmm.

'The story goes: The walrus feared the emptiness, the infinite emptiness of being forgotten. I could see that fear in the Old Gentleman's eyes too.'

Dmm.

'The story goes: The walrus did not want to be lost in time.'

Dmm.

'The story goes: Wandering.'

Dmm.

'The story goes: Lost in time.'

Dmm.

'The story goes:…' Manigan left a long pause. 'Forgotten.'

Dmm.

'The story goes:…' Again a pause, and Manigan said. 'This is where the wind and sea join in and tell their part of the story, for they know all about forgetting. They helped the Old Gentleman to understand it.'

He waited and they listened to the fire breathing like the wind and crackling like the sea on sand. Eventually Manigan nodded, and the drum spoke.

Dmm.

'The story goes: The walrus needed a name.'

Dmm.

'The story goes: A name gives immortality.'

Dmm.

'The story goes: A name is a bond with the namer that lives on beyond death.'

Dmm.

'The story goes: A name is written into the heart.'

Dmm.

'The story goes: The walrus knew that if he had a name, he would not be lost in the iced wind of time.'

Dmm.

'The story goes: The walrus will do anything to avoid that.'

Dmm.

'The story goes: The void.'

Dmm.

'The story goes: Anything.'

Dmm.

'The story goes: The walrus needs to escape the void.'

Dmm.

'The story goes: The walrus asks to escape the void.'

Dmm.

'The story goes: The walrus seeks to be remembered.'

Dmm.

'The story goes: The walrus pleads to be released from being forgotten.'

Dmm.

'The story goes: The walrus blinks.'

'Did he blink?'

'He blinked.'

Rian remembered what Badger had told her, the stories within stories within stories, of which this was the innermost tale, like a capercaillie stuffed with a seagull stuffed with a cuckoo stuffed with a sandpiper stuffed with a wren. And inside the wren, what is there? The name.

Manigan shifted one hand off the walrus's head and gestured down the animal. 'The Old Gentleman gave a sharp flap of his rear flippers and all the other walruses knew what that meant. Those that were awake headed for the water, which woke the others, and in the way they do, they stampeded to the safety of the sea. But the Old Gentleman stayed with me, because he wanted to be remembered.'

Dmm. The drum urged him on.

'The story goes: The walrus is given his name.'

Dmm.

'The story ends.'

Dmm. There was silence.

Dmm, the drum demanded.

'The story ends.'

Dmm. The drum sounded greedy.

Manigan paused.

Rian could tell he was struggling with an old vow, revealing what he must not say to anyone else except the next Mutterer. He took a deep breath.

'I wrote his name in sand with the point of my spike. It is a simple name, just one letter. But Old Gentlemen like him do not read well, so he had to study it for a while. And then he blinked again and I wrote it on his heart.'

'The name?'

'His name.' He nodded.

'What is his name?' Shadow's voice was a cold stone.

Rian closed her eyes. Surely they shouldn't force him to reveal such a magic secret? But she couldn't keep herself from watching Manigan for long.

He sighed. 'Old man.' He patted the walrus gently on the head and its whiskers seemed to move as if it would speak. 'I promised you would be remembered. Here are my witnesses. The name I gave you is the only name I have to give. His name is I.'

He bent down and wrote a symbol in the dust on the floor with his finger, a line with 5 perpendicular slashes across it, a yew leaf, the second letter of Rian's own name. She looked at the walrus. Its name was part of her own.

'Death,' said Shadow. '*Iadh*, last letter of the alphabet, the tree of death.'

'Aye,' Manigan smiled wryly. 'Now you know.'

Rian felt her stomach churn. This was unpalatable food and she knew she must carry it inside her forever.

Dmm, the drum said suddenly.

'The story has ended,' Manigan said to it, softly. '*Iadh*, the great and noble walrus, will be remembered.'

Dmm, the drum agreed, and then for a while only it spoke, a slow pulse, as everything in the chamber absorbed and ruminated on what they had heard. Its slowing heart beat ebbed into the stones.

Duh Dum.

Duh Dum.

Duh Dum.

The fire was dying, hungry for food. When the drum stopped, Rian looked at Shadow and Manigan to try to gauge what she should do about it, but she couldn't make out what they might want. Shadow seemed locked in a drum-induced trance. Manigan just looked miserable, his hands now taken off the head and hanging limp beside him, his head drooping. She took it upon herself to feed the fire. It was the one thing in the world she could do. Some small sticks first, which she coaxed to life with her breath. Flames flickered and darted and seemed to stir Manigan. He rubbed his face and smiled at her. He looked so young in the firelight she wanted to stroke him. She put three bigger sticks onto the little blaze and sat back while the fire tasted them.

'I ask the sea spirits for advice. I ask the Old Gentleman for forgiveness. I ask the Death Stone for mercy.' He touched the three-faced stone lightly, then put his hands back on top of the walrus head. 'The old Gentleman's friends had left him to his naming ceremony, because they are polite and perhaps also a little scared of me. Bonxie and his men slaughtered them. I had told them not to. There was blood in the sea. Spears. It was wrong. I shouted at them to stop. There was nothing else I could do. They made a sacrilege of the muttering. I am ashamed to be a man among such men.' His voice was cracking, thick with emotion.

Rian hung her head. She had thought only of Jan Bonxie and the other men. Now she saw that Manigan carried the weight of this tradition and that what they had witnessed was a desecration of it. To survive combat with the walrus, great ocean spirits must be appeased and willing. This was his life. What Jan Bonxie and the others had done jeopardised everything.

Shadow was still trancelike, but something in the tilt of her head showed she was listening.

'Tell me what to do to make amends. If I must avenge his dead friends I will do it.'

'You have made the great sacrifice of your story. It is enough.' Rian breathed out with relief.

Shadow beat the drum. 'The ocean has avenged itself.'

'And what about the Old Gentleman?'

'What about him?'

'I should make his heart mine.'

'So do so.'

'I have no knife.'

'You have teeth.'

So Manigan hunkered down beside the animal, lifted the hide, inside which the inner organs lay, took the gory heart out with one hand and let the skin fall back. Grasping the bloody flesh in both hands, he chewed into it like a dog, worrying it until a piece tore off. As he swallowed, a trickle of red juice ran down his chin. He bit again.

After his third bite, he thrust the heart, unceremoniously, towards Rian. Her first instinct was to refuse but there seemed no option for rejecting it and the bloody flesh was oddly compelling. Manigan's hands were stretched out to her, so she leaned in towards the fire and took the dripping organ from him. He grinned, wiping his chin. She put the heart to her mouth.

She had eaten raw flesh before, even heart once, when Danuta killed the old cow at the winter solstice. But that had been hot from the body, and soft. This was cold and hardening. She had to tear at it with her teeth like a fox and she found herself smiling, a toothy predatory grimace, as the blood squirted into her mouth. It was the bloodiest meat she had ever encountered, as if all the walrus's blood was stored there in his heart. She chewed and swallowed and bit again. And then again. It bit back: her mouth was shocked with the nettle-sharpness of the flavour, but it was an exultant moment, to feast on the core of the great animal, to share its blood with Manigan, to put her mouth where his had been and taste the full red flesh.

She couldn't pass it directly to Shadow without crossing the fire, so she got up and stepped around. She held her bloodied hands out but instead of taking it, Shadow bent and licked it. Rian stood with the heart as big as a baby's head in her hands, while Shadow tore a shred of meat off with her teeth, then licked again, three symbolic bites, as if the blood disgusted her.

Rian wondered if she should be ashamed of her greed, the beast-like way she had chomped, but she couldn't rid herself of the satisfaction it had given her. She looked at Manigan, to see what he wanted next. He beckoned and she reached over to hand the heart back to him. Their hands touched as the organ slithered from her fingers. He leaned towards her and smeared blood across her forehead and in a stripe down each cheek. His finger lingered at the corner of her mouth. His eyes were pools, tempting her. Her head swam as she returned to her stool.

Shadow said, 'It is good that a child has been nourished by the Old Gentleman.'

Rian stared at her, head up, back stiffening. How could she know?

Manigan frowned, not seeming to comprehend.

'And it is good that you have marked its mother as a warrior. She will need that power.'

Rian blushed with shame but the moment passed. Manigan was intent on dribbling blood into the hollow on top of the three-faced stone.

When he had finished, Shadow banged the drum again. 'We have brought his spirit to the fire and sung the peace of our ancestors with him. We have brought his flesh to our bodies and given him a home into the future. What else does the Old Gentleman require of us?'

'He will be content now, I think. We should enjoy the rest of the delicacies, if you'd be willing to let us cook them?' He opened the skin and began laying the organs back onto the wooden trencher.

'You're welcome in my home.'

'Thank you. There are three more things I must do. The skin is for the water. I will take it, cure it, use it on the boat. The little old man, I cannot share with women what I do with that.' He set the penis aside. 'I'll take off the tusks tomorrow and the head is yours.'

'I want only some whiskers.' Shadow leaned over and tickled

the walrus's whiskery lips.

'Then let the birds have the head, so his mind flies free over the ocean. His brains are powerful medicine, I'm sure you know.'

Shadow nodded. 'Given what has happened, the birds can have them. And what about you?' She turned to Rian. 'What do you want from him?'

'Nothing. I just want to go home.'

'Home.' Shadow nodded. 'We'll talk tomorrow.' She tilted her head towards Manigan. 'You can stay another day?'

He shrugged.

'And so...' Shadow brought her beater down on her drum with a boom and let it resound.

'We thank the sea spirits.'

They murmured thanks.

The drum boomed again.

'We thank you, Old Gentleman of the Sea.'

They murmured again. Shadow dipped a little cup in a copper bowl of powder and handed it around the side of the fire to Rian, nodding for her to sprinkle it. She scattered it into the embers and it sparkled, then smoked. Little flames flickered and the smoke had a scent of such pungent sweetness that it made Rian close her eyes as she breathed it in. She remembered honeysuckle and the taste of clover flowers and the feel of sunshine on her skin.

Then the sound of water made her open her eyes, but there was no water, only Shadow with a bundle of sticks that had a trickling waterfall held by some magic inside.

'Now we bid you goodnight.'

The drum boomed for the last time and its long vowel reverberated around the chamber and into their bodies. Rian felt it fill her and subside.

Shadow put down the beater, got slowly to her feet and bowed to the walrus and the fire. Manigan and Rian did the same. Then Rian gathered up her fire box and followed Shadow out, aware of the heft of Manigan close behind her, as if the drum and the blood had opened up a sense of touch in her that could reach beyond physical contact and absorb the presence of his body into hers.

Outside it was night and cool sea air greeted them. Pebbles hushed and gave gentle applause as waves alternately washed them and let them settle. A few stars poked out from between clouds. A dog barked twice to their left and Shadow said, 'Aye, aye, dog. We're coming.' The dog fell quiet.

She took the trencher from Manigan and led the way up to her house. Rian followed. The path was narrow and he was silent behind her. When they reached the hut, she felt his touch on her arm.

'Thank you. Are you still angry with me?'

She thought about it but her fury had dissolved. She put her hand on his. 'No.'

DOLPHINS

They feasted on walrus meat which Badger and Kino had already started cooking with Gessan, Shadow's man. There was ale and bread. Rian managed only a little before a wave of tiredness hit her and she accepted Shadow's offer of a corner to sleep in.

She woke in the night, her bladder tight, and lay listening to the snuffles and snores of the others, and the stamp and snort of the cow. She needed to go out and relieve herself if she would ever get back to sleep. She crept up from her bed. The dog, silent, followed her to the door, but did not go out. She stepped around to the back of the house. Beside the peat stack she squatted, looking up at the stars. The clouds had broken up and the Star Hunter strode the horizon.

As she came back round the side of the house she stopped. One of the men was there. She hung back in the shadow, feeling herself vulnerable and exposed. But instead of turning back into the house, as she had hoped, he came towards her.

'Rian?' It was Manigan.

She didn't speak, but took a step towards him. It seemed to be all that was needed to close the distance between them to nothing at all, to allow him to wrap his arms around her and draw her even closer. She clasped her arms around his waist, pushed her body into his and lifted her head to seek his kiss. He was as greedy for her as she was for him. It was so simple, like running down a slope after hauling a heavy back-basket up a hill. All her burdens slid from her and scattered among the stones.

She kissed him, at first experimentally, tasting him. Beyond the beery flavour he was richer than mushrooms, a new taste she loved instantly. Somewhere in it must be the taste of the walrus blood they had shared. He pulled her even tighter and they broke off the kiss to laugh in delight at each other. He started to speak, but she stopped his mouth with hers. She had no desire to speak, no need for words, wanted only for them to be quiet enough to be undiscovered and undisturbed.

His hands started to explore her body. A fire inside her needed to be fed and the fuel was his body. Her hands sought his skin under his jerkin. He was warm on her cold palms, smooth as birch bark, supple as salmon. She kissed him more deeply, their tongues like seals, rolling together in shallows.

His hands were on her, his touch on her nipple as sharp and hot as bronze.

Then they were stripping away clothes, fumbling with each other's belts. She helped with a button on her skirt. When they stood naked, bare flesh to bare flesh, their skins talked love to one another.

Only touch remained, only the language of stroking. She pushed, to see if it was possible to be closer and he pulled her into him again. There was an ocean of intimacy to explore and she dived into it, wanting to lose even the sense of herself as skin, separate from him. She pulled him down onto the peat stack and abandoned herself to the muscled wave of him. They rode the storm that possessed them, bucking until they crashed to foam, soaked with sweat, panting and kissing.

But it was impossible for them to stop. The waves soon had them away again, but this time it was a gentler sea and Rian could see him as well as feel him. His eyes shone in the starlight as their bodies writhed like dolphins at play. They kissed a lifetime's longing into being, then let it wash them away into frenzy.

When they stilled, waves were still breaking on the shore. The cold air lapped them, evaporating sweat. He kissed her face, her eyes, her forehead, then lifted himself off her and started to dress. They giggled as they hunted for discarded garments and belts in the dark, stopping over and over to let their mouths fall together and to hold themselves against each other.

Once dressed, Manigan said, 'Let's go down to the sea.'

They walked down the path, arms around each other where they could, hand in hand on even the steepest sections, to the stony beach where the sea clapped at them with every wave and chased them away when they ventured too close. As the dawn opened out the world, Rian knew that the rest of her life would always be different now, that they had woken something between them that was surely unparalleled.

They sat on a ledge of rock, watching. No morning had ever been lovelier. Manigan spoke to her of the ocean, and she told him what it was like to be a slave.

'Never, never let me hurt you.' He held her shoulders, staring at her, insistent that she promise him.

IVORY

A drum beat drew them back to the Whale House. The door of the great temple was open and Rian said, 'Shadow is back with the…' She nearly said 'walrus', but checked herself, 'Old Gentleman.'

'Let's go!' Manigan jumped to his feet. 'There's ivory to salvage and a sea to sail on.'

He tugged her to her feet and they scampered up the path to the cliff top and across the narrow land bridge to the temple. Shadow was at the doorway with a small drum, beating in time with the waves on the shore as the sun rose over the sea. She gave a wry, knowing lift of her eyebrows at their beaming smiles.

Inside, everything smelled different: musty. Manigan wiped the hollow on the three-faced stone and returned it to its bag. Shadow helped them carry the Old Gentleman's head out and down to a big flat rock overlooking the sea.

'Rian and I need to talk today,' Shadow said. 'You are all welcome to stay here. There is no hurry to leave, is there?'

Manigan and Rian tried not to smile too widely, but Shadow looked between them and though her face was inscrutable, Rian knew there was no secret from her of what had happened in the darkness.

'We can stay another night.' Manigan patted the walrus head and ran his hand down one tusk. 'These'll take a while.'

'Come with me then.' Shadow led away back up the slope to the house.

Rian tore her gaze from Manigan, then turned her back and

followed Shadow, conscious of his eyes on her. She walked tall, feeling her body move as smoothly as a cat.

The house was tucked into a hollow above the cliff. Its back entrance was covered in ivy that sheltered a honeysuckle, humming with bees. Shadow stopped to fill the dog's water bowl from a stream that trickled, glittering, down to the edge of the crag via a fern-fringed pool. Rian stood, feeling the sunshine's warmth on her skin.

Inside it was dark and full of sleep-smells. Kino, Badger and Gessan were groping their way into the day. Shadow chivvied them outside with oatcakes and crowdie cheese and told them to take some down to Manigan. They went off, talking about fishing.

Shadow left the door open. 'Let's have some breakfast now.'

She poured some water from a barrel into a pot, which she hung from a hook above the fire and lowered it down so it almost sat on the peats. She patted a low stool near her.

Rian said, 'Should I fetch some more water?' The barrel had seemed low.

'No, no, we'll do it later. You need to eat.'

But Rian felt queasy and didn't like even the thought of crowdie cheese. She sat down cautiously on the stool.

As if reading her mind, Shadow said, 'No doubt you're feeling a bit sick. It's normal. If we get that water hot, a cup of raspberry leaf tea will work wonders for you. And I've some honey bannock that'll maybe go down a bit easier than fishermen's food.' From a cupboard in the wall she produced a pottery jar of blaeberries and some honeycomb. She unwrapped bannocks from a cloth. 'I saved you this after you went to bed last night.' Some sorrel leaves, dandelion and a bowl of pignuts, curd and a jelly completed the spread.

Rian really did not feel like it but Shadow was insistent. 'You must eat. Let's get that kettle boiling.' She passed Rian some sticks from a bundle of driftwood against one wall and Rian chivvied the fire into flame with a few breaths and encouraging words.

'You're a good fire-keeper. Who taught you?'

'Danuta. My foster mother.'

'Will that be the Danuta I saw at the Brodgar gathering at summer solstice?'

Rian nodded.

'I knew her brother, Sorok. He was a fine smith. So you're the one who was taken as a slave by Ussa?'

Rian couldn't look at her, or speak, but she managed to nod again.

'And now you've run away.'

So she knew. She might not be safe here after all. Ussa could appear at any moment. She could be beaching in the shallows right now. She felt her store of hatred for Ussa, like venom.

'I'm surprised she didn't come after you. It's not like her to let any of her possessions get away without profit.'

Rian didn't know what to say, but the water was coming to a boil so she was saved the need to respond by Shadow's preparation of a raspberry-leaf brew. As soon as she began to drink it she understood it was the right thing, exactly, for her. Sweetened with honey, it was an elixir. Her shoulders let go, the muscles in her forehead eased, tension she had not realised she was holding relaxed. She looked about her with eyes adjusted to the gloom and saw all the paraphernalia of a medicine woman's home: the herbs in bundles, drying, hung from rafters, a shelf containing neat rows of pottery jars, lidded or stoppered with wood, many with woollen plaits tied around them to mark their contents. The range of cooking pots and implements for grinding, pounding and cutting was even greater than Danuta's collection. A whole wall of bronze and copper hung glowing in the firelight.

'I expect Ussa will pass by here again soon,' Shadow said. 'I don't suppose yourself or Manigan will relish that.'

Rian stared at the floor, then looked across at Shadow who merely passed her a bannock.

'I can show you where to hide. She never stops for long. To be honest, I can't stand the woman.' She allowed a conspiratorial grin to sneak past her gruff demeanour. 'All that trafficking and gambling on people's lives, it's not right. But who else can you get these things from?' She gestured to the wall behind her and to the row of small jars that Rian knew must contain spices and herbs from other lands.

She chewed her bannock slowly, allowing it to ease her hunger, supping her tea with each mouthful. The nausea subsided. This woman reminded her so much of Danuta. There was a pause as she considered what Shadow had said. Was she being made an offer to stay there?

Thinking of Danuta, and home, but also the need to hide from Ussa or anyone else who might want to pass her back to her owner, she finally acknowledged the thing she had been refusing to think. Drost would not want her back nor could she trust him not to betray her if she was in hiding somewhere nearby. Not even Danuta would be able to protect her.

'How was Danuta, when you saw her in the summer?'

Shadow smiled. 'You want to go back to her, don't you?'

Rian had held Danuta's hearth inside her as her destination, the home she would return to, for so long now that she almost couldn't bear to recognise that she couldn't go back. It was a gravitational pull. All her life it had been her refuge, from bad weather, from any danger. But it was no longer safe. Drost had sold her and he would not want her back. If or when Ussa passed by again, he would have no hesitation about whose interests he would favour.

Shadow was waiting patiently for her answer, sipping at her tea.

'I can't,' Rian said, eventually.

Shadow nodded. 'Where will you go?'

Here was the void. The only hiding places she knew were in Assynt and although none of them were now guaranteed safe, perhaps if she could sneak her way into the area she could make her way there undetected. But winter was coming and she would need help; not least food. And that would involve danger to anyone she could persuade to give her secret support. Other than this part-formed idea she did not know where else she could go.

'I will go with Manigan.' Her heart pounded as she formed the words for what she had not known until that moment.

Shadow nodded again, more slowly. 'Have you thought about what it will entail?'

Rian didn't care what it entailed, other than nights under the stars with him. 'A lot of sailing.' She laughed.

'You're pregnant, Rian,' Shadow was sober. 'You can't have a baby out on the northern ocean or on a beach beside a herd of walruses. If you have nowhere else you can go, you will be safe here, and welcome. I can help you with the birth and I would enjoy your company through the winter. We can share our knowledge of plants. I can also let you have some warm clothes that fit you.' She smiled.

Rian swallowed, frowning.

'But I can't...' She couldn't finish the sentence. The idea of staying here while Manigan sailed away was poison.

'You need to think about the baby.' Shadow offered another bannock.

Rian declined.

'Is it Manigan's?'

She shook her head.

'Oh.' Shadow held her gaze and she did not need to say anything for Rian to know she was wondering what had happened. 'You'll need someone, a woman, to help you with the birth. It'll be the lean time of the year. Think about who will take care of you.'

There was an uneasy silence.

Rian got up. 'Can I go to see what they are doing with the walrus?'

Shadow shrugged. 'Take the bannocks.' She proffered the basket.

Rian took it and made her escape back down to the shore, nearly slipping in her haste to get away from the dilemma that now faced her. But seeing Manigan crouched beside the great head did nothing to ease it. She showed him the warm honey-bread and he put down the saw he was working with to take a piece. He kissed her, then stuffed the bannock in his mouth like a hungry boy.

'Mmm.' He munched happily and pointed at the tusk he had already sawed off. 'That's for you.'

She looked between the ivory and him, not comprehending. 'What?'

'It's for you. To buy your freedom.'

'You said you don't buy women.'

He looked put out. 'I'm not buying you.' He took another piece of bannock. 'It's a gift. From the Old Gentleman. Consider it as payment for the ceremony, for helping. You'll need it when Ussa finds you. I think the Old Gentleman would be happy if one of his tusks could buy your freedom.' He kicked it towards her. 'It isn't worth as much alone as with the other one but I need that for the boat, for the men. But it's a good tusk, it's still valuable. More than a sword.'

He picked up the saw again and resumed cutting the second tusk. Rian stood nearby, watching. After a burst of vigorous strokes of the blade, which squealed, he paused.

'Fucking thing. Blunt as a butter paddle.' Another burst, then another. Rian was amazed how hard it was to cut, much tougher than bone. 'Is it the Chieftain who gave you the child or the Greek? Or someone else?'

She blushed and looked at her feet.

'Pretty as you, I guess you might not know. Must have been plenty of men wanting the favour.'

Now it was her turn to look put out. 'I know exactly. It wasn't like that. I didn't want...' She couldn't go on. The memory of the night when Pytheas did what he did was like a sudden submersion in cold water. She turned away and tears spilled over and trickled down her cheeks.

Manigan wrapped his arms around her and turned her to him, lifting her face to look at him. 'You were raped?' He crushed her in a hug, his head bent so she could feel his breath in her hair. 'I'm sorry, Rian. I'm a stupid bastard. I didn't think what it must be like to be a slave, to be someone's possession.' He pulled away to look into her face again.

She was crying hard now. Somehow his sympathy was even more painful than the memory. The word 'rape', the naming of it, was like a knife cutting her, yet it also released something in her that had lain pent up, stoppered, ever since that night at sea. She couldn't speak for crying.

'The Greek?' He was holding her away from him, his eyes raging.

She nodded, and he wrapped his arms around her and rocked her as she wept. 'You poor, poor little one, my own little fish, little pretty thing.' He murmured away to her, crooning like a child with a pet animal as she cried.

She felt raw. Snotty and wet-faced, she pulled herself away and wiped her nose and cheeks on her sleeve. There was emptiness in her now, and relief to have let the poison out.

He was kissing her eyes and her forehead and her cheeks, his big hands around her head. Between kisses he said, 'I'll kill him.'

'No. It only happened once and he hated himself afterwards.'

'How can you possibly forgive him?'

'I don't. But I don't wish him dead.' She looked up at him. 'I don't know why.'

'I'll never let anyone hurt you ever again.' He sought her hands with his and held her at arm's length, making a declaration. 'I'll look after you.'

Of course he could not keep her safe, not from the likes of Ussa, but Rian loved him for wanting to.

She looked at him and smiled through her tears. She turned towards the sea and leaned against him, his arms still wrapped around her. He leaned his chin on her head. She wondered what he saw, and whether it was the same as she did.

The sea was like a ruffled cloth woven from threads of many shades of blue and grey. The breeze rippled its surface and where the sun cast a beam across it, sparkles glittered in a ribbon so bright it was blinding to look at. Somehow, although the breeze seemed gentle and consistent, a band of clear, smooth water was spread across the surface. It writhed as if some creature under the surface was present there, turning slowly in its sleep, absorbing the ripples into its skin. She pointed it out to Manigan and said what she thought it was.

'The sea tells our future if we know how to read it.' The weight of his chin was comfortingly heavy on her head. 'There is a serpent in the ocean bottom – bigger than this one, and when it shifts about it makes storms and heavy weather. They say when it dies, which eventually it must, all the seas will go calm and then the walruses and whales will go down to the ocean floor where they do not dare to go while the serpent lives, and they will bring to the surface all the boats that have sunk and wrecked since ever we people began sailing, and all the ships will be transformed into harps and all the sailors will sing like seals and they'll sail happily into the sunset together, escorted by the walruses and dolphins and whales.'

'So if we kill all the walruses...' She didn't need to finish the statement.

'My old granddad used to say there's a sailor drowned for every walrus we take unless we plead well with the spirits. I'm not sure pleading would stop them, to be honest, though it might encourage them to take a different victim. What do you think?' He squeezed her. 'You talk to them with your fires. Do they listen to us, do you think?'

'Of course. The fire spirits do, anyway. I don't know about the sea spirits so much. But surely everywhere they're keeping balance for the Great Mother.'

'Tidying up for us when we make a mess.'

She elbowed him in the ribs and he laughed and squeezed her again.

'So has Shadow finished with you or what? Can we head off tomorrow?'

'Where are you going?'

'We, you mean. You're coming too.'

'I may not.'

'She wants you to stay here?'

'It's the baby.'

'So what? I don't care whose it is. It'll be part of you. I'll love it just like I love you. Can you not feel this glow between us? From you into me, from me into you. It will infuse the child.'

He was holding her tight, her back rubbing up against the length of his body, arms crossed over her chest, as if he would never let go.

'The birth…' She petered out. Now the tears had eased she was feeling a bit sick again.

'It's your choice.' Now there was a note of huffiness in his voice.

'Where will you go?' What she wanted to say was, 'Will you come back if I stay?'

'To the Faroes. Perhaps further north if the ice will let us. We need one last hunt in the north before the season's over.'

She imagined the slow drifts of pack ice on the sea, and then thought of a storm and what the ice must be like then, bucking and rearing on waves.

'Then south to trade ivory and work on the boat while the days are short, and back north again in spring. Same as every year.'

The honey bannock did not seem to be suiting her stomach at all. A wave of nausea rose up and she tried to breathe deeply but it wouldn't pass. She pulled away from Manigan and suddenly she was retching. She staggered a few steps away and kneeled down to empty her stomach among the stones.

'You're in a bad way.' Manigan stroked her back. 'Maybe Shadow's right. I don't know anything about these things.'

Rian wiped her mouth. She needed a drink.

Manigan, solicitous, pointed out a nearby stream. Ashamed, but relieved to put some space between them, she cleaned herself up and washed out her mouth.

'Perhaps you should go back up to the house, take a rest.' Manigan had returned to sawing the tusk. 'Do you need a hand?'

She shook her head. She needed to lie down.

The crag seemed twice as steep returning as it had done earlier.

Shadow seemed unsurprised to see her and was unfussy but motherly in suggesting she rest for a while. It felt good to lie down, to let the rhythm of her breath slow, and the kind hand of sleep draw a curtain over her mind and all of its questions.

Just before she slept she remembered that Manigan had still never told her how he came to have the stone and what it was, nor had he finished the tale he had begun about his own life, when and why he became the Mutterer and what the problem was between him and Ussa. There was so much she needed to ask him. And then there was the story that the Sage was going to tell Red the smith. All these unfinished stories, like threads unspooling from spindles, rolling away from her. And the Sage's face on the stone seemed to come to her mind, smiling. He was speaking. But his voice was so quiet she could not hear him, listen as hard as she might.

DEPARTURE

She woke to a confusion of men's voices and sat up, rubbing her eyes. She was bleary, not fully conscious. Manigan was giving instructions to pack up their tools, to whom she was not sure. Then he was beside her.

She sat up. It was dusk outside. She had slept the day away.

He was giving her the walrus tusk. 'Keep this safe. Don't part with it until you are absolutely sure of your freedom.'

'What's happening?'

'We're going.'

She started to get to her feet. 'Shadow says you should stay here.' He pressed her shoulder. 'I told you about my mother, didn't I? She died, Rian. I can't let that happen to you.'

'But I'm fine. I want to come with you. Why are you going?'

'Ussa's coming. Badger saw her when they were fishing. We have to go now.'

He slung the bag with the stone head across his shoulder and leaned down to kiss her.

'Come o-o-n,' Badger yelled, sticking his head around the door.

'I'll be back in spring. Or sooner. I love you.' And with that he was running out of the house.

Rian tried to collect herself, found her boots and the clothes she had taken off to sleep, and struggled into them. Her frantic rush to follow Manigan was more of a hindrance than help. She grabbed her coat and strapped the firebox around her waist. She bumped into Shadow coming into the house.

'Go if you must, child, but think of how sick you are. Your baby is trying to tell you to stay on land and take care of it.'

Rian passed her and ran. She was halted by Shadow's shout of her name, and looked back. She was holding the tusk.

Rian ran back, took it, thanked Shadow and set off again after the men. They were stowing their kit on board as she came into view of Bradan. The tusk was heavy and she shifted it to her other arm, and ran on. But she was dizzy and by the time she reached the beach she was feeling sick again.

The look on Manigan's face when he saw her told her everything she needed. He lit up. 'You're coming!'

But his glee melted away as she shook her head.

'I can't. Will you come back?'

He walked up the beach to her, pulled her to him. She kissed as if she was giving him her life. He took it and repaid.

Then Badger was shouting, 'Fucksake Manigan. Are we going?'

'Spring,' he said, and she nodded.

Then they were all lifting and heaving Bradan down the beach until the water held her. Kino, Badger, Manigan and Gessan were jumping aboard. They were instantly at oars, and the boat skimmed away, Manigan's eyes on Rian's until the boat was all the way around the headland and out of view.

She cradled the tusk. Its crescent moon heaviness was all that she had of him. He could not keep her safe, but he had given her back her freedom.

She walked back up the beach, bitter tears on her cheeks, her heart tearing as the choice she had made settled its claws in her chest. It was a long, slow plod up the hill where the strange woman's house stood, a long, slow plod towards winter.

IMBOLC

Out on the hill behind the broch, Rian wandered along with Shadow's cow and calf. The moon had waned and waxed again since the midwinter solstice and there was little forage to find. The cow was resorting to chewing tough heather while the calf snuffled at grass, wispy and desiccated by cold. They might fill their bellies to keep hunger at bay but there was little goodness in this vegetation. Rian hoped Shadow would spare them some hay when it was time for milking. It was starting to feel cruel to take milk away from the suckling, although he was a sturdy enough little thing now. Rian had come to bring them home and whenever the cow lifted her head from the sward, Rian edged them on towards Shadow's hut.

It was a bright, blue day, cooling now as the sun sank towards the south west, its beam a silver ribbon across the Sound to the Mainland, as they called it, even though it was actually just another island, albeit bigger than all the others in the archipelago.

A boat was heading towards Whale Island. It passed into the stream of glitter thrown down across the water by the sun and emerged within a few moments out the other side. Such rapid movement no doubt meant it was being swept along on one of the formidable tides that helped or hampered the sailors in these waters so much. It sometimes seemed to Rian that fishermen, like Gessan, Shadow's husband, never talked of anything else.

The vessel carried a big sail the reddish colour of well-tanned hide and above it was a smaller top sail like the one Manigan flew on Bradan when the wind was light. Rian took a sharp in-breath and stood watching the boat, staring and staring as if wild hope and a determined gaze might be enough to materialise what she longed for.

The cow eventually nudged her with its forehead. She pushed it away. It paused to munch again, lowed to its calf, then lumbered off in the direction of home.

Rian turned back to the sea. It was Bradan, its approach fast enough to confirm that leap of wishing. There could be no mistaking its narrow form, pointed prow, tall mast and dark-haired helmsman.

She didn't feel her bare feet carrying her across the springy grass. She forgot the huge bulge of her pregnant belly. She was oblivious to the chill insinuating itself inside her unbuttoned coat.

At the line of seaweed thrown up by the most recent storm she stopped. The boat bore on as if drawn towards her. The top sail came down. The main sail was turned, wind spilled from it to slow the boat's progress, and then, at the moment the hull touched pebbles on the shore, it was bundled down and one after another three men clambered over the side to haul the vessel up out of the water. She didn't recognise the other two men. From nowhere, it seemed, although presumably from the broch, other people appeared, jogging along the shoreline to help carry the curragh. They heaved it up away from the danger of waves.

Manigan said something to the others and separated from them, striding up the beach towards Rian. She stood, arms stretching downwards, legs frozen to the spot until he pulled her out of her daze into the hug she had been dreaming of for months: that smell of seals and walrus, her selkie mariner, his oceanic smile, the ripples of his laughter.

'Green eyes.' He stroked her hair with one hand, the other around her waist. Leaning back, he dazzled her with his sea blue sparkle.

She could only grin, tongue-tied. Eventually she mustered, 'You'll be hungry.'

'Ravenous!' He laughed an open-mouthed guffaw of delight and her cheeks ached with the pure joy of seeing him.

'I've got a plan. I'm going to take you to Ictis.' He patted her belly. 'Once you're ready, the two of you. You'll be safe there. The Queen Bitch won't get you there, the Keepers will make sure of that. What do you think?'

She beamed back at him. 'Where've you been?'

He laughed again. 'Put me by a warm fire. I've got stories for plenty of long nights. These boys...' He gestured down towards the boat. 'Do they know how to handle the tides?'

'Who are they?'

One of the strangers was approaching.

'They belong here. Stron, they're called. Father and son. Couldn't wish for better crew. I found them on the Long Island and they volunteered to come up here with me while Badger and Kino went home for the winter.' He detached himself from Rian and turned towards the short, bearded man. 'Is there a noust free we can lay her up in?'

The man nodded. 'So we'll empty her?'

'Every last thing. Take it all off. I'm not going anywhere for a while.'

'Right.' The bearded man turned back to the boat.

Manigan pulled Rian closer in to him and kissed her. 'I've got a barrel of oats and bags of nuts and mushrooms for you.'

She didn't think it could be possible to grin more broadly. For months she had been feeling guilty about eating Shadow's winter supplies.

'I thought you'd be missing the woods by now.'

She felt she might burst. 'Not as much as I've been missing you.'

He kissed her again. 'Where did your cow go?'

She giggled. 'Home, I hope. To Shadow's.'

'Will I be welcome?'

'A barrel of oats, you said?'

The bearded man was back. 'Are you going to put her down

and help us with the boat, or what, skipper?'

Manigan stuck a lewd finger out and carried on kissing Rian.

She made a half-hearted effort to prise herself away. 'You'd better help them, surely.'

He squeezed her tight to him. 'I've waited months for this.'

She shuffled sideways a little to give the baby space. She could feel it kicking as if it wanted to get out. It was sure to come soon. A memory intruded of Pytheas, that thin foreigner whose offspring it was, and then she dismissed him from her mind. Her breath filled with Manigan's sea scent instead.

She hugged him fiercely. At last, after all that she had been through, Rian could embrace the freedom she'd been longing for.

AUTHOR'S NOTE

The Stone Stories trilogy is set in 320 BC, around the British coastline, north into the Arctic and east to the Baltic Sea. It takes as its trigger the journey of a historical explorer and scientist, Pytheas of Massalia, who made an epic voyage of discovery from his home in one of the western Greek colonies. He is credited with being the first Mediterranean person to circumnavigate and map the island of Alba (Britain), and he coined the phrase *Ultima Thule* for the northernmost land he reached. This intrepid traveller encountered a land of monumental coastal architecture built by matriarchal tribes who worshipped liminal spirits. He was in search of the origins of certain high-value materials in short supply in the Mediterranean (tin, amber and walrus ivory) and he travelled with traders of these goods and other commodities, including slaves. He was awed by the northern ocean and those who sailed and hunted on it.

The book Pytheas wrote of his travels, *On the Ocean*, is lost, so where exactly he travelled is something of a mystery. However, his book was widely quoted, and from these fragments of text academic historians have pieced together the outline of his voyage, although many details are contested or simply unknown. Yet from one fragment we can be sure that Pytheas travelled up the west coast of Britain and made landfall at the latitude of Clachtoll Broch, an impressive Iron Age building in Assynt, which was at the heart of a sophisticated maritime society between the Western and Northern Isles and northern mainland.

ACKNOWLEDGEMENTS

It all began with Clachtoll broch, so my first thanks must be to the Iron Age architectural genius who worked out how to build a 15-metre-high, double-walled dry stone tower. John Barber of AOC Archaeology calls him Ug, so thank you Ug. You not only left a remarkable legacy on the shore of my home parish, but you sparked in me a fascination with your period and with the people who built, inhabited and visited your implausibly wonderful building. Along with John, I must also thank Graeme, Andy, Alan, Charlotte and all the other dedicated members of the AOC team who have helped to bring the Iron Age (and indeed other periods) to life through their work in Assynt and indulged my wonderings about what Pytheas may have found here when he came, way back in 320 BC.

Huge gratitude also to Gordon Sleight, who has repeatedly hired me to hang out with this brilliant team on their various digs, and to pick their brains while ostensibly writing blogs and media releases for them. Gordon has also read these books with a meticulous care and pointed out the many mistakes, anachronisms and pieces of wishful but implausible thinking that I wove into earlier drafts.

Professor Barry Cunliffe was also very helpful in his insights about Pytheas and in encouraging my ideas about what he might have been getting up to in this neck of the woods. Professor Donna Heddle was similarly key in helping me imagine the cultural world Pytheas would have found here. Staff of several museums, including the National Museum of Scotland in Edinburgh, Kilmartin, Stromness, Kirkwall, Wick, Inverness, Pendeen, Penzance, Copenhagen, Oslo, Krakow and Longyearbyen, helped me in my research over the years. Particular thanks to Neil Burridge for showing me his bronze-smithing magic, to the captains and crews of the Ortelius and the Noorderlicht, for amazing adventures in the pack ice and northern ocean, and to Ian Stephen for sailing wisdom and stories about the sea-past. And thanks to everyone else who has talked to me about the Iron Age and helped me to time-travel back to when Pytheas made his amazing journey. All remaining historical inaccuracy is entirely my fault.

The book could not have been written without the chance to take some time out of the day job, and this was made possible by a generous bursary from Creative Scotland, for which I remain hugely grateful. It came about as a result of urging from staff at Moniack Mhor, who also gave me retreat space and moral support by simply believing in the project.

Margaret Elphinstone was my first reader, critical friend and mentor, and the long conversations and convivial times with her and Mike were priceless waypoints on the journey to the finished books. Jane Alexander and John Bolland were crucial readers of early drafts, so thank you both for the encouragement and vastly helpful suggestions about story and characters. Thanks also to all my other writing buddies: Romany, Jorine, Anna, Maggie, Becks, Anita, Graham, Kate, Alastair, Phil and everyone else who has come to join in writing events in Assynt, not forgetting Ed Group, Helen Sedgwick, Peter Urpeth and Janet Paisley. I'm grateful to Lesley McDowell for editorial advice, and to all at Saraband, especially Sara Hunt, for bringing it to fruition.

My Mum sadly didn't get to read this book, but her pride in me lives on and I'm grateful for it every day. Thankfully I have my Dad and my uniquely wonderful sister, Alison, offering endless support. Thanks to you both and to all the rest of our far-flung tribe.

This book was largely written at sea, thanks to the crew of Each Mara, the most precious of whom is Bill, my patient mate and co-skipper, to whom buckets of love and hugs, onshore and off.